Sunset Lullaby

BY ROBIN JONES GUNN

Christy & Todd

THE BABY YEARS

BOOK 3

Sunset Lullaby

First printing November 2017

ISBN 978-1-942704-09-6

Published by Robin's Nest Productions, Inc.
P.O. Box 2092, Kahului, HI 96733

Edited by Janet Kobobel Grant and Julee Schwarzburg
Cover Images by Jenna Michelle Photography
Cover and interior design by Rachel Schwartz and Ken Raney

Printed in the United States of America by Bethany Press
Bloomington, Minnesota 55438

For the Bridegroom
who has invited all of us to the Wedding Feast
and patiently waits for us to RSVP.

One

Christy closed her eyes. She felt the tingling sensation rush against her skin as her slender frame dove beneath the frothy wave and came up on the other side with glistening dots of seawater clinging to her eyelashes. She smoothed back her long, nutmeg-brown hair so it cascaded over her shoulders like a mermaid's veil.

Christy looked across the shimmering saltwater and there he was. Only a few feet away, watching her with his familiar heart-crushing grin.

Todd.

He swam closer and his hand reached for hers. Their fingers knit together effortlessly as they had done a thousand times. He pulled her close. His screaming silver-blue eyes were lit by flecks of the golden California summer sunshine as they floated together and he whispered, "Forever, Kilikina."

Her heart melted every time she heard Todd say her Hawaiian name. He smiled at her and tilted his head the way he always did when he was about to kiss her. Christy anticipated the salty taste of his lips and the soaring feeling that still lifted her after all these years of being Todd Spencer's one and only.

She waited, eyes closed, heart ready, lips expectant.

Nothing happened.

Todd?

Forcing her eyes to open, Christy squinted and blinked. Todd was nowhere to be seen. She was alone. At home. On the couch.

On the floor in front of her was a box of newborn diapers. On the end table was an empty carton of key lime yogurt and an A, B, C puzzle missing the L and the X.

To Christy's right was an oversized chair, and wedged securely between the arms of the chair was a portable bassinet. Inside the bassinet was a baby. Her baby. Todd's baby. Their second child. A boy.

Cole.

The reality of her true life rushed over her like an invisible gust of ocean sea spray. All the bliss from her twenty-minute nap vaporized. Christy drew in a deep breath.

Still squinting, she forced her weary body to rise from the sofa. She shuffled over to the bassinet and smiled at the treasure nestled inside. Ever since Cole Bryan Spencer entered the world seven weeks ago on April 13 at nine pounds, eleven ounces, he had let his presence be known.

At this moment, though, he was asleep and appeared to be contentedly floating in the fairyland Christy wished she could return to. Sleep had become a luxury. Dreams were rare these days, as were any real-life dreamy kisses or intimate moments with Todd.

Christy leaned closer and smoothed her fingers over Cole's round head and his barely there fuzzy blond hair. The sensation reminded her of the baby chicks she loved to hold when she was a little girl growing up on the farm in Wisconsin. She hoped her son didn't mind her gesture of motherly affection because she loved his little noggin and everything else about him.

"Cole, you are the cutest chubby-cheeked, bright-eyed baby boy who has ever entered the world. You know that, don't you?"

He released a slight flutter of a breath. An "infant purr."

A toddler-sized thump sounded upstairs. Christy waited for the familiar squeak of Hana's bedroom door. At two and a half years old, big sister Hana seemed to be still deciding what she thought of this bundle of tough competition.

During Cole's first week, Hana discovered that her tiny brother could outwail her. Even during her worst meltdown moments, Cole's boisterous cries rose above hers. Hana took the challenge and increased her volume. The times when both Hana and Cole went into weeping and wailing mode in tandem were Christy's worst moments of motherhood.

Christy hadn't heard Hana's door open yet, so she started to get up to go check on her when her cell phone vibrated on the end table, sounding like a flustered bee. She reached for it and walked over to the foot of the stairs as she read the text from Todd.

WON'T BE HOME TILL SIX. HOW'S EVERYTHING GOING?

"Six?" Christy frowned and kept muttering to herself. "You said you were going to come home early today."

She tapped out a message reflecting her exasperation. It was the third night that week that Todd had stayed after hours at the high school where he taught in order to work on the upcoming missions trip to Africa. The group of seventeen students was leaving for Kenya in less than a month, and the full responsibility of organizing the trip was riding on Todd's shoulders.

WE HAVE NO GROCERIES HERE, REMEMBER? I SENT YOU A LIST EARLIER. YOU SAID YOU'D GET FOOD AND BE HOME BY FOUR TODAY. WHAT HAPPENED?

Just before hitting the Send button, Christy paused. She heard Hana's bedroom door open and the padding sound of Hana's little feet coming down the hall to the top of the stairs.

Christy knew Todd was drowning in details. There was no grace in the message she'd written. Her words would only ignite all the wrong kind of communication between them. They'd already floundered through two quarrels that week. Was it worth it to start a third one?

Deleting her text letter by letter, she retyped her reply.

OK.

That was all she wanted to communicate to him right now. His coming home late again was going to have to be OK. Having an empty fridge was OK. The baby was OK. Hana was OK. Everything was OK. Nothing was great. But everything, including Christy, was just *oh-kay*.

Todd texted back. THANKS FOR UNDERSTANDING. I LOVE YOU.

Christy pressed her lips together and frowned again.

If you knew how NOT understanding I feel right now, you would not be thanking me.

Hana appeared at the top of the stairs with her stuffed bunny under her arm and wearing her pacifier on her finger like a ring. "Mommy, I wake."

"Yes, I see." Christy kept her voice low and motioned for Hana to come join her on the couch. Christy sat down first and then welcomed Hana into her arms and up on her lap. "Did you have a good nap?"

Hana nodded. Her tousled blonde hair tickled Christy's neck as she cuddled up close. It seemed Hana realized that her baby brother wasn't occupying the prime real estate in Christy's arms, and she was determined to make up for the many lap cuddles she'd missed out on.

Christy hummed quietly and rocked Hana side to side. Christy loved Hana's tickly hair. It was beachy blonde like her daddy's and fell into feathery curls that skimmed the top of her shoulders. She had her daddy's silver-blue eyes, whereas Cole's eyes seemed to be staying closer to Christy's distinct blue-green mix.

"I your baby," Hana said happily.

"You're my big girl," Christy said softly.

"No, I your baby," Hana repeated. She stuck her pacifier in her mouth and kept swaying even though Christy had stopped.

What did that advice blog say about regression of the older sibling? Am I supposed to let her act out being a baby, or am I supposed to get her to focus on all the advantages of being a big sister? I can't remember.

Before Christy could select a course of action, another text from Todd redirected her attention.

OK IF I BRING 2 GUYS HOME WITH ME AT 6? WE'LL HAVE TEAM LEADER MEETING AT OUR HOUSE INSTEAD OF HERE.

All her frustrated feelings returned. With both her arms around Hana on her lap, Christy typed a concise summary of what she wanted to say to him earlier.

WE HAVE NO GROCERIES.

Todd replied with, WANT ME TO BRING PIZZA?

Before she could think through how she wanted to reply, another text popped up on her screen.

LASAGNA OVERLOAD AT MY HOUSE. YOU GUYS WANT SOME?

Christy stared at the message. The timing was just a little too perfect.

The text was from Jennalyn, her neighbor and new friend. More than once Jennalyn had shown up at just the right moment during their fledgling friendship. Christy responded to Jennalyn with a YES PLEASE!

She then tapped a reply to Todd. NO PIZZA. JENN IS BRINGING LASAGNA. SEE YOU AT 6.

Todd's reply was a hasty thumbs-up emoji. Christy was still frowning. She wasn't sure what had just happened, but she knew she and Todd needed to talk. They needed to sit down, look at each other, and have a real conversation with complete sentences. For weeks now their communication had been clipped messages, assumptions, and bits of information delivered on the go. Now they were down to a smattering of emojis. It made Christy feel hollow inside.

No wonder I dreamed about being loved by my husband. Right now, that sensation feels so foreign to me.

Christy put her phone down and gave Hana a squeeze. "Auntie Jennalyn is coming over."

Hana popped up from her cocoon position. With a gleeful look she said, "Baby Eden?"

Christy nodded and put her finger to her lips, hoping Hana wouldn't wake Cole. She was trying something different with her second baby by putting him down for naps in the middle of the living room instead of in his bedroom. She'd read about how to train babies to sleep anywhere by not isolating them at bedtime. Todd was all for trying it because they still had trouble getting Hana to go to sleep if all the conditions weren't just right.

Hana wiggled free of Christy's hug and scampered across the tile floor to the front door. She stood with her face pressed against the screen with her bunny under her arm. The pacifier had been cast aside along the way.

Christy got up and self-consciously tried to tuck the ends of her hair back into the messy bun on top of her head. It was her standard hairstyle these days: up and back and away from little fists that liked to grab the long strands and hold on. Christy's loose knit pants and even looser cotton top were also standard apparel these days.

She didn't feel like she needed to change because Jennalyn was coming over, but she still felt twinges of insecurity in spontaneous moments like this. It wasn't that Jennalyn made her feel that way. If anything, she had made Christy feel at ease from the beginning.

Jennalyn Marino had reached out to Christy six months ago. She came to Christy's door with a handmade invitation to a Christmas tea party and bravely said she was on the hunt for other moms in the neighborhood now that she just had a baby. She'd introduced herself as "Jenn," but Christy noticed that she'd written "Jennalyn" on the invitation.

When Christy asked if she preferred to be called Jenn or Jennalyn, her reply was, "Jennalyn. I usually introduce myself as Jenn because my husband, Joel, says it's easier for people to remember."

Jennalyn had paused a moment. Her dark eyes seemed to be searching Christy's to determine if she could share something deeper. She lowered her voice and confided, "My mother's name was Lyn. She passed away almost a year ago. I don't mind if people call me Jenn or Jennalyn. But for those who understand, when I hear Jennalyn, I feel a little closer to her."

Christy's heart went out to her and from that moment on, Christy felt invited into Jennalyn's life and into her inner circle of friends. They were young moms together. Neighbors and wives. Best of all, as Christy soon discovered, Jennalyn and Joel were God Lovers, as Todd called it. They made it clear that they loved God and were committed to living their lives as Christians.

When Jennalyn arrived with the lasagna, Christy was quickly clearing dirty dishes from the kitchen counter. She called out, "Come in," and Jennalyn entered carrying a large box and wearing her classy-looking sunglasses.

"Hi." Hana followed Jennalyn into the kitchen. "Hi."

"Hello, Hana girl. I like the pretty butterfly on your top."

Hana looked down and patted the butterfly. She scampered into the kitchen, following Jennalyn to the counter where she put the large box.

"You have no idea how much I appreciate this," Christy said. "Thank you for feeding my family tonight. And a few others."

"Baby Eden." Hana crawled up on a kitchen stool and tried to peer into the box.

"No," Jennalyn said, "Baby Eden isn't in the box. She's at home with her daddy. She's sleeping right now."

"My baby sleeping." Hana held up her bunny.

"Then I should be quiet, shouldn't I?" Jennalyn whispered. She gave Hana a smile and a kiss on the top of her dandelion head before turning her attention back to Christy. "How's your day been?"

"Good."

Jennalyn tilted her head and examined Christy more

closely over the top of her sunglasses as if she wasn't convinced.

Christy caught a whiff of the lasagna and shifted the attention to the gift inside the box. "It smells wonderful."

"Joel made it. He's trying out a new recipe. As I've told you before, the problem with being married to a chef is that he always cooks as if he's feeding a full restaurant on a Friday night and not just the two of us."

"Well, you know that Todd and I don't mind all the times you've shared the bounty with us." Christy lifted a large covered bowl from the box.

"That's a Caesar salad. There's chopped up anchovies in the dressing, so if you guys don't like anchovies, you might want to skip the salad. I think Joel put some garlic bread in there, too."

Hana scampered off to play with her toys and Christy put the salad in the nearly vacant refrigerator. "I need to start paying you guys for the ingredients, at least. This is the fourth time you've brought dinner to us this month."

"I've told you before, Christy. It's what my husband does. He loves to feed people. He won't accept payment of any sort, so you can drop that idea for good, okay?"

Christy met Jennalyn's gaze and offered her most sincere smile. "Thank you."

"You're welcome, but it's not a big deal. Really." Jennalyn slipped her sunglasses up and used them like a headband. Her dark hair had been long, like Christy's, up until a month ago when she took a big step and had it cut short for the first time since grade school. Jennalyn was able to donate her hair to a local organization that crafted wigs for cancer patients. Her new short style elongated her oval face and curved in just under her chin line. It gave her a flattering, sophisticated look.

"It is a big deal to me. Especially tonight."

"What's going on tonight?"

"Todd is bringing some guys home and we're low on groceries and . . ." Christy wished she hadn't started down this road. She tried to pull up a convincing smile. "Let's just say your timing was perfect."

"Do you need anything else? I've got lots of vegetables right now. Do you want me to go get some for you?"

Christy declined the offer, even though she didn't doubt that Jennalyn had an abundance of vegetables to share. Jennalyn and Joel had created a terraced box garden on their deck. It was an impressive design in the small space and had produced some of the sweetest carrots Christy had ever eaten.

"Unless," Christy added. "You have any more carrots. They were so good."

"No. We picked all the carrots last week. Weren't they good? We're definitely planting those again."

A piercing cry filled the house as Cole sounded one of his I'm-starving-come-feed-me-or-I-shall-perish alarms.

Jennalyn gave Christy the knowing nod of a fellow nursing mother and said, "I'll see you at my Summer Soiree next Thursday night, if not before."

"Thanks again. See you!" Christy called over her shoulder, giving a wave. She had already begun walking into the living room because her body was responding to the call of the wild child.

Jennalyn waved back and let herself out. Hana came over and planted her feet on the shaggy rug in the center of the living room. She put both her hands over her ears and filled her little chest with a gust of gumption. Christy caught her out of the corner of her eye and said, "Hana, no yelling!"

As soon as she said it, Christy realized she had just yelled at Hana in order to be heard over Cole's cries. As Christy lifted Cole, Hana ignored Christy's warning and let loose with her best competitive effort to match the decibel level of Cole's wail.

Christy went into multitasking mama mode. She tried to get Cole attached as quickly as possible, but as long as Hana was screaming, Cole wouldn't stay latched on. He cried even louder and that only sparked Hana to tune her pipes to a higher pitch.

The struggle was real.

Christy finally got both of them settled by resorting to a tactic she hated using. But at moments like this, it was the only thing that worked. She pressed the buttons on the remote as quickly as she could. All was calm as long as the man in the big yellow hat and his mischievous monkey were on the screen.

Christy cringed. A murmuring voice had invaded her thoughts.

You are a terrible mother.

Instead of ignoring the voice or putting the moment into perspective, Christy let the lie rest on her spirit. Her lips moved in an inaudible reply.

I know.

Two

The cloud of emotional discouragement floated over Christy for the rest of the night. Todd came home at six with two high school guys. They all helped themselves to the warmed-up lasagna, bread, and salad and then gathered around the fire pit on the deck to discuss the many unfinished details for the trip to Kenya.

Christy got Hana ready for bed and read her a story. All the while, she was wearing Cole strapped across the front of her in a comfortable baby sling. Christy placed her hand on Hana's forehead and prayed for her and blessed her before kissing the tips of her fingers and pressing the kiss to Hana's soft cheek.

"I want Daddy."

"I know, honey." Christy felt like saying, "So do I." Instead she said, "I'll ask him to come up and kiss you good night."

Hana rolled on her side, cuddled up with her bunny, and smiled sweetly. She didn't look like a child who was capable of throwing a shrieking tantrum the way she had that afternoon. Christy told herself for the tenth time that she needed to come up with a solution to that scenario before Hana got used to using her screaming to get what she wanted.

Christy clasped her hands as a support to the underside of the sling and took her time going down the stairs. She stepped out on the deck and Todd looked up. He raised his eyebrows, silently asking if everything was okay. His short hair seemed to take on a silvery white glow under the café lights that lined the deck.

"Hana was hoping you'd go up and tuck her in."

With a nod, Todd hopped up. He turned to the high school guys who had their phones out and were tapping away. "If you finish the checklist, could you go over the letter and make sure we didn't leave anything out?"

"Got it." One of the guys opened the binder on his lap and flipped through the many pages.

Christy thought of all the various outings she'd gone on with Todd over the years. He'd relied on her to be the organizer, and she often used binders to keep all the details in one place. It felt strange not to be involved in this huge endeavor and to have no idea what was on those many pages in the binder. No one had asked her to be involved or to help in any way with the trip, and she realized in the moment how sad and left out that made her feel. She reverted to her familiar role as a happy hostess.

"Can I get you guys anything?"

"No. I'm good."

"Me, too. Thanks, Mrs. Spencer."

Christy went back inside, feeling even more off balance. Todd's students were the only ones who ever called her "Mrs. Spencer." She hadn't spent much time around his students this year and had only visited his classroom twice. The first time was when she'd surprised Todd with cupcakes on his birthday, and the second visit was when Cole was a month old and Todd wanted her to bring him in for the first few minutes of a faculty meeting.

She knew so little about the everyday people and moments in her husband's life.

I can't even remember the names of the two guys sitting out on our deck right now.

Christy headed upstairs, feeling an urgency to be with Todd and find a way to connect with him, even if it meant simply being in the same space he was in for more than five minutes. She stopped outside Hana's open bedroom door and listened. Todd was singing to their little girl.

A softness settled on Christy's frenzied thoughts. It sounded like a lullaby, but Christy didn't recognize the tune and she couldn't quite hear the words. What she did hear were the sweet, "I love you forever and evers" the two of them exchanged.

A lump gathered in her throat.

I need you here for moments like this, Todd. It's going to be so difficult to do all this by myself while you're gone for weeks in Africa. And what if something were to happen to you? I don't want to raise our children by myself.

As Todd withdrew from Hana's room and quietly closed the door, Christy moved down the hall and tucked into their bedroom. She wasn't sure if Todd had seen her or not, and she knew he probably wouldn't want to see her now because an army of tears had collected along the ridge of her lower lids and were ready to take the field.

She wished she could control her emotions right now. Everything felt so overwhelming.

Christy stood just inside their bedroom waiting in the shadows as silently as she could. Todd didn't pass by and bound his way downstairs as she thought he would. Instead, he stopped and it seemed as if his large frame filled the doorway.

"You okay?" he asked softly.

Christy shook her head in the darkness but couldn't pull up a peep. Her throat had swollen and the tears were now charging down her face, throwing themselves over the cliff of her chin. The battle was on.

"Christy?" Todd turned on the light.

She squinted and turned her head as if she could still hide. Todd's strong arms were immediately around her, holding her, sheltering Cole who was bivouacked between them.

"What is it? What's wrong?"

"Nothing." The single word found its way out of her mouth in a squeak.

Todd looked dubious. "I'll tell the guys we're done for the night." He let go and headed for the stairs.

"Todd, no. I'm okay." She caught her breath. "It's nothing." Her voice wobbled. "Don't stop because of me."

Todd's expression seemed to be a mixture of relief and disbelief. He stepped closer and dried her tears by running his thumb under each eye. It was a gesture Christy had thought romantic and endearing in years past. Tonight his rough skin on her face irritated her. She pulled away and went to the nightstand to grab a handful of tissues.

"What's going on?" With waning patience, Todd stood with his arms folded, waiting for Christy to blow her nose.

"Sorry," she offered as a hopeful benediction to her frustrating burst of emotions. "Postpartum stuff. I'm fine."

Christy thought of how she used to hate it whenever Todd would question if a sudden burst of emotions was hormone related. Now she gladly used the excuse as a cover. But Todd wasn't buying it.

"You're mad at me, aren't you?"

Christy blinked and shook her head vigorously the way Hana used to during the potty-training phase whenever she was asked if she needed to go to the bathroom.

"Christy." Now Todd was the one who was clearly angry. "What is it?"

"I'm frustrated. But we can talk about it later."

"Let's talk about it now." He stood his ground. "You only use the word frustrated when you're trying to find a polite way to say you're ticked off at me."

Christy knew he was right, but she didn't want to admit it.

"Just tell me. What are you mad about?"

Cole seemed to pick up on the tension and started squirming in the confined sling. He let out a squawk, and Christy was certain one of his Goliath wails would soon follow. In her calmest voice Christy said, "I need to feed him. After the guys leave, we can talk."

Todd didn't move right away. He seemed to be waiting to see if Cole was going to follow through with his wailing or if Christy was only using their son as an excuse to put off their necessary discussion.

Cole bellowed loudly and Todd left the bedroom, closing the door behind him. Christy lowered herself into her snuggle chair in the corner and got Cole settled before he got too worked up. She thought about what she was going to say to Todd once their conversation took place.

How can I tell him that I'm mad that he's going to Africa? Christy shifted in the chair and smoothed her palm over Cole's fuzzy head. *Why did we all think this big missions trip was such a great idea anyhow?*

Christy knew the answer. Last summer their closest friends, Eli and Katie, had stayed with them for several months. They lived in Kenya and served with an organization that brought clean water to remote villages. Katie had come to California for her father's funeral and ended up staying because she was experiencing difficulties during her first trimester of her first pregnancy and it wasn't safe for her to travel.

The four long-time friends spent many evenings sitting around the fire pit, and one of those nights one of them started dreaming like a teenager and they all said, "Yes! Let's do this! It's going to be amazing!"

But last July Christy had no idea she was going to have a baby the following April. Nor had they estimated how busy Eli was going to be with all the group trips he'd set up while he was in the U.S. Todd took on more responsibility than most group leaders because he knew how much it would help Eli and Katie if he set up all the travel details .

Christy drew in a deep breath.

If I tell Todd tonight how much I'm struggling right now and say to him, "Please don't go. I really, really, really need you to stay home with me," would he consider my needs to be his greatest priority and pull out of the trip?

She wasn't sure he would. It seemed likely that the only way Todd would pull out of the trip would be if he found someone to take his place.

But who would that be?

Christy remembered how discouraged Todd was two months ago when three of the other adult leaders pulled out, all for good reasons. Eight of the high schoolers who originally signed up had backed out, but that was helpful because the group was a bit more manageable with only seventeen students traveling together, especially now that Todd was the only adult leader.

What if they postponed the trip for a year? They could all go next summer. They'd have more time to plan, and I'd be able to help out more. Maybe I could even go with the group.

Christy liked her idea. She was formulating the best way to present it to Todd when the bedroom door opened and Todd entered carrying two glasses of water. "I thought you might be thirsty."

He placed the glass on the end table and lowered himself to the edge of the bed. His voice was low and his expression one of concern. "I know that sometimes crying makes you thirsty."

Christy looked at the glass of water. It was an unusual gesture from her husband. A cup of cold water.

A Cup of Cold Water in Jesus' Name. That was the slogan for the missions trip and had been the theme for the fund-raisers.

Christy stared at the glass of clean water waiting for her and she knew.

She couldn't jeopardize this trip by begging Todd to cancel it. Not after all the heroic efforts the entire school had made to support the teens. And she certainly didn't want to be the reason that the people in the assigned village had to wait another year before having access to clean water.

No. Todd needed to keep his promise. That was the kind of man he was. And Christy needed to be brave and find contentment because that was the kind of woman she wanted to be.

"Thank you," she whispered.

"You're welcome." Todd stretched out on the bed on his side, gazing at Christy. "What do you need, Kilikina?"

His question, like the unrequested glass of water, caught

her off guard.

"What do you mean?"

"I mean, how can I be a better husband? What can I do to help out with the kids? You have been doing everything lately. You have good reason to be mad at me. I just now remembered that you asked me this morning to get groceries on the way home. I completely forgot. I'm sorry."

"It's okay." Christy thought of how everything that day had been OK. "It all worked out. Jennalyn brought the lasagna and salad over. But we are low on diapers."

"I can get groceries tomorrow after school and get all the big stuff—diapers, laundry soap—whatever we need. I'll drop it off before the Gathering."

Christy had forgotten about the Friday Night Gathering for high schoolers that Todd had been leading for over five years. For some reason she was thinking today was Wednesday.

"What else can I do?" Todd asked. "Do you want me to call your mom and see if she can come help out on Saturday?"

"No. I wanted to hold off asking her for a while because she did so much for us the first few weeks after Cole arrived."

"It's been a few weeks. I don't think she'd mind coming over on Saturday."

"Why on Saturday?"

"It's the Senior Awards Breakfast. I agreed to present the awards this year. Otherwise I would have tried to get out of going. I wrote it on the calendar in the kitchen, but I don't think we've talked about it."

"No. We didn't talk about it."

"Right after the breakfast is the final meeting with all the parents of the students who are going on the trip. We should be done around one o'clock. Hopefully sooner. That's why I thought you should see if your mom is available."

"Okay. I'll ask her." Christy thought Todd sounded more concerned than he should.

"And then a week from Sunday I'm speaking at baccalaureate. I know I told you about that."

Christy nodded. She could see the stress lines beginning to deepen across his forehead. Her heart went out to him. Todd was dealing with so much right now. She wasn't the only one who was exhausted.

For some reason her thoughts went to an image she held in her memory of her husband on Saturday mornings. He'd be the first one up. From her cozy side of the bed, Christy would watch him with one eye open as he pulled on his swim trunks and grabbed his Rancho Corona University hoodie from the closet. Todd had no worry lines across his handsome face on those Saturday mornings. He was always happy when he headed out on "dawn patrol" to surf with his friends and get his energy renewed from the ocean waves he loved so much. It had been months since her surfer boy had found time to go to the beach.

Cole had finished and released one of his cute, quivering-lip, contented purrs.

"Here." Todd got up from the bed and reached for Cole. "I'll take him." With experienced pats strategically administered to his son's back, Todd got a nice burp out of him.

"Are we okay, then?" Todd asked as he cradled Cole in his brawny arms. "Is there anything else?"

"No. We're okay. Everything is okay." Christy didn't feel the same sense of discouragement she'd felt earlier when the hissing accusations that she was a terrible mother had settled on her spirit. Nor did she carry any more anger about Todd's schedule and the fact that he was going to be away for so long. It all changed inside her when Todd offered her the cup of water.

Another memory came to Christy and she smiled to herself.

"What?" Todd stood in front of her, rocking Cole but watching her expression.

"I was just remembering something Katie and I used to say to each other when we felt the opposition coming on strong."

"What was it?"

Christy quoted the line. "'When the enemy comes knocking at your door, step back and say, "Jesus, it's for you."'"

Todd grinned and nodded. "That's good. I needed to hear that."

Cole lifted his head, bobbled a bit, and then rested his cheek against Todd's shoulder.

"I think I have been trying to answer too many knocks on too many doors this week," Todd said. "I'm going to remember that."

"Me, too," Christy said.

"By the way, did I tell you that David agreed to lead the Gathering for the rest of June and July?"

Christy was surprised. She hadn't seen her brother for several weeks and knew that he and his girlfriend, Fina, had been having a hard time trying to work out their schedule so they could see each other. Fina had come over earlier that week and told Christy that between her classes at Long Beach State and David's two jobs, the only time the two of them saw each other was on Sundays.

"I'm amazed he's got the time."

"He said his work schedule changes next week and he wanted to do it." Todd's handsome face took on a lopsided sort of grin. "I'm sure my begging and pleading with him only slightly influenced his decision."

"What did you say to him?"

"I told him I needed to spend time with my family."

Todd's sincere expression comforted Christy. She knew the next few weeks were going to be difficult. But Todd was trying. And right now, that meant the world to her.

Three

Christy and Todd's conversation on Thursday night helped her uneasiness a lot. But what helped even more was that she made herself stop everything and take a nap while Hana and Cole were napping on Friday.

Todd made good on his promise to pick up groceries, and while he was at the Gathering, Christy gratefully restocked the pantry and organized the refrigerator. It was crazy how much this simple chore had felt overwhelming to her since Cole's birth. She'd only gone to the grocery store twice with both the kids in the last month, and both times her anxiety was way more than it should have been for such a simple, familiar task. She now felt like she could handle her next trip with aplomb. They were well stocked thanks to Todd so trips to the grocery store would now yield only two or three bags of items instead of the big box sort of shopping Todd had done.

On Saturday morning Christy made smoothies for herself and Hana with fresh fruit and yogurt. They sat together at the kitchen counter, giving each other playful side-eyes while they slurped through their straws.

Christy had made good on her promise to ask her mom to come over later that morning. Just knowing that she had backup coming that day had put her in a more relaxed mood.

Todd came tromping down the stairs and said, "Call me if you need anything."

He gave Christy a kiss on the cheek and brushed a quick peck on the top of Hana's head. Unleashing his phone from the charger, he checked the screen. "I'm late. I love you both."

"Daddy!" Hana slid off the counter stool. "Wait! Daddy! Come back!" She ran to him and Todd scooped her up and hugged her close.

"I have to go for a little while, Sunshine. I'll be back. We'll have the whole day to spend together tomorrow." He put her down and strode to the back door.

"No, Daddy. No." Hana started crying.

Todd gave Christy a pained look and made his escape, locking the door behind him so Hana couldn't turn the knob and follow him. Hana put her hands over her ears and let fly with her newly crafted siren of a shriek.

Not surprisingly, Hana's outburst woke Cole and now he was wailing from his portable crib in the downstairs guest room. Christy dealt with Hana first by bending to her daughter's eye level, getting her attention, and with a stern expression holding up her hand like a crossing guard. Hana knew the signal because Christy used it to get Hana to stop in parking lots and before crossing the street.

Christy held her firm expression and her palm-open stop sign in front of Hana. Hana caught her breath and was about to release her second round when Christy cupped her open palm across Hana's open mouth, stifling her scream. Cole was at full force now in the adjoining guest room.

"Hana, no. No screaming." Christy removed her hand.

"I want Daddy!" Hana wailed.

"I know, honey. He'll be back. You need to go finish your smoothie while I go take care of your brother." Christy pointed to the counter and waited to see that Hana remained subdued and was complying with her strict instructions.

Once Hana was seated and had not attempted another shriek, Christy hurried into the guest room. She picked up Cole and immediately discovered he'd had a diaper blowout that had gone through everything.

"I can see what kind of day this is going to be." The buoyancy she felt earlier was quickly draining away.

Christy completed the toxic waste cleanup like the pro she'd become. With Cole fresh and friendly once again, she started the washing machine, strapped Cole into her handy front sling and got Hana going on a new project of sitting on the rug in the living room and putting all the blue balls in one mixing bowl and all the red balls in another bowl. Sorting things up was one of Hana's favorite things to do lately.

A knock sounded at the front door. Hana jumped up and tried to open the door. Christy thought it was too early for her mom to be here. She had a feeling it might be Jennalyn and Eden. They usually went for a walk in the mornings and often stopped by to see if Christy wanted to join them.

To Christy's surprise, it was her brother, David.

"Hey, Christy. Do you have a minute? Sorry to drop in like this."

"Of course. Come in."

"Hi, Hana."

Hana turned shy and trotted over to the mixing bowls

where she proceeded to dump out all the balls.

"Would you like something to drink?" Christy asked. "Are you hungry?" It was her automatic response whenever anyone came to their home. She always wanted to make sure they felt comfortable.

"No. I'm heading to work in about half an hour, but I need some advice. Is Todd home?"

Christy shook her head. "Senior brunch and then a meeting for the missions trip."

David nodded. He was tall and ruddy like their dad. He'd been working on a house-renovation demolition crew for the past four months and was more muscular than Christy had ever seen him. Ever since he graduated from college and started pursuing a serious relationship with Fina, David had seemed more like a friend to Christy and less like her baby brother.

"Sit down. What's going on? Or did you only want to talk to Todd?"

"No. I wanted to run something past both of you, but now that I'm here, I'm kinda glad it's just you." David bent his long legs and lowered himself onto the edge of the well-worn sofa. Hana scurried over and held up a book and then showed him a toy mermaid doll Aunt Marti had brought for her on their last Family Night Dinner.

"Come here, Hana," Christy said. "I'll fix a cozy corner for you and you can look at all your books."

"Cozy-cozy-corn." Hana hurried back to the basket to scoop up more books.

Christy spread the soft throw blanket over the comfortable chair by the window and got Hana set up in her special reading nook. This little mothering trick had helped Christy corral Hana many times over the past few months when people came to visit. Hana loved books and somehow associated the extra preparations as making the reading time a special treat.

Hana settled in and Christy sat on the other end of the sofa, waiting for David to reveal his mysterious questions.

"So, you know how Fina is going to be finished with classes next week?"

Christy nodded.

"And you know how she wanted to get into the graduate program in Indiana next year?"

Christy vaguely remembered. She'd been in and out of that conversation at the last Family Night Dinner because of Cole.

"Well, she found out she qualifies for a special accelerated program if she starts in August. It's exactly what she wanted."

"Wow." Christy had anticipated that Fina would get into a master's program at one of the universities nearby. She didn't realize Indiana was not only a serious consideration, but a better option for her.

David's face took on a warm glow as he raised his bushy eyebrows and said, "So, I think I want to marry her before August."

"Oh!" Christy hadn't expected that. "Wow! Well, have you and Fina talked it through?"

"A little."

"What do you mean, 'a little'?"

"She knows, I mean, we've talked about it."

"You've talked about graduate school or about getting married?"

"Both. But the thing is, I have to ask her dad. You've met her parents. They're sort of old world, and Fina thinks he'd like it if I approached them first in this traditional way before

I ask her."

Christy tried to let all the information settle in. When Fina decided to move to Newport Beach last August so she could be near David, she and David had come to Christy and Todd together and told them their plans for her to go to school in Long Beach and find a place for her to live. They had been straightforward, and it was clear they'd talked it through together ahead of time. This plan of David's felt quite different.

"It would be a really short engagement, but I think Fina would be okay with that. To me, it doesn't make any sense for her to go to Indiana and for me to be stuck here working when we could be married and I could work there while she finishes school."

"So, what exactly did you want advice on from Todd and me?"

"What do you think about us getting married? I mean, I haven't talked this through with anyone else yet. Not Mom and Dad or anyone. I need advice."

"Okay. Have you or Fina said anything to Bob and Marti?" Christy had to ask because when Fina moved to Newport Beach, she moved in with Christy and David's wealthy aunt and uncle who lived nearby in a large beachfront home.

The room-and-board arrangements had been ideal for Fina because she was rarely home. Aunt Marti, however, had often expressed her disappointment over Fina's busy life. Marti's hobby was renovating. She liked to redesign houses as well as people. Christy had been Marti's frequent remodeling focus until she started having babies. Marti wasn't especially interested in babies or in young moms who seemed to have forgotten how to wear makeup or style their hair.

Fina, on the other hand, was striking with her high cheekbones and short caramel-colored hair. She was a fit volleyball player and an especially polite young woman. Christy felt sympathetic toward Marti over the many hoped-for lunches and shopping trips with Fina that had never happened.

Knowing how much Marti would want to be involved in every detail of David and Fina's wedding meant that the timing of when Marti would be brought into the plan was going to be another factor David needed to consider.

"Good point," David said. "I'm sure Aunt Marti will be a big help with the party stuff. She's good at all that. But the proposal is just between Fina and me."

"That sounds good," Christy said with a nod.

"So what can you tell me? How was it with you and Todd? I wasn't paying attention much when you guys got engaged."

"Do you mean, how did Todd propose?"

"No, I know it was with candy hearts or something. But I don't know how you guys knew you were ready to get married. All I remember is that Todd told me once that 'when you know, you know.'"

Christy nodded. That sounded about right. It also sounded like something her husband would say. "Do you and Fina 'know'?"

"Yes. No doubt. We want to spend the rest of our lives together. I mean, she's the one for me. I'm pretty confident if she were sitting here, she'd tell you that I'm the one for her."

"Just pretty confident? Not completely confident?"

"Well, yes. I mean, we haven't talked through what all the steps would look like. But we both know we want to get married one day. She's just really focused on finishing school. So this way we can do that. It's the only way we'd go to Indiana together."

Christy felt a tenderness for her man-child brother. David was younger than Christy, and somehow she kept being surprised at his milestones. He had graduated from college last year, and now he was talking about getting married. In only a few weeks!

"I love her, Christy. She knows I do. She's told me she loves me. I just don't know if I'm doing this the right way. Tell me. What do you think?"

Christy reached over and gave her brother's big, rough hand a squeeze. "I think you and Fina make a wonderful couple, and I love the thought of you getting married before she starts school in August."

"You do?" David's expression brightened.

"Yes. I do."

"You don't think I'm been impatient? I mean, that's the only thing I keep thinking. Love is patient, right?"

"I think it doesn't really matter what I think. The only thing that's important is that you find out what Fina is thinking."

"I don't want to ruin it. I wanted to kinda surprise her when I propose."

"But you need to prepare her a little bit, don't you think?"

David furrowed his eyebrows again. "How do I do that?"

Christy remembered the way her brother was often blunt and uncomplicated in his opinions, his taste in food, and in his decisions. Maybe he wasn't wired to navigate a major discussion like this without simply coming out and asking Fina to marry him. All or nothing.

"Tell me what you were thinking. What's your plan?"

"First I'd call her dad, like I said. I'd tell him I promised to take care of her and love her and ask for both his permission to marry her and his advice."

"That sounds wise. And it's sweet of you to do that, David. It really is."

"I'm not trying to be sweet. I'm trying to honor her family's way of doing things."

"Right. So, then, what about Fina? Would you get a ring and just surprise her and propose? Or do you think she'd want to pick it out?"

"She has the ring."

"She does?"

"It was her great-grandmother's wedding ring. Her mom gave it to her. She showed it to me once. She doesn't wear it. She said she wanted to save it because she wanted it to be her engagement ring one day."

Christy was thinking that was a good sign. If Fina was letting David know she already had a ring and had shown him where the ring was, it was likely that a proposal was on her mind as well.

"Fina probably doesn't want an elaborate proposal." Christy realized she'd said her thought out loud. In the past year that David and Fina had been dating, Christy had gotten to know her pretty well, and she loved her like a sister already. "But I'm guessing she would want a big wedding in Glenbrooke since her family is there."

"Actually, we talked about that one time. She said she always wanted to have a small ceremony at the beach at sunset and then a big reception in Glenbrooke after the honeymoon."

"She told you that?"

David nodded. "She asked what I thought and I said it would be a pain to have to wear dress shoes 'cuz they'd get filled with sand."

Christy grinned. "She's ready."

"Ready?"

"Yes. She's ready for you to propose. If she's talked about

specifics like the location and the reception and the ring . . ."

Christy felt so happy for her brother. "Fina is ready for you to propose."

David looked both relieved and nervous. "I guess I'll call her dad then. And try to figure out how to get the ring."

"Is it in her room at Bob and Marti's?"

"Yeah, she has this music box that opens and it's in there. The music box was her grandmother's or great-grandmother's. It's a little Swiss house."

"A chalet?"

"Yeah, I guess. You lift the lid and it plays music."

"I've seen it on her dresser." Christy sat up a little straighter. "Why don't you leave that part to me? I'll get the ring. Just let me know when you want it."

For the first time since their unexpected conversation began, David looked relieved. "Can you get it by Monday?"

"I think so. Sure. I should be able to." Christy wasn't sure how she'd pull it off, but she loved the thrill of the adventure. "Have you thought through how you're going to ask her?"

He confidently nodded. "We have this bench we like to go sit on to watch the sunset. It's in Corona del Mar up on the ridge. I thought we'd go there, like any other time when we meet up. That way she won't suspect anything. I already wrote out what I'm going to say. I think I have it memorized."

"You do? What are you going to say?"

David jutted out his chin. "That's for Fina to hear first."

If Christy had at all doubted her brother's maturity or the ability to honor and love and care for Fina as his wife, all hesitancy was gone. He was ready.

Now all Christy had to do was figure out how to get the ring by Monday.

Four

"So?" Katie's freckled face filled the screen of Christy's phone. "How do you plan to pull off the heist?"

Christy turned down the volume, feeling like a teenager who was trying to hide out in her room to make her phone calls. Her mom had arrived about an hour ago, and as soon as Christy got Cole down for his morning nap, she went upstairs to do the same. At least, that was her plan until Katie texted and asked if Christy was available for a call. It was the middle of the night in Kenya where Katie and Eli lived at the Brockenhurst Conference Center near Nairobi. But Katie's life with an infant meant she was up at all hours.

A baby-sized squeak of a cry came through Katie's end of the phone.

"Is he still awake?" Christy asked. When their call began almost ten minutes ago, Katie said her little guy needed to get his wiggles out before going back to sleep.

In a swish, the view changed from Katie's face to her six-month-old son lying on the couch beside her. He was still kicking his legs in his feetsie pajamas and looking perfectly content to be doing his running-in-place exercises at midnight.

"Where does he get so much energy? That's what I want to know."

Katie moved his little arm in a wave to Christy and in a baby voice said, "Hi, Auntie Christy!"

"Hello, Jimmy. You are so adorable."

"To look at him, you'd never know that only a half hour ago he was screaming out all the high notes of the national teething anthem. He's got a second tooth coming in on the bottom."

"Already?" Christy tried to remember when Hana got her first tooth. "Jimmy sure likes to get a running start in life."

"I know. Did I tell you that Eli's mom is convinced I was pregnant earlier than all the calculations? She doesn't think he came early. Of course, we don't know his exact birth weight, but there was nothing preemie about him."

"I still can't believe you gave birth in a tent out in the tea fields, Katie. I told Sierra your whole story when I talked to her a few weeks ago, and she said, 'Only you, Katie.'"

Katie laughed. "The only reason she said that is because I was the one who was always saying, 'Only you, Sierra' back when we met in England. That seems like a lifetime ago, doesn't it? Our big missions trip to England. We thought we were so daring and independent. I just remember feeling like I was loud and annoying because I was so out of my element and so insecure."

"Who would have ever thought back then that you'd end up becoming a real 'Missionary Woman' in Africa and giving birth in a tea field?"

"Not me, that's for sure!" Katie shook her head so her red hair swished just above the top of her shoulders. "I hope you didn't make Jimmy's birth sound uncivilized. You told Sierra I had a doctor with me as well as a skilled midwife, didn't you?"

"I did."

"Because I think it was probably more pleasant than some hospital deliveries. Eli was a champion and Jimmy was fine. Plus, I definitely had the best view ever out the door of the tent."

"The only view that sticks in my mind is the picture of you in the wheelbarrow on that muddy trail back to the conference center the next day."

"I'm so glad Eli took that picture. I told him I'm going to frame it and put it in Jimmy's room. When he grows up and tries to give me a hard time about anything at all, I'll point to the picture and remind him of what I endured bringing him into this world."

Christy had heard the details many times about the early morning walk Katie and Eli had taken into the beautiful, expansive fields that bordered the ministry conference center where she and Eli as well as his parents made their home. According to all the dates and measurements Katie had been given, she still had at least three weeks before she should expect to go into labor. The original plan was that she'd go into Nairobi and stay with friends a week or so before her due date so they could drive her to the hospital when the time came.

Instead, Katie's water broke on their morning walk, and it was clear that she couldn't trot herself back to the conference center, let alone be driven down the bumpy, curving highway that would take them into the congested morning traffic in

Nairobi.

One of the overseers of the tea field had set up a tent on one of the hills since it was rainy season. When the first contraction overwhelmed her, the overseer willingly let Eli and Katie take over the tent while he rushed back to the conference center to bring help.

Christy could picture it all vividly because when she and Todd had gone to Eli and Katie's wedding in Kenya, they had all taken a leisurely morning stroll through the tea fields and had a picnic on the highest knoll.

Christy also knew that with all the medical missionaries who came to Brockenhurst on breaks from their various villages throughout Eastern Africa, it wasn't difficult to find experienced assistants who brought everything they needed to the tent and attended to Katie with special care.

But still, Christy found it so fitting that her favorite Peculiar Treasure would give birth in a tea field in Africa. Of course she would.

The image on the phone screen swooped around the room as Katie readjusted. When the image settled, Christy could see that Katie was holding Jimmy so his strong little head rested in the curve between her neck and shoulder.

"Okay," Katie said. "Enough reminiscing about my birthing story. We've talked about that too many times already. Let's get back to a much more important topic. Christy. Do you have enough rope and one of those metal claw things so you can break in through Fina's bedroom window and steal her ring?"

"What?"

"It's a simple question. Yes or no? Do you have enough rope?"

"No." Christy grinned. "I'll have to find a reason to go upstairs and slip in and out of her room when no one is watching."

"Good thing she's living at Bob and Marti's house. You wouldn't be able to pull off your *Mission Impossible* skills like that if you had to pick the lock on the front door of her apartment or scale down the wall from the roof."

"Katie, it's not as cartoon crazy as you're making it sound."

"Oh, come on. Let me have some fun imagining you wearing a stocking-cap mask and toting around a flashlight the size of a loaf of French bread. Ooo. French bread. Doesn't that sound good right now?"

Christy agreed that it did. Their phone calls usually included lots of sharing about their mutual struggles with sleep and weight loss and all the other changes pregnancy had done to their bodies. Talking about food had become a recent addition to their conversations. It often included Katie dreaming about foods she'd decided she should no longer eat or foods she couldn't find in Africa.

"Warm French bread with melted butter. No, melted garlic butter." Katie tilted her head back as if she was in agony. "Why didn't you tell me I'd be starving all the time once I turned into a human food truck?"

Little James Andrew Lorenzo squirmed. Katie kissed him on the side of his head and said, "You were worth all the agony and deprivation, my son. Hush now. Go to sleep."

Katie lowered her voice and said, "So, I don't think you told me. When are you going to pull off the heist?"

"I don't know. Probably this weekend. I'm beginning to regret that I offered to do it."

"I wish I were there. I'd do it. I've always wanted to give my Cat Woman skills a try. And getting to wear a turtleneck with black Spandex pants would be the best. They'd call me Muffin Top the Cat Burglar."

Christy laughed. "I wish you were here. I'd gladly turn the assignment over to you."

"Call me as soon as you can and tell me how it all goes down with the thievery and the proposal," Katie said.

"I will." Christy could hear Cole crying downstairs. It was about time for him to be fed again. "I should go, Katie."

"Okay. Call me. Love you."

"Love you, too, Katie girl."

Feeling revived from talking with Katie, Christy went downstairs where her mom was doing her best to rock baby Cole and convince him to try the pacifier. He wasn't turning into a Binky Baby the way Hana had been and at times still was.

Christy took over with the real stuff and her mom took Hana into the kitchen to finish their Play-Doh art project on the counter. Christy's thoughts were still percolating about how she was going to get Fina's ring. Everything in her wanted to spill the whole plan to her mom, but Christy had promised David she wouldn't say anything. She probably shouldn't have been so chatty about the details with Katie. But who would Katie tell? Besides, David planned to tell their mom and dad on Sunday, after he'd made the call to Fina's dad.

As Christy listened to her mom's soothing voice going over the four colors of Play-Doh to Hana, she thought about how good it felt to have this inside connection with her brother. She and David had never shared something close like this. Even though it felt foreign to be keeping the secret from her mom, being included in David's grand plan had definitely lifted Christy's postpartum gloom.

Christy wasn't the only one going through the day with a more hopeful expression on her face. Todd came home a little after two o'clock. Christy's mom had just left and both kids were down for naps. While her mom was there, Christy managed to finish the laundry and the dishes, cut up vegetables for dinner, and take a long shower. The almost waist-length strands of her wet hair, split ends and all, fell over her shoulders as she let it air dry.

Todd entered the kitchen with a grin and with one hand behind his back. He smiled at his mermaid of a wife and pulled out a big bouquet of white carnations.

With a happy, "ohh!" Christy rushed to him and put her arms around his middle. She lifted her chin and received a very nice kiss. And then another and another.

Drawing back and taking the flowers from him, Christy smiled broadly. "You didn't have to do this."

"Yes, I did." Todd leaned in to give Christy another kiss. "You deserve flowers every day. Thank you for being my wife."

"Thank you for being my husband."

Todd reached behind Christy and grabbed a handful of grapes she'd washed and put out for snacking.

"How did everything go?" Christy placed the flowers in the clean, empty sink and went on the hunt for a vase.

"Good. We had four more girls drop out. We're down to thirteen students and me. I don't think we'll have any more changes." He bobbed his head as he munched on the grapes. "Seems like this is it. It's a good number. We're okay without another leader. We can all fit into one van. It's lookin' good."

The relief in Todd's expression and outlook were obvious. Christy told him how glad she was to see him this way.

"There's just one thing I wish were different." He gave her a lingering gaze. "I wish you were going."

"I know. Me, too."

Todd kept gazing at her. "You're beautiful."

Christy felt her face getting warm. First the flowers and

now the compliments. It had been a long time since she'd felt this kind of affection from her husband.

"Come here." Todd wrapped his arms around her and held her close, kissing her tenderly on her eyelids, nose, and lips. "I've missed this," he murmured.

"Me, too."

They held each other for a long moment. Christy found herself memorizing all over again the scent of her husband's skin and the strength of his arms. She knew her wet hair was leaving marks on his cotton shirt and water on his arms. Todd didn't seem to care.

"What do we have going on tonight?" he whispered in her ear. "After the kids go to bed?"

"This," Christy murmured back.

"Good." Todd kissed her earlobe and asked, "Do we have any plans for dinner?"

Christy reluctantly pulled back, untangling her hair from his embrace. "Well . . ."

Todd drew back and tried to focus on her at arm's length. "What? Did I forget something?"

"No. You didn't forget anything. I was just thinking that since we had to cancel going to Family Night Dinner last month, Uncle Bob said we should come another time. Anytime, is what I think he said. So, maybe we could ask him if tonight works for them."

Todd seemed surprised at Christy's suggestion. "Are you sure you're up for it?"

"I am. I'm doing well. No emotional meltdowns on the horizon. At least, none for me. I can't promise what your children will do if we go to Bob and Marti's, though."

"*My* children, huh?" Todd reached for another handful of grapes. "Does that mean when they both behave like angels, they're *your* children?"

Christy grinned. "Sure. Why not? I like that arrangement."

What Christy was really trying to do was figure out how to get Fina's ring. She needed a natural reason to show up at Bob and Marti's beachfront house since she hadn't been over there since Cole was born.

Todd shook his head at Christy's banter and seemed to be warming up to the idea of going to Bob and Marti's for dinner. "Do you want to call your uncle? Or should I?"

"Do you mind calling? I'm going to put these beautiful flowers in some water. Thank you again. I love having fresh flowers in the house."

Todd made the call and with very little hassle, their dinner plans were made. "All set. Bob said he has chicken and green beans but asked if we could stop by the store and get some bread."

"Perfect! Let's get French bread with garlic butter." The suggestion tumbled out of Christy's mouth.

Todd seemed amused at the preciseness of all her requests all of a sudden. For weeks she'd barely been able to rub two thoughts together to form an opinion, let alone a decision. And here she was, suggesting dinner plans and deciding on what kind of bread they'd take, before they even got to the store.

"Okay. French bread with garlic butter it is."

Hana came downstairs from her nap, and Todd scooped her up and had a sweet forehead-to-forehead conversation with her. Then Todd fell into his usual routine of kicking off his shoes, going into the living room, and turning on the TV. When it came on, Christy could hear that it was still set on the home-decorating channel she liked to watch and not the news channel Todd liked to watch for their detailed surf report.

It surprised her that he wasn't changing the channel. She glanced over and saw that Hana had climbed up in his lap and he was staring at the TV as if there were an advertisement for a monster-size burrito and he hadn't eaten for two days. He pointed the remote at the screen and called out, "Christy, you have to see this. Come quick."

Christy recognized the voice on the television before she saw the screen. She stood beside the couch and stared with Todd at the commercial for a new show called "Diner Do-Overs." She pointed and looked at Todd. No words tumbled out of her mouth.

He turned up the volume even more, and together they heard the end of the commercial.

"I'm Rick Doyle. Join my wife, Nicole, and me as we crisscross the nation and bring dilapidated diners back to life." A montage followed of handsome, dark-haired Rick wearing a construction hat inside a tiny café and pointing to a wall that was falling down. Nicole was at a soda fountain counter, laying down paint chips like playing cards, and a large cook in a dirty apron was shaking his head at all of them.

The final clip was of the outside of a beautifully renovated diner with tall Rick standing proud with his arm resting on Nicole's shoulders, their little girl standing in front of them, and a line of townsfolk lined up ready to go inside.

The commercial ended with the day the new show would air running across the bottom of the screen.

Speechless, Christy turned to Todd. She had dated Rick in high school, Todd had been roommates with him in college, and Katie dated and broke up with Rick soon after Christy and Todd were married. Rick and Nicole had been in their lives right after Christy and Todd moved to Newport

Beach, but then a job opportunity for Rick took them to New York. They kept up through Christmas cards and sometimes through updates on social media.

"Did you know?" Todd asked.

"No. I can't believe it. Their own television show?"

"Apparently so."

"They look happy," Christy ventured. "And look how big their daughter is. I can't even remember her name."

"Don't look at me. I can barely remember our own daughter's name." He leaned in close so that their noses touched as she looked up at him. "What's your name again?"

"Hana!" she shouted and then started giggling.

"I thought your name was Sunshine." Todd teased.

"No, I'm Hana."

Christy loved watching them play this way. Her mind replayed the commercial she had just seen.

The camera sure loves Rick. He looked like an experienced movie star already. And Nicole looked so good! She's lost a lot of weight. And her short hair is so flattering.

Christy tried to let it all soak in.

I've gotta tell Katie. She won't believe this.

Five

"Todd, could you rewind it?"

He pushed the button on the remote control, and Christy hurried to get her phone. "That's good. You can stop there. Keep the volume up." She videoed the end of the commercial where it was easiest to see Rick's face and the shot of Rick with Nicole and their daughter.

"What are you doing?" Todd asked.

"I want to send this to Katie. She's never going to believe this."

"Do you want me to record the series?"

"Sure."

Katie responded to the video text right away and the two of them went back and forth with a stream of texts that were a patchwork of their collective memories of what it was like to have Rick Doyle in their lives.

JUST THINK. YOU CAN HAVE RICK AND NICOLE VISIT YOUR LIVING ROOM EVERY WEEK! WOW. AS

DOUG WOULD SAY, THAT'S AWESOME.

Christy was pretty sure Katie was being her normal, sarcastic self. She still seemed a little bruised over her relationship with Rick. Of course, Katie and Rick had gotten much more serious than Christy ever had during her sophomore year of high school. Rick had started talking of marriage when he and Katie were together. Katie was the one who broke it off, and yet sometimes she still referred to him as "Slick Rick."

Katie rallied with her final text. LET'S JUST SAY YOU AND I ARE BEYOND BLESSED THAT WE ENDED UP WITH WHO WE DID.

I AGREE.

That evening Christy realized that the easiest part about her covert operation to nip Fina's ring had been Todd's call to Uncle Bob to arrange the time for them to go over there. The hardest part was managing to get all their pieces together, get out the door, get the kids strapped into their car seats, and then make the stop at the nearby grocery store.

When they arrived almost twenty minutes late to Bob and Marti's lovely home, they had to park two blocks away because to Christy's surprise, her parents' car and Fina's car were already in the narrow driveway.

"I didn't know everyone else was coming, too." Christy waited beside Todd holding Hana's hand as Todd unlatched Cole's infant carrier from the car seat and adjusted the handle so he could carry it in one hand.

"I guess Bob put out the word that we were coming. Do you think I should go get more bread?"

"I don't know. I guess you can always go back after we find out who's here."

Marti opened the front door sporting a bright-orange

sweater. Undoubtedly it carried a designer label, but it wasn't along the lines of the neutral classics Marti usually wore. The image of fashionable, petite Marti looking so snazzy struck Christy because Christy's mom was standing beside her, and for one of the first times Christy could remember, her mother outshone Aunt Marti.

Christy's mom looked lovely in the long, flowing, beachy top Christy had talked her into buying over a year ago when her parents moved to Costa Mesa. They'd lived inland about an hour and a half away in Escondido ever since the family had moved to California when Christy was fifteen. Now that they lived near the beach, Christy's mom had let her completely white hair grow a little longer and had started dressing more like a coastal living woman and less the way she always had as a dairy farmer's wife from Wisconsin.

Uncle Bob and David emerged from the kitchen. Todd had lifted Cole out of the carrier and handed him over to Uncle Bob, who was smiling and stretching out his hands in a "hand-him-over" gesture. Hana immediately latched on to Christy's dad, as she usually did, and was in his arms with her shoulders shrugged, playing her adorable little shy game with him. Christy's dad was eating it up.

"I saw Fina's car," Christy said. "Is she home?"

"She had a clinic today," David said quickly. "I dropped her off and I'm going to go pick her up in about ten minutes. We should both be back here by six o'clock. Six fifteen at the latest."

Christy picked up the clue. David seemed to be trying to communicate a time frame for how long the coast would be clear in Fina's upstairs bedroom.

"She's at a kinesiology clinic," Marti added with an air of intimate knowledge about all things related to Fina's education toward a career in the field of physical therapy. "She was looking forward to it very much."

"Oh. That's interesting," Christy said.

"We thought we'd eat when David gets back with Fina," Marti explained. "Will that work for everyone?"

Without waiting for an answer, Marti continued. Because as they all seemed to know, it didn't matter if it was convenient, it was what they would be doing.

"We have beverages ready on the kitchen counter. I thought we'd eat inside since it's so windy this evening. We'll have to wait until the summer weather catches up with the West Coast before we eat out on the front patio."

David caught Christy's eye and motioned for her to follow him into the kitchen. The two of them were the only ones at the counter, selecting a beverage from the assortment of bottles and cans lined up next to the tall glasses and ice bucket.

"He approved," David said under his breath.

It took Christy a moment to grasp the cryptic code. She looked up at David with a cautious smile. "You called Fina's dad already?" she whispered. "You asked him?"

David nodded, looking relieved.

"Have you talked to Mom and Dad yet?"

David shook his head. "Tonight or tomorrow."

Christy opened a bottle of agave-sweetened lemonade and held it up to her lips. It provided a convenient camouflage for her smile, now that the rest of the family had gathered around the counter.

She subtly gave her brother's forearm a squeeze. Then because she felt so elated for him, she followed the first squeeze with two more. Squeeze-squeeze-squeeze meant "I-love-you" to Christy and Todd. She hoped her brother would decipher the message as well.

"You know what to do," David murmured. He slid past Christy and she gave him what she thought was the slightest of nods.

"Excuse me." Christy put her opened bottle on the counter and hoped to make quick work of her trek upstairs. She got as far as the bottom of the stairs when Marti called out to her.

"Christina? Where are you going?"

"I need to use the restroom," Christy answered quickly.

"The downstairs powder room is available."

"I um, I thought the exercise would help if I used the upstairs one."

Marti's snapping dark eyes gave Christy an inquisitive look. Her hair was styled in a new way tonight, combed to one side making her look a bit more daring than usual. Christy hoped she could keep her cool and be daring as well in getting upstairs.

"But Christy darling, I thought you moved the nursery downstairs at your home so you wouldn't strain yourself on the stairs."

"We did. When Cole was first born."

"Are you climbing stairs at home now?"

"Yes. Every day. I'm much better now than I was the first month or so. I really am. I'm sure you'll agree that I need to get whatever exercise I can." Christy chuckled nervously, hoping that anything related to an attempt to lose weight would ring all the right bells with her calorie-conscious aunt.

"Well, that's good news, then. I hadn't heard that you'd moved the baby up into his nursery. Now, tell me again, when does Todd leave for Africa?"

"June 19."

"That's what I was afraid of."

Christy really wanted to start up the stairs but Marti's

statement dangled in the air between them. She couldn't help herself. She took the bait. "Afraid of what?"

Marti brushed aside the sweeping bangs that crossed her forehead. "That means Todd will still be gone during the first week of July."

"Yes. They'll be gone until July 11."

"I was hoping to surprise you but I had a feeling the dates might not work. You see, Robert has booked us for a week-long golf tournament in Idaho over the first week of July. We've rented a house on the lake. We both loved the idea of you and Todd coming with the children for a few days. We could celebrate the Fourth of July together. It's been such a long time since the two of you have had any time to relax. "

"That's really kind of you. Thanks for thinking of us."

"Your parents and David and Fina have already said they wouldn't be able to come. I was hoping you and Todd were available. You could come alone. Well, with the children, of course."

Christy tried to picture herself getting on a plane with Cole and Hana and taking them to Idaho. She felt her blood pressure rising. "I think a trip like that would be better when the kids are a little older or when it works out for both Todd and me to go."

"I understand. Another time. In the fall, perhaps. Robert and I have a lot of getaways planned for the remainder of this year. It's ideal having Fina as our built-in house sitter. We can pack up and go anytime we want."

Christy hoped she was doing a good job of hiding her initial expression at Marti's comment. Things around Bob and Marti's home were certainly going to change once David and Fina made their engagement official.

But first, I have to get the ring so David can propose!

Christy pointed to the stairs and gave a by-your-leave sort of dip of the chin, hoping to make her escape.

"Christy, if you are in that much of a hurry, please use the powder room." Aunt Marti motioned at the open door of the half bath only ten feet away. "We all know what having children can do to a woman's body. Don't attempt the stairs when it's a matter of urgency."

Christy caved. She reverted to her fourteen-year-old self as a skittish guest of her aunt and uncle for the summer. The persuasive ways of Marti were not to be ignored.

With small steps, Christy went to the powder room, closed the door, and tried to plan her next attempt to slip upstairs undetected.

The golden moment of opportunity came after dinner. David returned with Fina and everyone gathered around the large dining room table. He shot glances at Christy all throughout dinner while Christy returned an ever-so-slight shake of her head on his third questioning glance and watched his expression droop.

No, I haven't gotten it yet, David. But I will. Be patient.

David's puppy-dog look fueled Christy with even more determination. She waited for Cole's first squeal of hunger and, without a word, excused herself from the table. Certainly everyone would know that she was more comfortable nursing her son in another room.

Instead of going into the downstairs den, though, Christy held Cole close and as quietly as possible headed upstairs without anyone seeing her. He was squirming but not crying loudly yet, which was good. After catching her breath at the top of the stairs, Christy headed for Fina's room.

She turned the handle on the closed door and eased it open. Fina's bed was made but it was covered with clothes that appeared to have come from the dryer. Christy tiptoed over to the tall dresser and scanned it quickly for the Swiss chalet music box.

It wasn't there.

She looked around and slipped into the en-suite bathroom to see if Fina kept it on the counter by the sink.

No. Not in the bathroom.

Christy returned to the bedroom just as Cole started to get serious about his supper. The music box wasn't on the bookshelf. It wasn't on the nightstand.

Christy heard someone coming upstairs. It was Fina telling someone she'd be back in a minute. Her athletic, long legs seemed to be bounding up the stairs two at a time with resounding stomps.

Quashing the panic that washed over her, Christy engaged her crying son to his desired goal with record speed. She quickly lowered herself into the rocking chair in the corner just as Fina's feet seemed to hit the top of the stairs. Christy's heart was pounding. She shifted her top and her arms to make Cole comfortable. Hopefully it looked as if she planned all along to bring Cole up to this quiet corner and feed him in the rocking chair.

That's when Christy's eye fell on the music box. It was hidden on the end table next to the rocking chair. Tented over the music box was a text book titled *Ligaments and Tendons*.

With a one-handed awkward movement, Christy slid the book to the edge of the table, lifted the roof of the chalet, pulled out the only item inside, and closed the top with one finger. A single musical note sounded just as the bedroom door opened.

Fina stopped short, one hand still on the doorknob, the other flying to her chest. "Oh! Christy! You startled me."

"I hope you don't mind." Christy's voice came out squeaky. "I thought it would be quieter up here. I should have asked you first. I'm sorry."

"No. You're fine. No problem. You surprised me, that's all." Fina's shoulders relaxed. She was tall and slender with high cheekbones and dark, distinct eyebrows. Her caramel-colored short hair had grown out so it was long enough to put up in a clip, and that's how she usually wore it.

"Christy, you're welcome here anytime. You know that." Fina stepped closer. "I just need to get a book. I was telling Bob about the way a bone spur can mess up the Achilles tendon. He has a golf buddy who's considering surgery."

Fina stopped short again. This time she stood unmoving in front of the side table right next to Christy. Fina's gaze fell on the book that was no longer opened and tented over the top of the music box. She tilted her head a moment.

Christy tried to keep the best poker face she could muster, barely blinking.

Fina bent over to pick up the book. Did Christy imagine it, or was Fina looking at the music box?

She knows!

Christy fixed her gaze on Fina as she scooped up the book, gave Christy an easygoing glance over her shoulder, and left the room, closing the door behind her.

Christy rocked back and forth, hearing only the ruffled sighs coming from her son as he nursed. She smiled to herself and closed her fist a little tighter. She'd done it! Her Frodo moment was accomplished. The ring was in her hand.

Now all she had to do was slide the precious treasure to David without anyone suspecting a thing.

The opportunity to make the handoff came when Christy and Todd were getting ready to leave. David seemed to catch on that the ideal cover-up would be during the normal gathering up and strapping in and hunting down a shoe or dolly that always happened when they got ready to leave. It was a chaotic process when they had only Hana. Now that this was their first outing with two kids, the added details and motions provided a great smoke screen.

Todd left to go get the car and pull it up to the front of the house. David came over to the front door, offering to help in any way he could. Christy casually said, "Here. Hold this for me so I don't lose it." She realized her voice and tone carried added dramatic emphasis that probably wasn't necessary.

With her back to everyone else, Christy placed Hana's pacifier along with the valued ring into the palm of David's large hand. He glanced down and immediately closed his fingers. She caught a dash of relief and happiness blitz across his face before he looked away. Transferring the pacifier to his left hand, David slid the ring into the pocket of his jeans and kept a straight face, as if nothing out of the ordinary had just transpired.

Todd arrived with the car so the procession began. Christy carried the diaper bag and folded-up travel bassinet. Her dad was carrying Hana and David was muscling Cole's infant seat with Fina close behind him. Todd hopped out to strap in the baby, Christy got Hana secure in her car seat, and David and Fina stood back, waiting, it seemed, for a final wave good-bye.

"We'll see you guys later," Christy said, hoping her smile wasn't too overdone.

"Yeah, later," Todd called out over the roof of the car before getting into the driver's seat.

Christy was about to slide into the passenger seat when her brother reached for her elbow. It was a gentlemanly gesture and not unusual, but definitely not something he normally did. Christy felt his warm fingers pressing into her arm.

Squeeze. Squeeze. Squeeze.

A cluster of happy tears gathered in the back of Christy's throat. She swallowed and offered a closed-lip smile as David shut her door. She didn't want Fina to catch any of her emotional expressions.

David put his arm around Fina's shoulders and the two of them waved as Todd pulled away from the curb, leaving Bob and Marti's house as they had done hundreds of times over the years. Only this time was different. Christy would always remember this as one of the very best moments she and her brother had ever shared.

Todd turned at the corner, heading the few short blocks to their home. He cleared his throat and said, "Well?"

"Well, what?" Christy kept looking straight ahead.

"Christy . . ."

Six

"Todd, you have to understand. David was trying not to say anything. Not to anyone."

"Not even me?"

Christy shook her head. "Sorry."

"I thought you said you told Katie."

"I did." Christy slid under the covers on her side of the bed and realized she was frowning. They'd been home for less than two hours, and between Todd's clever trick questions, a few leading comments, and even a tickle attack while she was trying to brush her teeth, he had managed to drag all the details about David and the ring from her.

Christy rolled on her back and let out a long sigh. "I owe my brother an apology."

Todd didn't agree or disagree. He crawled into bed and leaned on his side, looking at Christy with a cute half grin. It seemed as if he was enjoying all this way more than Christy was.

"Todd, what made you suspect something was going on between David and me?"

"Your face."

"What about my face?"

Todd kissed her cheek. "You have a very cute face, but it always turns red when you're trying to hide something. And when you don't want me to know what you're thinking, you stop blinking and your eyes get round. Like this." Todd opened his eyes as wide as they would go and didn't blink.

Christy swatted his shoulder. "I don't look like that."

"Well, maybe not exactly like that. More like this." He lowered his chin and took on a coy expression with a subtle, closed-lip grin.

"Now you look like Hana when she's trying to talk me into singing her a song at bedtime." Christy mimicked the sweet baby-doll, pleading look.

"She gets that look from you, you know."

"When do I look like that?"

"I just told you. When you're trying to keep something hidden from me."

Christy wasn't sure how serious he was and how much he was teasing.

He scooted closer and with a sincere expression said, "Just so you know, you'd make a terrible spy."

"I know. I would."

"Glad to know we agree on that." Todd reached under the covers and gave her a playful tickle around her middle.

All Christy could think about was how wobbly her midriff was and that if there was anything she'd been trying to deliberately hide from her husband, it was her body. She felt much more chunky and flabby after this baby than she had after the first one. Christy kept hoping the bulges would melt away quickly, as they had when she was nursing Hana. The thicker parts of -her were a lot more belligerent this time around.

"Come here." Todd stretched his arm under her so she could snuggle up against his chest.

"I love you just the way you are." He kissed her just above her ear.

"And I love you just the way you are." Christy bit her lower lip. Todd's statement could have still been referring to her lack of keen abilities as a spy. Or since he seemed to know when she was trying to hide something, did he perceive that she was trying to hide her waistline from him? Was that why he was cuddling up and telling her he loved her just the way she was?

"So, David is getting married." Todd's voice rumbled in his chest.

"I know. Although, Fina hasn't said yes yet."

"She will."

"I think so, too." Christy wiggled closer and tried to get more comfortable.

"And they're moving to Indiana. Didn't see that coming." Todd shifted his position in response to Christy's wiggling. Her hair was in its usual knotted bun on top of her head and seemed to be bumping against his jaw.

"Can you undo this thing?" Todd slid his fingers into her clump of hair and tried to release the tangled strands. "I like it when you wear your hair down the way it was this afternoon when I came home."

Christy quickly took over what he was trying to do. She sat up and untwisted the bun. Instead of letting her hair stay down, though, she automatically folded it into a loose, messy braid and flung it over her shoulder.

"I meant just let it go free," Todd said.

"It's too . . ." Christy couldn't decide which word to use for her tangled, frizzed-out, aggravating hair.

"Too what? I love your long hair."

"It's all gone to seed."

Todd laughed.

"What?"

"Gone to seed."

"What's so funny?"

"You, Christy. You come up with stuff sometimes that sounds just like your mother."

"I do not."

"Yes, you do. Like what was it you said the other day about fish?"

Christy repeated the saying she remembered hearing from her grandmother. "'Wishes and fishes.'"

"What is that supposed to mean?"

"It means with wishes and fishes you need to put them to use. Because if you let them sit around too long, they'll stink up your life."

Todd laughed again.

"Why are you laughing?" Christy was still sitting up, facing her entertained husband. "It's cute. Wishes and fishes. It's clever."

"It is." Todd's handsome face took on a more serious expression. "Cute and clever. Like you."

"I always knew what my grandma meant when she said it. It meant I was supposed to get busy."

He pulled her braid back over her shoulder and loosened the ends with his fingers. Giving her hair a shake, the braid came undone. "Guess it's true." Todd's tone was low and melodic.

"What's true?" Christy loved the way she felt right now. It had been a long time, too long, since she'd felt close to Todd like this.

Todd leaned in and kissed her neck.

Christy closed her eyes and tried to remember what they were talking about.

"Wishes . . ." Todd's voice trailed off.

Christy knew what her husband was wishing. She was wishing the same thing.

Without another word, they got busy and made each other's wish come true.

The next morning Christy was still in bed when the scent of bacon wafted upstairs and prompted her to open her eyes. She'd been up at three o'clock for Cole's usual diaper change and feeding, but then she tumbled back into bed and slept soundly, knowing that for the first morning in a long time, Todd didn't have to be out the door before seven thirty.

She stretched and tried to see the time on the digital clock on the nightstand. "It can't be eight forty-five." Christy sprang to her feet and padded into the hallway. She quietly opened the door to the bedroom across from theirs that had been turned into Cole's nursery. He seemed to still be asleep, which was unusual.

Creeping closer to the crib, Christy saw that he was stirring. She leaned over and Cole opened his eyes, meeting Christy's gaze in the shadowed room.

"Good morning, Little Bear. You certainly had a good sleep." She twisted the knob on the teddy bear lamp on the table next to the glider. Soft yellow light filled the room.

Cole seemed to have suddenly figured out that he should be starving by now. At the sound of Christy's voice, he let out a wee cry and then followed it with a more conscientious effort. Christy lifted him and held him close.

"Yes, yes, I'm here. I will feed you. Shhh. All is well."

"Mommy!" Hana called out from the open nursery door. "Mommy, look!"

Todd stood behind Hana with a breakfast tray. "We were going to surprise you." He was wearing an old surf T-shirt and board shorts. It had been a long time since Christy had seen him in anything other than his usual teacher garb of khaki slacks and short sleeve shirt and tie that he wore every day.

"Wow!" Christy called out over the din of Cole's cries. "I am surprised. Thank you."

The room fell silent as Cole helped himself to his breakfast while Christy calmly glided in the corner chair. Hana scampered up next to Christy, leaning on the arm of the chair. She patted Christy's leg and said, "Bekfest."

"Yes, Cole is having his breakfast."

Todd stood over her with the tray. Christy could smell the bacon again and saw the rest of the offering of scrambled eggs and toast. She particularly liked the single carnation popping its frilly white face up from a jelly jar vase.

Todd cleared space under the teddy bear lamp and placed the tray next to Christy. "Hana made the toast, didn't you, Sunshine."

Hana grinned and nodded and swayed from side to side as if trying to get the glider to go faster.

"Then I will eat the toast first." Christy gave Hana a big smile. It was so nice to see her daughter happy and getting lots of attention from her daddy. This cheerful version of Hana was so much better than the screaming, stomping version.

Todd went downstairs and returned with a second tray with lots more food. He and Hana had a picnic on the nursery floor rug while Christy ate. It was one of the sweetest

Sunday mornings she remembered having in a long time.

The rest of the day rolled out at the same leisurely pace. After breakfast they took a long walk along the beach with Hana carrying her bucket and shovels and Todd carrying Cole in the front sling. It was a first for Todd and Cole and made Christy appreciate her husband even more. It meant Christy was free to sit with Hana in the sand and build a sand castle with her. They ate popcorn, apples, and cheese for lunch, and all four of them managed to get in a nap during the quiet afternoon.

At Christy's request, they had burgers and fries for dinner. Todd took Hana with him to pick up the fast food. When they returned Hana couldn't wait to show Christy the special prize she'd gotten. It was a small bottle of bubbles and she tried using all her words and jibbers and glee to express what that treasure meant to her.

They ate on the back deck even though the June-gloom weather meant it had turned beachy cold. Todd blew bubbles for Hana and she danced around on the deck, trying to catch them. The hood of her sweatshirt was over her head and her feathery blonde hair seemed eager to escape by sticking out in every direction around her face. Christy thought she looked like a little sunflower that had bloomed today while basking in the love and continual attention of her daddy.

I wish we could have more days like this. Our children need more time with their daddy. I need more time with their daddy.

Christy went into the kitchen to throw away the trash and put on the kettle for some hot tea. She looked at the calendar on the wall and pressed her lips together. At her request, Todd had written in details of what he had going on over the next few weeks. The days were marbled with his scrawling letters. Finals, baccalaureate, graduation, the wedding of a former student, last day of school, teachers' meeting, retirement lunch for one of the history teachers, and on the nineteenth, in big letters, LEAVE FOR KENYA.

The ghostly depression that had floated in and out of Christy's life over the past few months seemed to return and stand beside her, silently staring at the calendar with her.

Today was a tease. Todd and I were given a lovely, sweet breath of fresh air. Tomorrow morning we dive back into the ocean of our real lives. What's going to happen when we add David and Fina's events to the calendar?

Christy's contribution to the calendar included Jennalyn's Summer Soiree on the eighth, an order for two throw pillows due to a client on the ninth, Cole's two-month checkup on the thirteenth, and their monthly Family Night Dinner on the twenty-fifth.

She felt a single tear forming in the corner of her eye. It stung as she blinked. *Why do I feel so overwhelmed? This month is not that busy. We've had much busier months. What is my problem?*

Christy didn't want to end this perfectly wonderful day with an emotional crumbling.

It has to be a hormone thing. I've already settled the issue of Todd leaving for three weeks. It's going to be okay. I'm going to be okay. Everything is okay. Just be thankful.

She drew in a deep breath and blinked back the copycat tears that rose to follow the first one.

I am thankful, Father God. I'm very thankful for today.

She heard the scurrying of Hana coming in from the deck along with Todd, who was carrying Cole.

"We're heading upstairs. Cole needs a clean diaper and Hana is going to play in the tub, aren't you, Sunshine?"

Without looking over at them, Christy said, "I'll come

up with you guys." She didn't want Todd to see how wide her eyes were right now and think she was hiding something from him.

"No word from David?" Todd asked as Christy followed him up the stairs.

"David? Oh. No. I think he planned to talk things over with Mom and Dad today."

"Did he give you any idea of when the wedding might be?"

"No."

"You don't think it will be while I'm gone, do you?"

Christy hadn't considered the possibility. "It seems like they'd at least wait until late July or early August. They can't get married while you're gone. You have to be at the wedding."

"I don't have to be at their wedding. But, of course, I'd like to." Todd took Cole into the nursery and lowered him onto the changing table. Hana went over to the teddy bear light and tried to turn it on. She couldn't reach the knob so Christy turned it on for them.

Todd started the diaper change while Christy sat in the glider and welcomed Hana into her lap. Christy thought about how Todd was officiating at the wedding of the former student next week. He had completed the licensing requirements years ago when he was on staff at a church as a youth pastor. He'd only done a few weddings. Was he asking about their date because he wanted to perform David and Fina's ceremony?

She asked and his answer was, "If they want me to."

"Once they make their announcement official, we should let them know you are qualified to officiate," Christy suggested.

Todd finished the diaper change and held Cole up to his chest so their son's little face was peering over Todd's shoulder.

"Hi, baby," Hana said gleefully. She waved at her brother and scooted down from Christy's lap so she could dance around Todd's legs and try to get Cole's attention.

It was one of the few times since Cole was born that Hana had taken an interest in him, and Christy wanted to encourage the playful moment. "Here, Hana. Let Mommy pick you up so you can see your baby brother."

"You okay lifting her?" Todd asked.

"Yes."

"How about if you sit and I'll trade you?"

Christy returned to the rocker and took Cole from Todd. Hana reached up her arms to her daddy. As soon as Todd lifted her, Hana lost all interest in her brother and patted Todd's face.

"Sing, Daddy."

Todd burst into a funny made-up song about bubbles. He started dancing around the rug with Hana in his arms. She grinned and bounced along for a few moments but then patted his face again and said, "No. Not bubbles. Sing lullaby."

All of Todd's fancy footwork halted. He glanced at Christy.

"Which lullaby?" Christy asked.

"It's something I've been working on."

"Sing it, Daddy."

"Okay. I will sing the lullaby song to you and bunny and you can play the bongos. Do you know when?"

Hana shook her head.

"After you take your bath."

Surprisingly, Hana didn't protest about the bath or having to wait to hear the lullaby sung to her while she did her favorite thing, which was playing her own little bongo drums. All she said was, "Bubble bath! Bubble bath!"

Todd exited with Hana in his arms. He paused in the

doorway and shot Christy a big smile. "You know what, Hana? You have a beautiful Mommy."

"I know." Hana's little voice sounded as cute as it could be. She waved at Christy and Christy blew her a kiss back.

By the light of the glowing teddy bear lamp, Christy rocked her son and fed him, listening to all the happy sounds and splashes echoing from the bathroom. It was all such a contrast to several nights she'd experienced that week when Todd wasn't home and she had been alone, wrangling both children at bedtime.

I know that every night can't be like this, but thank You, God, that tonight is so peaceful and that today was completely wonderful in so many ways. Thank You.

Seven

The routine around the Spencer household continued as usual for the next few days, and Christy felt less wobbly. She'd started a list in her journal titled, "Thank You, God" and added to the list almost every day. The result was that her emotions weren't dipping into that dark, shadowy place as frequently. Whenever the woe-is-me feelings started to creep in, she'd return to the list and remind herself of the many things she had to be grateful for.

One thing Christy was determined to do was schedule a few more days or at least some nights when she and the kids could have Todd all to themselves before he left. She penciled in the possible times on the calendar and hoped no other events or last-minute meetings would pop up for those days.

On Wednesday afternoon the best sort of pop-up moment happened when Christy got a text from her brother. It might have seemed cryptic if anyone else saw it, but Christy understood completely.

TONIGHT. SUNSET. NERVOUS.

She texted back, EXCITED FOR YOU!

David replied, THX.

And then the waiting began.

Christy wondered if David had talked to their parents as he said he was going to. If he had, then Christy wondered if it was okay for her to call her mom. She was about to make the call when she remembered how she'd told her brother she'd keep his confidence.

I've already told Todd. Katie, too. That wasn't fair to my brother.

It would only make her credibility with David worse if she called her mom to discuss his plan.

I owe my brother an apology. I wish I kept everything quiet the way he asked me to. I'll tell him the next time I see him.

The evening seemed to drag on as Christy kept checking her phone. She knew that her brother's first priority this evening was not going to be sending her an update text. But the waiting was driving her crazy!

Christy could barely keep her eyes open after Hana was asleep and Cole was tucked in. Todd was heading to bed so Christy joined him. She checked her phone at 3:00 a.m. when she got up to feed Cole. No word from David. She checked again when Todd got up and was showering for work. No updates.

Finally, when the kids were up and Todd had left for school, she sent David a one-word text. WELL?!?

He replied within seconds. SHE WANTS TO THINK ABOUT IT.

Christy stared at her phone in disbelief. *She wants to think about it?*

A half-dozen questions came to Christy's thoughts and

she started to type the first one but then deleted it. She only asked the most important question of the moment. ARE YOU OKAY?

David replied with two emojis. A thumbs-up and a sad face with a tear.

Christy sent the same sad face with a tear emoji back to him and put her phone down on the counter. Hana was in the chair next to Christy, coloring with a big purple marker.

"What did she have to think about?" Christy asked aloud.

Hana looked up as if the question had been for her.

Christy leaned over and gave her daughter a kiss on the top of her head, then got up to start a load of laundry.

Is Fina thinking about her decision because of school? Does she want to finish the program first and then get married? Or is she having hesitations about how she feels about David? Poor David!

She pressed the button on the dryer and felt another wave of sadness for her brother. Rejection of any sort was painful. Rejection from someone you'd fallen in love with had to be the worst sort of pain.

David sounded like they both knew their relationship was heading toward marriage. If Fina doesn't feel the same way, why didn't she say something to David before now?

Christy went to work on the sewing project that was due on Friday. The throw pillows were for an interior designer friend of Aunt Marti's. She ordered custom pieces from Christy about every other month, and the extra income really helped.

These pillows were a different style than usual. They had piping around the edges in a contrasting fabric, which Christy was having a hard time getting just right. For the next hour while Cole slept in the bassinet beside her and Hana flitted around, playing with her toys, Christy sewed. All the while she fought the urge to call her brother.

A buzz vibrated her cell phone and to her surprise, the text was from Fina.

ANY CHANCE I CAN COME OVER?

OF COURSE.

It took Fina only a few minutes to arrive. As soon as she stepped inside, Hana ran to her and enthusiastically showed Fina her toy car with the little plastic figures that fit inside.

"That's nice, Hana." Fina's voice sounded hoarse. "Aunt Marti told me you have a new mermaid doll."

Hana scurried off to find her mermaid doll and Fina turned to Christy. "Thanks for letting me drop in like this."

"Of course." Christy gave her a sisterly hug. "How are you doing?"

"Not good. I didn't sleep all night."

The electric kettle clicked off. Christy motioned to the two mugs and box of tea she'd put on the counter right after Fina called. "Would you like some tea?"

"No. Thanks."

Fina slid onto one of the kitchen counter stools and ran her fingers through her short hair. Christy made herself a cup of tea and waited for Fina to start the conversation. She didn't know if David had let Fina know that Christy was involved in the proposal plan or not, so she wanted to let Fina be the one to do the talking.

And talk she did.

The whole story poured out about how David had texted her to meet at their bench for sunset and she showed up in workout clothes, never expecting him to propose.

"He was so nervous. I should have picked up on that clue. But I didn't." Fina's lovely face was shadowed by a scowl. "He said, 'I've been thinking a lot about this, Fina, and I think we should get married before your graduate program starts.'"

Christy felt a twist of agony in her stomach. She knew how blunt and seemingly unemotional the men in her family could be. Her brother had really missed the mark with the proposal.

"I thought he was just bringing up the topic, which was a good thing," Fina said. "I was glad he finally said something because we've only talked around the edges. I honestly thought he was simply tossing out his logical thoughts on marriage so we could discuss it."

Fina stared at her hands. "So I told David we should think about it. To me, that meant I was ready to discuss all the options. I mean, wasn't that the logical thing to do? That's how it was last summer when he and I talked about me moving here. We talked through all the scenarios and came to a mutual agreement. That's a good thing to do with any major decision, don't you think?"

Christy nodded her agreement.

"But you should have seen his face! He looked crushed. I didn't understand why he was so defeated. So I said something about how the first thing we should talk about was whether or not I was going to enter the program in Indiana."

Christy was surprised that Fina had stated that detail as still being up for discussion. "I think my brother was under the impression that the plan for you to go to school in Indiana was already locked in."

Now it was Fina's turn to look surprised. "Why did he think that? Nothing is final yet. I applied over a year ago, before I even met David. I was wait-listed. Now that I've been accepted, I don't know if I want to commit to the program. I'm not sure what I want to do. I need time to think things through and pray about it."

Christy let out a slow breath and rubbed the back of her neck. "It sounds like you and David need a rewind on all this. You need to have a long talk about everything."

"That's what I thought we were doing last night. It was the perfect time to sit and have an important long conversation about school and our future. But then David pulled out this ring."

Fina held up her right hand and showed Christy that she was wearing the ring on her little finger. Christy hadn't gotten a good look at it yet. It was a dainty gold band with an inset ruby in the center flanked by two tiny inset diamonds. Obviously it needed to be sized by a jeweler. Another detail David hadn't considered.

"Christy, this is my ring. My grandmother's ring. David had it in a plastic sandwich bag in his pocket!"

Christy thought Fina was going to cry.

"I have no idea how he got a hold of my ring. When he pulled it out of that crumpled bag, I was in shock. Actually, I was mad. Really mad. It was the last thing I expected to see. I kept thinking, 'What are you doing? Why do you have my ring?' He just held it in the palm of his hand and looked at me with those big puppy-dog eyes. He didn't say anything. Not a word. It was like he froze and was waiting for me to hit the *Play* button."

Christy winced. "What did you do?"

"I grabbed the ring out of his hand like a monkey snatching a peanut. I thought he was going to drop it. I didn't want to lose it." The tears spilled over and Fina quickly wiped her eyes.

Christy pulled a paper towel from the roll on the counter and handed it to Fina in lieu of a tissue. "Fina, I'm so sorry."

"It was awful, Christy. I was so confused and upset. I jumped up and told him I had to go. I didn't know what else to do. I started jogging to my car and then I realized maybe he was trying to propose."

Fina pressed the paper towel to her forehead, covering her face. Her voice came out in squeaky tones. "I thought he might come after me. Or call me. Or at least text me. But he didn't. And I don't know what to do."

Christy had moved to Fina's side of the counter. She wrapped her arm around Fina's shoulder. "Oh, Fina. I'm so sorry."

"You don't have to apologize." Fina lifted her head and cleared her throat and seemed to be trying very hard not to release any more tears. "It's not your fault. It's mine. I knew he was nervous. I should have gone back."

"Fina." Christy drew back and tried to look her in the eye. "I think part of all this is my fault. I contributed to the confusion."

"You? How?"

Christy told her how David had come to her for advice and how she had been the one who took the ring from the music box.

"I thought you'd figured out what I'd done when you came up to your room and I was there with Cole," Christy said.

"No. I didn't suspect anything. You took the ring?"

Christy nodded. "I'm afraid my own romantic inclinations prompted me to encourage David more than talk through the plan with him. Especially the proposal part. When he told me he'd gotten permission from your dad, I thought everything was going to be smooth as could be."

Fina's lips parted and her eyes opened wide. "Wait. Did you just say that David asked my dad if he could marry me?

Is that what you just said?"

Christy instinctively covered her mouth. She felt sick inside. She'd just revealed another significant piece of information that wasn't hers to tell. In a quiet voice all she could say was, "Yes."

Fina stared at Christy. She blinked several times and finally released a half-question, half-declaration sort of sentence. "My father gave David his blessing?"

"I shouldn't be the one telling you this."

Fina kept staring, processing the information out loud. "My father must have said yes, then. He must have told David he could marry me."

Christy cautiously placed her hand on Fina's shoulder. "I wish you weren't finding out this way."

Fina seemed to snap out of her moment of shock. She reached inside her shoulder bag. She pulled out her phone and started texting. "I need to talk to David."

Christy nodded and pulled back.

Fina's expression had changed from looking stunned and hurt to a look of strength and resolve. Her phone sounded a chirp, indicating that her text had a reply. She quickly typed out her answer and tossed her phone back into her bag.

"He's going to meet me at Julie Ann's Café."

"Good." Christy still felt like she should be apologizing for the confusion she added to the situation. "I hope . . ."

Fina stood and wrapped her arms around Christy in a sisterly hug. "Thank you. I love you, Christy."

"I love you, too. I hope . . . well, I just . . ."

Fina drew back and offered Christy a gracious look as if there was nothing Christy needed to apologize for. "I think it's all going to work out. I'm so glad I came over and that you told me everything you did. You really helped me." Fina scooped up Hana on her way to the door and gave her a squeeze. "I've got to go, Hana. Give Auntie Fina a kiss."

Hana pressed her lips to Fina's cheek and made a cute "mwah" sound, the same way Fina always did when she gave Hana a kiss on the cheek. Fina returned the kiss and put Hana back down. She gave Christy a wave and left in a flurry.

Christy remained planted in the kitchen, her arms folded across her unsettled stomach. Her phone vibrated on the counter. The text was from Jennalyn.

JUST A REMINDER. SUMMER SOIREE TONIGHT! SEE YOU AT 6:30.

Christy tapped back a thumbs-up emoji in reply. She'd nearly forgotten about Jennalyn's get-together that night.

The reminder proved to be a small blessing because Christy's ruminating thoughts about David and Fina were put aside as she started working through all the logistics required in order for her to walk out the door at 6:25 that evening. She needed to plan Cole's feeding times for the rest of the day and check to make sure Todd would be home and/or ask her mom to come over to help. She needed to figure out what to do for dinner and make sure it was ready by 6:00 at the latest. She needed a shower and she needed to come up with something cute to wear.

Christy didn't know who was going to the Summer Soiree. That unknown along with the list of what she needed to accomplish made her feel a little anxious. However, the thought of an evening at Jennalyn's lovely cottage with yummy food and cheering conversation was worth every effort she needed to make in order to get out the door that night.

Eight

At 6:27 on Thursday night, wearing makeup and her cutest, newest summer dress, Christy opened her front door. She stepped outside into the golden light of the early summer evening and closed the door behind her.

Immediately, she heard Hana burst into a wail. "Mommy! Mommy!"

Christy paused. Every motherly instinct in her said to go back inside for one last hug and kiss, even though she had thoroughly prepared Hana and everything and everyone else in her life for this one rare night out.

She closed her eyes, remembering the image of Todd standing in the living room with toys all over the floor, a well-fed baby in his arms who was filling his diaper as Christy was reaching for her purse. And now, Hana in a full cloudburst.

Go. It's okay. Leave now. You can do this.

Putting one foot in front of the other, Christy lifted her chin and started down the street to Jennalyn's beach cottage.

She drew in a deep breath and reveled in the fine salty mist that filled her lungs.

This is good. Really good.

Christy reached the end of her street and opened the whitewashed plank-board gate that led to Jennalyn's front door. Their house, like many of the houses on that block, had a small patio between the sidewalk and the front door and a garage in the back. The garage could be accessed through a long one-way alley and the patio was the only "yard" space they had. Todd and Christy's house was unusual in that the garage was at the front of their house and the deck had been added on to the side. None of the houses had grass or even splotches of dirt where sod could be laid. Everything was concrete and all the houses were close together.

The layout of Christy and Todd's neighborhood wasn't considered a drawback because in exchange for grass and yards, the residents had to walk only a block or two and they'd be able to bury their feet into luxurious, fine sand that ran for miles to the north and to the south. And beyond the sand was the ever-stunning Pacific Ocean.

The most distinctive feature that set Jennalyn and Joel's house apart from all the other beach cottages was that they had turned their front patio into a garden. Christy paused to look at the progress of Jennalyn's green beans in the wooden planter and then checked out the layered planter where she had five different herbs growing. The mint looked like it wanted to take over. Christy plucked a few spiny needles from the rosemary and rubbed them between her fingers.

Mmm. I really need to get a planter going on the deck. I would love to use fresh rosemary on a roasted chicken or have fresh mint to put in water or to use to make tea.

Christy noticed that the row of colorful pink cosmos

flowers were starting to come up underneath the front window. And best of all was the arched trellis that curved like a rainbow over the front door. Two potted honeysuckle plants were wending their way up either side of the trellis and had almost met in the middle. By mid-August Christy guessed that the blooming honeysuckle would fill the house with a gush of sweet fragrance whenever Jennalyn opened the front door.

Christy wondered if she and Todd could try something like that at their front door. They didn't get as much sun as Jennalyn's house did.

Maybe I could try something else. Like jasmine.

Her parents had great success with the jasmine that grew in front of their house in Escondido. Christy decided she would get her dad to help her figure out what they could do at their house.

Just before Christy knocked on the lapis-blue front door, she pulled her phone from her pocket. Part of her expected to find an SOS text from Todd. She had no messages.

Okay, then. Here goes!

The door swung open and Jennalyn stood there smiling, with Eden on her hip. "Christy! Come in. You're the first one here."

"Well, that's probably because I didn't have far to go." Even though she said the words lightheartedly, Christy felt as if she'd just traversed the precarious bridge every mother of a newborn must cross in order to reestablish contact with the outside world.

Christy leaned closer to Jennalyn's nine-month-old and smiled. "Hello, Eden. You look like a sleepy girl."

"She is. Joel was just going to put her down. She's been crying, haven't you, sweetheart?" Jennalyn kissed her baby's cheek and motioned for Christy to come all the way into the living room. "She's teething. I think it's a molar because she's been unhappy all day long."

"I'm impressed you were able to pull all this together with a fussy baby." Christy looked up at the banner hung in front of the opening into the kitchen. The fancy cursive pastel letters said "Summer Soiree."

"That's so cute, Jennalyn. Did you do that?" Christy already knew the answer.

"Yes. I got some new pens I love. I had to play with them, and a banner for our evening seemed like something new and fun to try."

"It's so festive!"

"Thanks."

Jennalyn was especially gifted at lettering and graphics and doing watercolor images of flowers and leaves. The beauty that Joel created with food, Jennalyn created with her garden and her artwork.

On the coffee table between the two couches in the living room Christy spied a scrumptious-looking chocolate cake perched on a vintage glass cake stand. The cake was a single layer and had glossy dark-chocolate frosting that swooped down the sides in an elegant scalloped pattern. On top were a cluster of colorful pansies and a few sprigs of rosemary from Jennalyn's herb garden. It was a magazine-worthy work of culinary art.

"That's beautiful," she said.

"Joel is especially proud of that one. It's a new recipe of his. Flourless chocolate amaretto."

"Wow." It was the only word she could find to express her admiration because her salivary glands had gone into action. For months Christy had done a good job of staying away from sugar. She felt just fine about saying yes to a small slice and enjoying each decadent bite.

Next to the cake was a tray with four hand-painted glasses. They were slender and tall with a whimsical pattern of wildflowers painted along the bottom like a rolling arpeggio of musical notes. A glass pitcher sat in the middle of the glasses, plump and round and filled with what appeared to be pink lemonade.

Christy thought it looked as if the round ice cubes in the lemonade had something inside them. She stepped closer to try to figure out what it was.

"Strawberries," Jennalyn said as if anticipating Christy's question. "I froze them inside the cubes. I like the way the strawberries continue to sweeten the lemonade as they melt."

"Jennalyn, your creativity amazes me."

"It's not that much, really. When we were first married, I used to go a little Pinterest crazy every few months. Poor Joel had to endure all my attempts at being artistic."

"You mean, like the bonsai broccolini garden?" Joel, with a good-natured tease in his voice, entered from the hall.

"We're trying to forget my early efforts." Jennalyn handed Eden over to her husband. "Well, at least one of us is trying to forget them."

Joel gave Jennalyn a grin and turned to Christy. "How's everything with you guys?"

Christy gave a general update on the Spencer clan and noticed how different Joel looked when he wasn't wearing a hat of some sort. His receding hairline and extremely short dark hair made him look older than he was. She remembered hearing Jennalyn say once that the hair loss was heredity and she married Joel for who he was on the inside and not for what he had on the topside. He was good looking and reminded Christy of an actor she liked who had a famous scene where he drove a sports car down a curving road in the California wine country.

Joel asked when Todd was leaving for Kenya and then commented on how the summer crowds had arrived early this year at the restaurant where he worked.

"I noticed it when we were out on the beach last week," Joel added. "Lots more people this year. It's going to be a wild couple of months around here. Especially since we have rental units on either side of us and we have to share our garage with them."

Eden started to fuss so Joel made his exit. He closed the door that led down the hall to the two bedrooms and bathroom. The door was a unique feature in their small house and one that allowed for a lot more laughing and talking in the living room without disturbing those who were in the bedrooms.

Christy had been to two other get-togethers Jennalyn hosted. She only stayed for the first part of the last one because it was three weeks away from her due date and she was super uncomfortable regardless of whether she was sitting or standing.

Based on the number of women at Jennalyn's previous get-togethers, Christy was surprised that she was the only one at the Summer Soiree so far. She glanced out the front window and wondered if the other women were still trying to extract themselves from their homes and families.

"Did I come too early?" Christy asked. "You did say six thirty, didn't you?"

"Yes. I put six thirty on all the invitations." Jennalyn stepped into the kitchen and reached for her phone on the counter.

Christy watched as she quickly scrolled through the messages that had apparently come in while they were talking. Jennalyn looked up at Christy.

"Is everything okay?" Christy thought Jennalyn looked embarrassed. Her dark eyes looked away.

"Mia and Skylar just cancelled."

Christy was about to make light of the circumstances by saying something like, "That just means more cake for you and me."

But clearly, that wasn't the right thing to say at this moment. The problem was that Christy didn't know Jennalyn well enough to know if she could joke with her the way she would joke with Katie in the middle of an awkward situation.

Jennalyn leaned on the counter. "I only invited six women this time. I thought it would give us a chance to get to know each other better. Three of the six let me know right away that they couldn't come. That was fine because I thought the four of us would have a chance to have really interesting conversations."

Christy tried to think of what she would want someone to say to her if she was the hostess of a party and only one guest had come. The problem was that she was feeling awkward for being the only one who showed up.

"Jennalyn, I hope you're not taking it personally that the others weren't able to come."

"No. I understand how it is. I really do. Life is busy for all of us." Jennalyn slid her thumbnail between her lips and stared at her phone the way Fina had stared across Christy's kitchen counter that morning.

It's so difficult to watch other women when they're hurting. I never know what to say.

Christy wished she knew Jennalyn better. They hadn't

yet had the kind of friend-to-friend, heart-to-heart sort of moment where they could both feel comfortable walking around barefoot on the edges of each other's thoughts.

"You know what?" Christy decided to say what she thought and not be nervous about how Jennalyn might take it. "I'm really glad I came, and I think when things like this happen, it can turn into a God-thing."

Jennalyn nodded slowly as if taking in Christy's thought.

"I've told you about my friend, Katie, in Africa. She's the one who taught me to pick up on God-things like this. Maybe there's something you and I are supposed to talk about. It could be that we wouldn't have talked about it if the others had come."

Christy hoped she didn't sound like she was spouting clichés. She hated it when she was hurting for whatever reason and someone in her family or small circle of friends would toss a bunch of platitudes at her, and none of them even touched the pain she felt at the time.

"Thanks for saying that. I think you're right." Jennalyn's expression had changed. She no longer looked embarrassed. Her dark eyes looked vulnerable and sweetly humble. "I'm glad you came, Christy."

Not knowing what to do next, Christy awkwardly motioned toward the sofas, as if this were her home and she was trying to get her guest to feel comfortable. "Should we sit down?"

"Sure. Let's have some strawberry lemonade."

"Good. I want to watch the ice cubes melt." Christy tossed out the line without thinking about it. As she heard herself saying it, she was pretty sure it sounded as silly as she thought it did.

Jennalyn poured the beverage, ice cubes included, into

the elegant glasses. Christy examined the lyrical-looking band of wildflowers around the base. "These are so cute."

"Thanks."

"Have you ever thought about making some for specialty resale? Like for some of the gift shops on Balboa Island?"

"No, I've never thought of that. Most of what I do is spontaneous. I'm not sure I could duplicate it exactly over and over."

"You wouldn't have to make anything exact. That's what makes it a boutique item. You know how I sell decorative pillows? Some of them go to a shop I used to work at on Balboa Island. If you'd like, I could take one of these glasses in with me on Friday when I deliver the pillows I'm working on now. Or if you have anything else you think you'd like to make a bunch of, I'd be happy to present them."

Jennalyn didn't look enthusiastic about the idea. At least, not as enthusiastic as Christy thought she'd be. Perhaps Joel and Jennalyn were comfortable on Joel's income and didn't need a little extra the way Christy and Todd always did.

"Well, think about it." Christy took another sip of the refreshing lemonade, feeling the uneasiness returning.

Jennalyn reached for the long knife next to the cake. She held it over the decadent chocolate treat and let it sink into the frosting. She paused. "I have a confession." Jennalyn lowered her voice and looked over her shoulder, as if to make sure the door to the hallway was still closed. "I have been thinking about this moment all day long."

Christy wasn't quite sure what Jennalyn meant.

"My biggest dream today was about a piece of cake." A slow smile brought a glow to Jennalyn's face. She seemed to be inwardly laughing at herself. "I think there's something seriously wrong with me."

Christy smiled. "Then I must have the same disorder. Because ever since I walked in the door and saw this cake, I have been thinking, 'Get-in-my-belly!'"

Jennalyn giggled and gave Christy a gleeful expression as if the two of them now shared a delicious secret. She returned her attention to the cake and slowly lowered the knife until it hit the glass cake stand. After lifting the knife, Jennalyn paused before making the second cut. Her measurement would have resulted in a normal, petite-size slice of cake. With a questioning look at Christy, Jennalyn let her eyes ask if Christy wanted the slice to be larger or smaller.

Christy tilted her head to the right, giving Jennalyn a silent signal that she could go ahead and make the size of the slice a bit larger.

Jennalyn moved the knife and looked to Christy for approval. Christy nodded to the right again. Jennalyn moved the knife again. They repeated the wordless conversation regarding the flourless cake until Jennalyn was about to cut a slice approximately one-fourth of the entire cake. She looked at Christy again.

For fun, Christy nodded her head one more time to the right.

In a decisive move, Jennalyn moved the knife all the way over and gracefully sliced the cake right down the middle. She lifted the knife and with a straight face said, "Which one would you like?"

Christy and Jennalyn started laughing and couldn't stop. Whatever the mysterious, common-ground moments were that turned two people into Forever Friends, this was definitely one of those moments for Christy and Jennalyn.

Nine

Christy yawned as she plopped a scoop of scrambled eggs into Hana's smiley face bowl and put it on the tray of the high chair. "Blow on it, Hana. It might still be hot."

Hana had collected three of her stuffed animals and tucked them in all around her in the high chair. She daintily plucked the first bite and blew on it with puffed-out cheeks.

"Good job, Buttercup."

The sound of Todd's feet tromping down the stairs made Christy smile. She'd know that gait anywhere.

"Morning!" Christy smiled at him over her shoulder. "Eggs?"

"Sure." Todd gave Cole's kicking foot a shake in the baby chair on the counter. He kissed Hana on top of her head and went to the refrigerator. "Do we have any orange juice?"

"No. Just apple juice."

"Appo joo!" Hana called out. "Appo joo!"

"You have apple juice," Christy said. "Right there in your

sippy cup."

Todd pulled a plastic container from the top shelf and popped the lid. "What's this?"

"That, my wonderful husband, is half of the world's most incredible flourless chocolate amaretto cake. Minus about six bites. Well, maybe eight bites."

"Leftover from last night?" Todd pulled a fork from the drawer and took a bite.

Christy waited, watching him.

His eyes grew wide. He looked at the cake and dug in for a second bite followed by a third. As soon as he swallowed, he made the obvious declaration. "Joel?"

"Yep." Christy held up the pan of scrambled eggs so he'd take note of the original breakfast option.

Todd took a fourth bite before he put the lid back on and stuck his cake-laced fork into the eggs. He licked the chocolate off the edge of his lips before putting the first bite of eggs in his mouth. Wagging the empty fork at Christy and nodding, Todd swallowed the eggs.

"The next time you ask if I want a cake for my birthday or our anniversary or Flag Day, I want you to know my answer will always be yes as long as it's that cake."

"Did you just say Flag Day?"

He tipped his fork toward the wall calendar. "And Father's Day is this month, too. What about having another cake like that for Father's Day?"

"We've been invited to go to Bob and Marti's for lunch on Father's Day. I put it on the calendar, but . . ."

"Better make two cakes, then."

"I don't know if we should go. It's the day before you leave. You'll have lots to do so if you think we need to cancel, I should probably tell Bob and Marti now."

"No. Don't cancel. I'll make sure I'm packed before Sunday."

Christy held out a plate and serving spoon so Todd could dish up some eggs instead of eating out of the pan.

He obliged her unspoken request and sat at the counter, facing Cole and ginning at him. "How long has he been up?"

"About two hours."

"I didn't hear you get up. Did he cry?"

"Yes. He cried." She'd noticed that with their second child, Todd had somehow developed a middle-of-the-night hearing problem. He managed to sleep through everything. When she returned from Jennalyn's last night, the house was quiet and Todd was already asleep. He didn't stir when she slid into bed next to him.

"How was the sorbet?"

"Soiree," Christy corrected him. "The Summer Soiree. It was wonderful."

"What did you do?"

"We talked about the expectations on women in our generation and how we struggle with balance because we tend to get too focused on wanting to do a good job with everything in our lives."

Todd looked up at her.

"Jennalyn made some really good points about how we feel entrusted with so much ability and potential when we finished our college degrees. If we marry and take on the privilege of being at-home moms with our children, we feel like we've lost out on fully using the skills we were pursuing when we were in college."

Todd stopped eating and watched her as if trying to decide if she was being serious. "I thought when you went to these things at Jennalyn's you shared cookie recipes and tried on each other's makeup."

"Todd." Christy swallowed the laughter that was gurgling up. "We don't try on each other's makeup."

He studied her more closely. "Is that the way you feel?"

"Feel about what?"

"That you've missed your potential?"

"No." Christy wiped her hands on a kitchen towel. "I would never say that I missed my potential. But my life is different than I thought it was going to be. It's more limited now."

"What do you mean?"

"Kenya, for example. I'm not going with you and that's because I'm a mom. It's better for me to stay home with our little cuties."

"I knew you were bummed because you wouldn't get to spend time with Katie," Todd said. "But I didn't know you felt locked in here because of the kids."

"I didn't say locked in. I said limited. And of course I'm limited because of our kids. So are you sometimes. I'm not complaining. It's just that this season of life we're in is different than I thought it would be."

"That's what you and Jennalyn talked about last night?"

Christy nodded. She wondered if Todd had any idea at all what her early marriage dreams of their future life together had been. Christy had envisioned long strolls on the beach with their children chasing seagulls and lots of endless summer days with cupcakes and pinwheels and funny little works of art displayed on the refrigerator.

She knew marriage and having children would be a lot of work, too. But she never calculated the sheer volume of diapers and meals and, worst of all, the sleep deprivation.

"Did all the women there feel the same way?" Todd still looked a little astounded at what she was telling him.

"It was only Jennalyn and me. The other women cancelled." Christy shared how she and Jennalyn had both questioned why they ever went to college. "What was the purpose of spending all that money and investing all those years in education when we knew that we wanted to be married and pour all our best efforts into our families?"

Chomping on his last few bites of eggs, Todd seemed deep in thought. He carried his plate over to the sink and leaned against the counter. "Do you regret getting married when we did?"

"No. Not at all."

Todd folded his arms across his chest. "Do you think it would have been better if we had waited a few more years?"

"No, I definitely would not have wanted to wait any longer."

"What about having these two? Do you wish we would have waited until we were older before we had kids?"

"No, of course not." Christy wasn't sure why Todd was going down this path and dissecting their past. She reached for his arm, gave it a squeeze, and said, "I'm glad we got married when we did and I'm grateful we were able to have children when we did. I'm not saying I'd want to change any of that. My point is that my life is . . . what I mean is, it's not the same as . . ." Christy felt flustered that the thoughts weren't flowing the way they had at Jennalyn's.

Todd waited, watching her face and listening.

Christy stepped back and tried to get her sleep-deprived brain to form several complete sentences. "I feel grateful. I like our life. But having small children changes everything for me in more ways than it changes things for you. My priority, by choice, is to put my attention here at home with them. With us, as a family."

"And that choice limits you." Todd said it as one of his

definitive statements.

"In some areas, yes. I'm not complaining. I'm just saying that's how it is and it requires more adjusting than I ever imagined it would."

"So, you could end up resenting me in this stage of life." It was another statement, and from the tone in his voice, Todd was taking this much more seriously than Christy expected. "Getting married when we did and having children when we did kept you from freely pursuing a career."

"No. That's not what I'm saying, Todd, I don't resent you."

"Honestly?"

"I mean, it's true that I've struggled with feeling left out as you've been preparing for this trip. And yes, I would love to go with you and be with you and help out and spend time with Katie. But I don't resent you, Todd."

He reached for her hand and drew her close in a big bear hug. He murmured, "I missed that whole piece."

Christy drew back and looked at Todd. "What whole piece?"

"Fina and David."

Christy thought her mommy brain was the one that was fragmented, but now Todd was the one who was jumping topics at lightning speed. "What about Fina and David?"

"They came over last night."

"They did? What did they say? How are they doing?"

"They decided they're going to take a couple days to not see each other so they can pray about their future. Both of them plan to talk everything through with their parents separately. I told them it was a good idea. There's wisdom in a multitude of counselors."

Christy frowned. She agreed with Todd. She also agreed with the portion of the verse he quoted from Proverbs. What she didn't understand was why they were struggling with it. "Why do you think this is getting so complicated for them?"

"It could be what you were just saying. Fina has been focused on her future career and her goal to finish school for so long that I think David's proposal paralyzed her. She's worried she's going to make a choice she'll regret later."

Cole had been wiggling contentedly. All the motion stopped and he spit up down the front of his pj's. Todd reached for a paper towel and did a daddy-style mop-up job.

"Do you think Fina loves him?" Christy asked.

"Yeah. She loves him. They both said it last night. They're in love. That's not the problem." Todd opened the refrigerator and took out the cake again.

"What is the problem?" Christy pulled a fork from the drawer and handed it to him.

"Every couple's problem. Communication. Also, I think David and Fina know too much."

"About each other?"

Todd plunged the fork into the cake and let the bite linger in his mouth before answering. "I think they know too much about what marriage really is. That's a good thing. If they were simply saying, 'Hey, we're in love so we're going to get married,' I'd be concerned. But they both understand what they're entering into. They know the sacredness of the vows they'd be making to each other, and they're taking this decision seriously."

Todd popped the lid back on the cake and slid it onto the top shelf of the refrigerator. Christy was secretly glad he hadn't eaten the whole thing.

"I was going to call David today," Christy said. "I need to apologize for telling you and Katie about his proposal plan. Do you think I should wait?"

"It's up to you. He did mention that last night."

Christy cringed. "What did he say?"

"He said he assumed you'd tell me because we tell each other everything. And he didn't mind that you told Katie. He just didn't want you to talk to your parents or Bob and Marti about it."

Cole had started hiccupping while they were talking. His little face was so cute. He looked surprised each time a gurgle bubbled up, as if he couldn't figure out where it was coming from. Hana started imitating him and giggling at herself after each silly hiccup sound she made.

Todd gave Christy an especially tender look and said, "We have cute kids."

"Yes, we do."

"Thank you for being such a good mom." Todd stepped closer to Christy and stroked the side of her cheek. "And thank you for being an excellent wife. I don't want you to ever regret us or regret this."

"I don't. Honestly. I love our life. God has blessed us and I'm grateful for everything we have."

Todd kissed her, and the hint of chocolate on his lips sweetened their affectionate expression even more.

"It's rough when you realize you've run out of big firsts." Once again, Todd sounded like he was stating a fact.

Christy drew back. She hadn't said anything about firsts or running out of anything. "You lost me."

"I hope I never lose you."

Cole let out a squawk followed by another hiccup. In an effort to deter him from one of his earth-shaking wails, Christy quickly unlatched him from the baby seat and held him to her shoulder, calmly rubbing his back. He'd been fussy and burpy early this morning, too. Christy couldn't help but wonder if the intense chocolate had gotten to him.

With Cole in her arms, Christy followed Todd to the small kitchen nook table where he packed up his laptop and phone in his messenger bag.

"Todd? What did you mean about running out of big firsts?"

"The first big season of life is over. First love, first date, first kiss, first graduation, then engagement, marriage, first apartment, first baby. You and Jennalyn both checked off all the big firsts on your list before you turned thirty."

Todd's statement stunned Christy. She stood in the open doorway as Todd stepped into the garage and squeezed through the narrow space in front of the nose of Gussie the Bussie, their renovated VW Bus.

"Are you trying to tell me that my life is downhill from here?"

He stood on the edge of the driver's side of the van and looked at Christy over the top of Gussie. "No. Of course not. You helped me see life from Fina's point of view. Her long-term goals are important to her. I totally missed that part last night. Love you. Later."

Todd started to get in and stopped. Popping his head over the top of Gussie a second time, he said, "I told David I'd run the Gathering tonight. I'm going to stay at school to finish grading finals, and then I'll go directly to the Gathering. See you around nine. Or ten."

"Okay." Christy felt a familiar squeeze in her gut as it seemed her life was closing in while Todd's was as expansive as ever. His trajectory of success was widening the gap between them and once again lessening the time they had to be together. Ten minutes ago she told him she didn't resent him. Was that true?

If this isn't resentment, what is it? Loneliness? Abandonment? Is it linked to all the postpartum stuff? Or is this what Jennalyn and I were talking about last night? Our lives have shifted and we're trying to get our hearts established in our homes. We want to be here. But it feels like it's not enough.

Christy went back into the kitchen, patting Cole's back and feeling the churning effects of Todd's words.

Is he right? Am I struggling with all these feelings because I've run out of big firsts?

Christy shook her head as if she could shake off Todd's unsettling comments. Her hand had moved from patting Cole's back and was now under his diaper, supporting him more securely. His nimble body stiffened and he proceeded to overfill his diaper so it leaked out the side on his thigh and onto Christy's hand.

She went to the sink to get a paper towel and noticed that Cole had stopped hiccupping. When Christy glanced at her shoulder she understood why. He'd spit up all over her and it was running down her back.

I was such a dreamer when I pictured this season of my life being about days filled with cupcakes and pinwheels and our children doing cartwheels on the beach.

Ten

"Mommy. Look." Hana was busy trying to share her eggs and juice with her three high chair companions. Her absorption in her little game had been a great distraction because she hadn't noticed that her daddy left. It also had given Christy time to do a rapid cleanup and diaper change.

"Does your bunny like eggs?" Christy asked, returning to the kitchen.

"Bunny Wuv." Hana pulled the beleaguered plush pal out of the high chair. "Dis Bunny Wuv."

Christy thought Hana meant that her bunny loved the eggs. However, throughout the day Hana kept chattering about "Bunny Wuv" and clung to her little pal in a more attached way than ever.

By the time Christy got Hana tucked into bed that night, she caught on that Hana had named her favorite stuffed animal. It wasn't just her "bunny" anymore. It was now "Bunny Wuv." The delight of watching her little girl's imagination sprout brought Christy a deep sort of joy.

Deep joy had been another topic she and Jennalyn discussed at the heart-to-heart level at the soiree. They both agreed that being there for every moment of these early years of their children's lives was a gift. This was what they wanted. This focused life at home was what they had chosen.

She smiled as she went down the hall in her quiet house after bedtime and thought of the other deep joys that had punctuated this day. Her greatest accomplishment had been finishing the last throw pillow and delivering them to the gift shop on Balboa Island. She had packed up the pillows, the stroller, and both children and delivered the pillows with her baby parade in tow. The shop owner was tickled to see Hana and Cole and let Christy know that the pillows were selling well and she'd have another order ready next week.

To celebrate, and because Cole was doing so great, Christy bravely rolled the stroller across the street and ordered a Balboa Bar. She couldn't remember if she and Todd had introduced Hana yet to the treat the two of them discovered the summer they'd first met. Today seemed like the day to let the legacy continue.

Hana had managed four bites of the chocolate-dipped ice cream bar before the confection started melting down Christy's hand onto Hana's dress. A big chunk of the chocolate shell fell on one of Bunny Wuv's ears. That's when Christy knew they'd enjoyed this first Balboa Bar for as long as they could. She took one final bite and sadly tossed the remainder into the nearby trash can.

"Well, Hana? What did you think of your first Balboa Bar?"

"Yum!" Her blue eyes were open wide and across her chin was a skid mark of chocolate.

Christy grabbed her phone and snapped a picture. "Your daddy is going to like this picture very much."

The deep joy covered her, tickled her, and brought to mind vivid memories of the skid mark her first Balboa Bar had left on her cheek during a tandem bike ride with Todd. It was a fifteen-year-old memory but just as vivid in her imagination as when it happened.

Todd had looked at her oddly when they arrived at Aunt Marti and Uncle Bob's front door at the end of their ride. He grinned a curious, lopsided grin and looked like he was about to say something funny. All he said was, "Later" and got in his original VW Bus, Gus, and chugged off down the street.

Christy was still chucking at the memory as she got the kids in their car seats and drove home from Balboa. *Maybe not everything has changed in this new season. It's just shifting. That's the part that makes me feel unstable.*

All day long Christy had been sifting through Todd's morning comments. She was almost ready to admit that the fact that she'd be turning thirty next month was messing with her psyche every time her emotions dipped into the postpartum pool. His summary of all the "big firsts" had come back to her a dozen times.

By Cole's evening feeding, Christy was asking herself the deeper questions.

Why do I feel like I should be doing more? More what, I don't know. I feel as if I'm letting God down. Why is that?

Christy put Cole into his crib and made her way down the stairs. She pulled a throw blanket off the sofa and went out on the deck with the blanket wrapped around her shoulders. Looking up at the evening sky, she saw what she'd hoped to see—the colors of the early summer night sky tinged with clouds that were a pale-orchid shade of ivory with flecks of pink.

Drawing in a deep draught of the cool air, Christy settled into one of the deck chairs and rested her feet on the rim of the fire pit.

Is that true, Father? Am I letting you down?

Christy's mind had filled with thoughts of all the education and training she had worked so hard to complete during her college years. She knew it had been the right decision at the time, but what did any of that matter now? Her heart's desire had been to honor God and make her life completely available for Him to use her in important and effective ways in this world.

Have I missed the mark by not doing more missions work before we had children? Should I have gotten more involved with the teens Todd has been ministering to over the years? Did I put my own comfort and desires ahead of ways I could have been serving God?

She knew it wasn't supposed to be a contest to see who was the most accomplished before they turned thirty. Having the privilege of being an at-home mom was a high calling and a role in life she took seriously.

But seeing Rick and Nicole starring in their new TV show and thinking about Katie and Eli changing the lives of thousands in Africa made her life feel small.

"Father God," she prayed. "What can I do? Just tell me and I'll do it. Should I start a Bible Study this summer for teen girls? Or maybe a sewing class? What about foster care? We talked about getting signed up a while ago. Should we do that? I could do child care here at home. That would bring in a little more money. Or should I somehow make a heroic effort and go with Todd to Africa after all?"

A clear thought came to Christy and settled on her frantic thoughts.

Oh, honey. Stop buzzing and just bee.

She didn't know if God's Spirit spoke in whimsy, but the play on words made Christy smile. The thought calmed her buzzing heart and felt as warming to her soul as the blanket around her shoulders.

"Okay," she whispered.

Christy lingered on the deck, leaning back and watching the night sky as the stars came out one by one. The beach houses built close around them blocked much of the expansive sky. All she could see was straight up to the heavens directly over the deck. In a way, the narrowed view reminded her again of her narrowed life. Like everything else seemed to be lately, it was okay. A limited vision of the heavenlies was all she needed. It was all her weary, pondering heart could absorb right now.

Christy sat in the solitude for a little while until it became obvious that she was ready for bed. It was her turn to sleep. She had blocked out the calendar tomorrow morning for family time. Going to bed now was a good idea. She'd be more rested when Cole sent out his usual middle-of-the-night alarm.

The kitchen clock showed that it was only seven forty-five. Christy couldn't remember where she'd left her phone. She did remember when she stepped into the kitchen, that there were four more bites of chocolate cake left in the refrigerator. She got a fork and took one bite, letting it glide over her tongue and down her throat.

With a contented "Mmm," Christy closed up the container and left the last three bites for Todd. She remembered how he had once told the teens at the Gathering that the bricks that made his marriage to Christy strong were things like communication, faithfulness, and intimacy. The mortar that held those bricks together was small acts of affection. Christy knew he would consider the last bite of cake waiting for him when he got home to be an expression of Christy's affection for him.

She was about to lock up the house and go on the hunt for her phone when she glanced out the kitchen window and saw Fina's car pulling into the driveway.

"Hope you don't mind," Fina said a few minutes later when Christy welcomed her inside. "I sent a couple texts."

"I don't know where my phone is. I think I left it upstairs. Come in. Would you like something to eat?"

Fina looked like Christy had asked her a difficult question.

"We have baby carrots. Or I could make popcorn."

The indecisive expression seemed to be fixed on Fina's face.

"If you're really hungry, there's some meatballs and left-over green salad. Or watermelon."

"No." Fina appeared to be putting herself out of agony by saying the word that finally stopped Christy's list of options.

Christy could see the problem. Fina was on overload. Decisions about life, love, schooling, marriage, David, food, future. All of it. She had decision fatigue; something Christy remembered feeling far too often when she was younger.

"Come on. Let's go get comfortable on the couch." Christy made the decision for both of them and waited to sit until after Fina had subconsciously chosen where she wanted to sit.

She took the chair instead of the couch. Her expression still looked dazed. Her high cheekbones, one of her most elegant features, seemed to be turning pink. The blush rose from the edge of her narrow chin, all the way to the corner of her dark eyebrows.

"Christy, how did you know? I mean, really know, that you should marry Todd?"

It took Christy a few moments to form her thoughts. She didn't have a good answer. Not really. And she didn't want to say that she just "knew." Her journey with Todd had spanned many years, so she started with that point of logic. They had a lot of time together as well as months apart from each other. Through all those years, they continued to grow closer and closer.

When Christy saw that her winding journey wasn't helping Fina, she simply said, "I knew for sure when I got to the point where I couldn't imagine my life without him being in every part of it."

Fina crossed her long legs. She was wearing leggings and a T-shirt, and somehow managed to make it look like it was an outfit and not just workout clothes. "How old were you when you decided that?"

Christy tried to remember. "It had to be in my early college years. It's funny because at the time I thought I'd always remember every detail. Now it all sort of blends together."

"Do you remember when you knew you were in love?"

Christy nodded. "I remember when I first told Todd I loved him. He'd told me that he loved me but I was hesitant to tell him."

"Why?"

"Because I knew that would be the turning point for me. For us. He was sure about me and had been since we first met."

Fina folded her fingers together and rested her hands on her midriff. "That's what David said about me. He knew from the beginning."

"But you're not sure about him?" Christy felt hesitant. The only thing she was worse at than being a spy was being a counselor. She didn't want to be in a position where she was offering advice that wasn't solid or worse, that would be the cause for her brother's possible broken heart.

Fina let out a long breath. "I honestly don't know what I think or feel. These last few days have depleted me of all possible decision-making skills. Ever since my freshman year of high school, I have been on a track for graduate school so I could go into some form of sports medicine. That's always been the goal. I'm close to the finish line and . . ."

Christy waited for Fina to complete her thought.

"I didn't expect to get serious about a guy until after I was out of school. David came along and I think it's like you said. I can't imagine my life without him being in every part of it. I can't just walk away. I can't." Fina paused. This all seemed like such a painful revelation to her.

"But will I regret it if I marry him when I'm this young? My mom was young when she married my dad, and I watched them grow apart when I was in high school. I don't want that to happen to me. My mom thought I didn't know that they were heading for a separation, but I knew. Kids know. They can tell when their parents are faking their relationship and are both in a lot of pain."

Fina looked Christy in the eye. "I was away at college in Arizona, and I remember drilling it into my soul that I would never do what my mother had done by marrying young. I promised myself I would finish my education and get established in my career so I'd never be vulnerable like that."

Christy had met Fina's parents last summer, and they seemed very close. "Did your parents separate?"

"No. They got back together."

"What happened to bring them back together?"

"Do you remember hearing about how the Wildflower Café caught on fire?"

Christy nodded. She had been to the charming Wildflower Café that Fina's mother ran. She'd heard how it had been rebuilt and remodeled a few years ago.

"The turning point, my mom says, was when she started renovating the café. She asked God to renovate her heart at the same time. That's when she started falling in love with my dad again. It's kind of a beautiful love story. A second chance at love. It would make a great Hallmark movie."

Christy smiled.

"My dad made a lot of changes in his life as they were falling in love again. The biggest change was that he finally became a Christian. That altered everything for our family."

"That's beautiful. Having spent a little time with your family, I can see all the results now."

"That's why I was shocked that my dad told David we had his blessing. My dad is more protective of my sisters and me than he's ever been. When I talked with my parents today, they said they've been praying for David and me ever since we met. My dad thinks we're a good match because of the way we're opposites."

Fina looked as if she'd suddenly had a revelation. "I guess we're being opposite now, aren't we? He's ready to jump off into the deep end, and I want all the measurements and calculations and wind speed before I even consider taking the leap."

Fina uncrossed her legs and leaned forward. "I know there's nothing wrong with wanting to accomplish a goal. I also know that getting married at twenty-one is not too young if you have support and a clear understanding of what marriage is. It's an unconditional commitment to an imperfect person. That's how Todd described it last night, and we agree with that."

A pause hung between them.

Christy said, "I don't know if this will help, but last night Jennalyn and I were talking about how different our lives look now." She went on to do her best to summarize the big-picture image, the balance of career and family and what all those twenty-something priorities might look like ten years down the road. Fina seemed to be taking it all in.

"We are women of options, Fina. That's for sure. Sometimes I wonder if we have so many options, it dilutes our ability to fully ignite our passions in a single area. Jennalyn thinks all of our drive toward overachieving in multiple areas is making the women in our generation fractured. We're losing our ability to love well and listen deeply because our culture dictates that we must do more and be more."

Fina's expression was clouding over.

"What are you thinking right now?" Christy asked.

"I don't know. Everything you just said is kind of spinning in here." She tapped the side of her head.

"When was the last time you ate?"

Fina shrugged. "I had a granola bar."

"When?"

"I don't remember."

Christy decided that as a woman of options, she was going to stop asking questions and show Fina an expression of affection and coax her into the kitchen for a little something to eat.

Eleven

Fina followed Christy to the kitchen and sat at the counter while Christy began pulling food out of the refrigerator. She lined up the selection hoping something would appeal to Fina.

"Do you have any peanut butter?" Fina asked.

"Sure do. Smooth or crunchy?"

"Crunchy."

Christy grinned. "You're like Todd. He likes crunchy. I like smooth."

Fina gave a weak smile in return. "Opposites."

"Yep." Christy placed both peanut butter jars on the counter and pulled out a loaf of bread and a knife.

"Is it okay if I have that last banana?" Fina also asked Christy to warm up a few meatballs, and she ate all the salad that was left over from yesterday. Her eyes brightened and she started talking again, this time sounding as if she had a clearer understanding of all the areas that concerned her the most.

"I haven't exactly admitted this yet to anyone, Christy, but I'm terrified."

"Of what?"

"Of making a mistake."

Christy sidled up to Fina and wrapped her arms around her. In this moment there was nothing opposite about Fina and her. Christy knew about insecurities and fear that could turn paralyzing and make it feel impossible to make a decision about anything.

Sliding into the seat next to Fina, she asked, "Why do you feel that way?"

Fina looked down at her empty salad plate. "I'm afraid that if I allow myself to become passionate about David the way he is passionate about me, I'll lose my passion and drive to accomplish the goal I set all those years ago to finish school."

Christy had several things she wanted to say about that, but she had a feeling there was more Fina wanted and needed to say, so she waited, doing the hard work of keeping her thoughts to herself. At least for the moment.

"I'm also afraid that if we get married and go to Indiana, David will regret everything he gave up here. He'd resent that I delayed him from getting his own career established."

Christy didn't think that would be an issue for her brother, but she didn't know what he may have told Fina in the past. Perhaps having an established coaching position was a bigger priority to him than Christy realized. Once again, Christy held back from adding her opinion.

"I don't want to go through what my mom went through." Fina started to tear up. "I'm afraid of what would happen to my heart if David ever decided he didn't love me anymore." A rush of tears came and Fina wiped them away quickly.

Christy got up and returned quickly with a box of tissues. She tried to read Fina's expression to gauge if she was open to hearing any of the things Christy was thinking. If Katie were here right now, she'd be talking a mile a minute, showering Fina with insights and options. If Todd were here, he'd be nodding and thinking. His conclusion would be insightful and something Fina hadn't thought of yet.

All Christy could do right now, or at least all she thought she should be doing, was listening. A few moments of unhurried silence passed between them before Fina straightened her shoulders and made a final statement.

"There is one other thing I'm really afraid of, Christy. I'm afraid I might fail graduate school."

That comment caught Christy off guard, and she was pretty sure her expression showed her surprise.

"I'm not a great student. My mom always said it was my competitiveness that got me through school. She's right." Fina attempted a self-deprecating laugh. "Can you see why I'm such a mess right now?"

"You're not a mess. You're a woman who cares deeply. There's a big difference between the two."

Fina drew in a deep breath and wiped her eyes. "So, what do you think? What should I do?"

Christy offered the most comforting look she could give. "I don't know what you should do. I do know something you can't do."

"What's that?"

"You can't let fear make the decisions for you."

Fina drew back and looked at Christy without blinking. Christy wasn't sure where she first heard that line. Perhaps it had been from Katie. It had helped her more than once to get her heart back on track when she was overcome by indecision.

"You're right." Fina reached for another tissue. "When you said that, I thought of that verse that says, 'God has not given us a spirit of fear.' Where is that?"

"It's in 2 Timothy. I love that verse." Christy lowered her chin. "The next question you have to ask yourself is, if all of these fears aren't coming from God, where did they come from?"

Fina knew the answer. It was evident by the way her eyebrows rose.

Christy wasn't sure what to say next. It seemed pointless to pick apart the fears Fina had listed. They could come up with pros and cons to each of them. The real issue seemed to be the way fear had paralyzed her.

A memory came to Christy of when she and Todd were in Glenbrooke last summer. Fina was trying to decide then if she should move to Southern California. On the porch of their cabin, Todd had suggested the four of them pray together, and they did. That seemed to be the turning point for David and Fina.

"Do you think we should pray?" Christy asked.

"Yes. I'd love that."

Christy reached for Fina's hand and bowed her head. She asked God to send all of Fina's fears back to the pit where they came from. In place of the fears, she asked God to give her wisdom and power and a clear mind. She asked God to comfort Fina with His peace.

Fina looked up when Christy said, "Amen." A small smile tugged at the corners of her lips. "Thank you, Christy. I needed that so much. While you were praying, I kept thinking of David's favorite verse in Philippians: 'I can do all things through Christ who strengthens me.'"

Christy knew her brother often used that verse with the young athletes he coached in the afterschool sports program. For a moment she thought Fina was applying it to being willing to tough it out and push through and marry David in spite of all her fears. But Fina was thinking of that verse differently.

"I can get through school with God's help. I know I can. And if David is willing to put his career on pause, that only shows that he loves me, right?"

Christy smiled. "He definitely loves you."

"Todd told us that verse last night about how husbands should love their wives and be willing to lay down their lives for them the way Christ laid down His life for us."

Christy recognized that verse as one Todd often quoted and was pretty sure it was in Ephesians.

Fina's countenance had changed. Christy guessed it was partly from having some food, but mostly it seemed that the fear was gone. She looked different. She was no longer stuck.

"Thank you. Christy, you have no idea what this means to me. Thank you for letting me drop in all the time." Fina leaned over and gave Christy a big hug.

"Of course. Fina, you're always welcome. You know that." A knock sounded at the front door. If Christy had been the only one home, she might not have answered since it was almost nine o'clock. Then she remembered that Fina was parked in their narrow driveway. Todd may have had to park down the street and didn't have a key to the front door since he always came and went through the garage.

Christy opened the door and found her aunt and uncle standing on her doorstep. Uncle Bob was holding a big box of diapers. Marti had an oversized bouquet of mixed summer flowers.

"Hope you don't mind. I texted you, Christy." Marti stepped inside and turned toward the kitchen. She stopped short when she saw Fina. "Oh! Fina. I thought you were at the Gathering with David."

"No, I . . . I'm not. I'm here."

"Coming through," Bob said with his usual cheerful attitude. "Thought I'd contribute to the cause. I've got two more boxes in the car. I'll be right back."

Marti gave Christy and Fina a look of exaggerated bewilderment. "Why did I agree to go with him to that huge warehouse? It's exhausting. All we needed were trash bags and Greek yogurt. Your uncle thought we should peruse every aisle and we filled the cart, and now our car is overflowing. Then, of course, we had to stop for gas and the line was so long. It feels like the middle of the night."

"Thanks for the diapers." Christy hoped this was the right place to insert her expression of gratitude.

"You can thank your uncle for the diapers when he comes back." Marti laid the big bouquet on the counter. "You can thank me for these. I know how much you like fresh flowers. I hope these bring you some cheer."

"Thanks, Aunt Marti. I love them." Christy gave her an appreciative hug.

"You're welcome. I didn't like the idea of showing up here with just diapers."

Marti said the word *diapers* with as much indignation as if it had been dirty diapers they were talking about.

Marti turned her attention to the crumpled-up tissues on the counter and looked more closely at both Fina and Christy as if to see who had the reddest eyes. "Is everything all right?" Marti's voice went up a few notes on the tone scale.

Christy and Fina exchanged glances and both started

nodding in an easygoing way.

"Yes, everything is good," Christy answered for both of them.

"I've had a very full week," Fina said honestly.

"I knew you had a lot going on," Marti said. "Because we've hardly seen you at the house."

Fina nodded but didn't offer any explanations.

"How is David doing?"

"He's okay. Busy, as you know, with both jobs."

"I imagine it's getting more and more difficult for the two of you to spend lots of time together."

Fishing, Aunt Marti. Fishing.

Fina didn't reply because Uncle Bob bounded in the door with a jumbo box of diapers under each arm. Christy hurried to take one of the boxes from him and protested that he really didn't need to get diapers for them.

"It's something I wanted to do," Bob said. "We all know how it's those little, everyday things that can add up and take a bite out of a person's budget."

Christy had a feeling her chin-lowered appreciation grin at him was coming out looking like more of a smirk than a smile. Bob and Marti always seemed to have more money than they knew what to do with. They owned the house Christy and Todd were living in as well as two other beach houses, including the luxurious two-story house they lived in. He and Marti drove luxury cars and traveled first class to their favorite resorts. It was hard to picture him knowing anything about having a bite taken out of his budget.

Christy noticed that Bob's years were beginning to show in his face more than anywhere else. He still had slightly noticeable scars on his neck, chin, and ear from when his BBQ caught fire over ten years ago and burned him. His many hours on the golf course contributed to his tan forearms and face as well as the deepened laugh lines in the corners of his eyes.

Christy loved her uncle dearly and thanked him again for the diapers.

"You're welcome, Bright Eyes. Any time."

Marti tossed out another line with a wiggly question dangling from the hook. "Do you and David have any fun plans for the weekend?"

"Not yet."

Christy admired Fina's ability to remain truthful without giving away anything personal that she wasn't ready to share yet.

"Why don't you two have dinner with us tomorrow night? We've been eager to try that new Cuban-cuisine restaurant in Laguna Hills. I've heard it's a romantic venue with good food. If you like spicy Latin food."

Fina flipped her short hair behind her ear. "I thought you didn't like spicy food?"

"I don't, particularly. But I was thinking of you and David. The romantic ambiance, the live music. It might be something fun for the four of us to do together."

"I don't think tomorrow night will work for us. I appreciate you asking, though."

Marti looked at Christy, the box of tissues, and back at Fina. She lowered her voice and got right to the point. "You and David aren't having a falling out, are you?"

"A falling out?"

"An argument." Marti raised her eyebrows. "Are you two fighting about something right now? Is that why you can't go to dinner with us?"

"No. We're not arguing about anything."

"Well, I'm certainly grateful that you and Christy have

each other. You've become close, haven't you? Like sisters."

Fina and Christy exchanged subdued expressions, both of them trying to remain casual.

"Yes," Fina said. "Like sisters."

Bob reminded Marti that they still had refrigerated items in the car and needed to get going. Fina got up and said she needed to make one stop, but that she'd be home shortly. Giving Christy a big hug, Fina whispered in her ear, "It is well with my soul. Thank you."

Christy sat at the kitchen counter after they left, trying to unravel the clues. Saying that it was well with her soul was a beautiful benediction to their time together, but what did it mean? Fina said she was making a stop before going home. Was she going over to talk to David? Or had she decided that schooling was her top priority right now and she was going to ask David to wait for her?

Christy felt a common-ground sort of sympathy for her aunt right now. Christy was dying to know what was going to happen, but she'd have to wait like everyone else to see how the next steps unfolded.

Twelve

"We're in here," Todd called to Christy early on Saturday morning.

The sound of Hana giggling filled the house as Christy came down the stairs with Cole in her arms. She found Todd on his back on the fluffy but dirty living room rug. He was lifting Hana into the air as if she were a barbell. Hana loved it and kept asking for more.

"It's raining," Todd said. "Can you hear it?"

"Yes. I love it. Although, I hope it clears before you have the outdoor baccalaureate tomorrow at school."

"It's supposed to pass through this morning."

Christy opened the refrigerator and pulled out the fresh fruit and other ingredients she thought would make a good smoothie for breakfast. She noticed the container with the cake was still on the top shelf. When she opened it she saw one bite left.

"Todd? I left this cake for you."

"I know. I had some when I got home last night. I saved that last bite for you."

Christy smiled to herself. It was amazing how loved and cherished his simple gesture made her feel. She pulled a butter knife from the drawer and cut the small bite in half one more time before she took the smaller of the two slivers and popped it into her mouth. She savored the early morning bit of sweetness and returned the final wee bite for Todd to discover and hopefully feel equally loved.

Instead of making smoothies, Christy decided a rainy morning called for oatmeal with lots of cinnamon and raisins. She got the pan of water ready on the stove and carried Cole into the living room so she could hand him over to Todd and have both hands free to finish making breakfast.

Todd had put Hana down and was giving his full attention to the weather report on the local news. Christy could tell by his standing posture and expression that a south swell was coming in with the rain, and that meant great surfing at all Todd's favorite spots. Hana was sitting on his foot with her arms wrapped around his leg. At random intervals, Todd lifted his leg a few inches and put it down.

"Again, Daddy! Again."

Christy handed over Cole and watched her strong husband multitask. He patted the swaddled baby, gave Hana a wacky elevator ride, and tried to hear what the reporter was saying about the weather forecast.

"Do you want to go?" Christy asked.

Todd pulled his gaze off the TV and looked at Christy as if he didn't dare believe what he thought she was asking him.

"Go where?" he asked cautiously, as if he expected her to say, "Go to the garage and get the vacuum." Or "Go to the store and get a week's worth of groceries."

Christy dipped her chin, motioning to the weather report. "Do you want to go surfing this morning?"

Todd's expression reminded Christy of how her little brother used to look when the family was headed into town on a Saturday to run errands, and their dad had given a hint that a drive-through Dairy Queen might be in their future.

"It's calling for four to five at Huntington."

"Then you should definitely go." Christy didn't know a lot about Todd's world of surfing, but she did know that it was unusual for the waves to get up to four or five feet during the summer in and around Newport Beach.

"Are you sure you wouldn't mind? You put Family Day on the calendar."

"We'll have Family Afternoon, then. It's fine. Really." She knew this gesture of her affection for him would be a little more mortar to hold together a few more bricks in their marriage.

"Seriously, Todd. Go. Go hang ten or whatever you guys call it."

"Hang ten?" he repeated with a teasing look in his eye.

"That's what they called it on a kid's show Hana was watching."

Todd looked down at Hana. "You watched a kid's show about surfing? Wow! You'll watch it again with Daddy one day, won't you? Surf's up! Hang ten. Cowabunga, Dude."

Hana didn't seem to know what to make of her daddy's funny voice and comical expressions. She did, however, know how to cry herself into a tizzy when he dashed out the garage door fifteen minutes later in his board shorts and Rancho Corona hoodie.

Christy was able to distract Hana by starting a project with her. With Cole strapped into his baby chair, Christy put an apron on Hana and pulled a kitchen stool around to the side of the counter Christy used for food prep. Together they made a fine mess.

The original objective was to clean out the refrigerator and get some hearty, homemade vegetable soup simmering all day in the Crock-Pot. The ideal rainy-day meal. That goal was eventually accomplished, but Christy's idea of giving Hana a bowl and mixing spoon didn't hold her attention very long. She was more interested in putting her little teeth marks into every carrot, every potato, and even the wooden stirring spoon.

Instead of letting up, the rain came in a rush as Christy was clearing the counter. Hana had been moved to her high chair with Bunny Wuv and her bowl of oatmeal, which had now cooled. She reminded Christy of Goldilocks with her bowl of porridge and her big blue eyes opened wide as she listened to the pelting rain.

The deep joy of motherhood poured over Christy in rhythm with the rain, and she didn't mind at all that she'd encouraged Todd to go spend a little quality time with his favorite orange surfboard out in God's majestic creation. Surfing was what filled up Todd's emotional well. She had always loved that about him and didn't want that to be one of the things eliminated from his life during this season of change for them.

Just then, she heard the sound of the garage door opening. It was almost eclipsed by the deluge of the rain. Christy looked at the clock. He wasn't even gone for an hour.

She waited for the door to open, picturing that Todd would enter, give a shrug, a brief report, and head for a warm shower.

When he didn't appear, Christy hurried into the garage

and found him struggling to peel out of his wet suit.

"Zipper broke. Can you help me?"

Christy tugged, Todd pulled, and he was soon out of his surfer boy second skin. "Do you think you can fix it?" Todd asked, examining the demolished fastener.

"I'll try. I need to get the right kind of zipper. I might need a special expandable sort of thread." She made a quick overall assessment of the condition of the rest of his wet suit. "You might be better off starting all over with a new one. How long have you had this?"

"Ever since the summer I first kissed you." He playfully leaned toward Christy and shook his short hair. Only a few remaining salty drops were flung on her.

"Hey!" Christy put up her hands in defense and started laughing.

He grinned the best sort of grin. For the past fifteen years he'd gotten the same giggly response from Christy. It seemed to never grow old for him.

"I take it the surf sesh was a wipeout?" She smiled at her pun.

"Swells were choppy. Only two to three. Crazy undertow." Todd came close and planted a very nice salty kiss on Christy's lips. "I realized I'd rather be here."

"Well, then, welcome home. Do you want some oatmeal?"

"Sure." Todd followed her back into the kitchen where they discovered that Hana had "fed" most of her oatmeal to Bunny Wuv, and it was dripping down the side of the high chair and onto the floor. The mess barely fazed Christy.

"Oh, Sunshine! What are you doin'?" Todd was less familiar with the usual daily disasters. He sprang into action and pulled a long stretch of paper towels from the roll. "It's in your hair! Hana." His voice had changed to his stern daddy voice.

"I sawee." Hana's face was speckled with cinnamon-tinged oatmeal. She kept picking at the side of her nose.

As Todd pulled oatmeal globs out of Hana's hair, Christy leaned in and lifted Hana's chin. In her firmest voice she said, "Hana. You may not put raisins or anything else in your nose. Do you understand?"

"Sawee, Mommy. Sawee."

"She put a raisin in her nose?" Todd sounded panicked. "Can she breathe? Do I need to take her to the clinic?"

"No. I've got this." Christy pulled a small device from the utensils drawer and with a firm, experienced hand under Hana's chin, she easily extracted the soft raisin. She held it for Hana to see and repeated her firm words. "Food goes in your mouth, Hana. Only in your mouth."

The repentant look on Hana's face was enough for Christy to believe that she understood.

Christy gave her a kiss on her forehead and got a taste of cinnamon on her lips. She smiled a tender mommy smile. Was Hana actually old enough to grasp the concept of sin and grace, of messing up and experiencing forgiveness? She certainly had learned early on that saying she was "sawee" was the first thing to do when she'd done something wrong.

"What do you need me to do?" Todd still appeared to be a bit dazed and in awe at the same time.

Before Christy could answer, Cole started crying. His hearty wails echoed off the kitchen ceiling and reverberated around the open space.

"You can give Hana a bath," Christy said loudly. She smiled at her unhappy son as she took him out of his baby seat. "Come here. It's okay, Little Bear. I didn't forget about your breakfast."

Christy left Todd to deal with Hana and went into the

downstairs guest room to the corner chair. Cole latched on as if he hadn't eaten in a week. Christy chuckled at his ravenous sounds that seemed to be a mix of yums and squeaks.

On many days when she was alone with their children and didn't have enough hands to deal with both of them at the same time, Christy would plop down to nurse Cole with a rushed, anxious feeling. This morning she felt calm and drew in a deep breath.

As she exhaled, she thought of how Katie had inspired Christy to pray simple prayers during the many hours she spent nursing her newborn. Katie had developed the pattern when little James Andrew Lorenzo was first born. She had told Christy that all her new mommy brain could come up with was a single word at a time. So, while she nursed Jimmy she would take a deep breath, focus on the one word that seemed to be at the forefront of her mind, and pray that for her baby.

Katie said she prayed a lot for "sleep" and "peace" during the first month before she realized those were things she needed, too. So she expanded her simple prayers by starting with her son and then expanding the same prayer by including herself and her husband.

Katie's idea inspired Christy because when Hana was an infant, Christy had spent her early months nervous about whether Hana was getting enough milk or nursing the right amount of time on each side. During many of their nursing sessions, Christy used her free hand to scroll through her phone and read everything she could on the many mommy advice sites. She was more focused on what to do and what was considered "normal" than on her newborn in her arms.

With Cole she felt a deeper confidence and sense of contentment. He was her baby. As insightful as the deluge of info and advice had been at the start of her journey into motherhood, Christy had taken up Katie's idea and in moments like this, she took the first word that rested on her and prayed a simple prayer over Cole using that one word as the theme.

This morning the word that came to Christy was grace. She stroked her baby's cheek and whispered a simple prayer that God would pour out His grace on her son and daughter as well as on her and on Todd. She thanked God for all the ways He had extended His extravagant grace to her over the years and asked Him to continue to teach her how to show that grace to her children, her husband, her family, her friends, and where it was often most needed, to herself.

When she switched sides, Christy closed her eyes and leaned her head back. She hummed one of the worship songs Todd had written with their good friend Doug many years ago. They'd titled it simply "Psalm 84" because nearly all their songs were taken directly from Scripture. Todd and Doug shared a goal of committing as much of God's Word to memory as they could. For them, starting in their high school years, it seemed the easiest way to do that was to put verses to music and sing them often.

Christy kept humming Psalm 84 and thought about how Todd and Doug's goal had been accomplished in her life through their many songs. Christy had memorized far more verses through the music than she ever would have if she'd tried using flash cards.

A thought stirred in Christy. She could do the same with her children by singing all their daddy's songs to them. God's Word would fall on their young ears and settle like seeds in their hearts. Hana loved music. She already had favorite worship songs she wanted Todd to sing over her each night. It gave Christy a little shiver up her neck to think that she could begin now to have an impact on their little ones by planting God's Word in their hearts.

Clearing her throat, Christy began singing softly. Cole looked up and stretched his mouth into the sweetest little quivering-lips expression. Christy grinned at him. All the experts said that anything that resembled a smile at this age was merely a muscle twinge or even a response to a gas bubble.

"They're all wrong," Christy said to Cole. "That was a smile, wasn't it? You like it when I sing to you."

She sang the melodic tune again.

"For the LORD God is a sun
and shield;
The LORD bestows
favor
and honor.
No good thing
does he withhold
from those
who walk uprightly."

Todd came downstairs and bent low to clear the doorway into the guest room because Hana was riding on his shoulders. He lowered Hana to the guest bed. She bounced with a happy smile on her freshly bathed face.

"What can I help you with around here? You need me to vacuum, right?"

"That would be great."

"Do you need me to take Hana and go get groceries so you can nap when Cole goes down?"

"That would be really great."

"Could you get a list together for me?"

"Sure. We have chicken vegetable soup in the Crock-Pot. Hana and I made it while you were out getting rained on and watching your wet suit disintegrate."

Todd paused and gazed at her. "I don't know how you do it, Kilikina. This two-ring circus of our lives is crazy. You amaze me."

The tune from the song was still floating through Christy's mind, as was her simple prayers for grace. She sang a line of the song as a response to Todd's comment. *"The LORD bestows favor and honor."*

Todd grinned and sang the last line back to Christy. *"No good thing does he withhold from those who walk uprightly."*

He leaned over and kissed her. "Thank you for walking uprightly."

Christy kissed him back, a lingering, happy-wife-happy-life sort of kiss. "And thank you for being my no good thing." She paused, rewinding in her mind what she'd just said.

"I mean my good thing. Well, not my thing. My good husband. Thanks for being . . . thanks for being you."

Christy realized she must have looked sweetly silly when she tried to retract her odd words because Todd watched her until he couldn't hold back any longer. He tilted his head back and laughed heartily at Christy's fumble.

Todd's outburst startled Cole. He stopped feeding and looked to his mommy to make sure everything was all right. She met his gaze with an assuring look, and he resumed his eager efforts. Hana rolled back and forth on the bed, laughing in an exaggerated way as if she was in on the joke and should laugh loudly, too.

"Come on, Sunshine." Todd picked up Hana. "Your no-good-thing daddy needs to go find the vacuum."

He turned around to look at Christy. His expression was

the best. The dried saltwater had left a faint pattern of white etchings across his forehead. His unshaven jaw looked indomitable, and his distinct silver-blue eyes were screaming across the room to her that she always was and always would be his one and only.

I love you, too, Todd. I love you with all my heart.

Thirteen

The sweet, silly, romantic moments Christy and Todd shared as a family in the guest room on Saturday morning were the happiest and nearly the only calm moments of their weekend. It was as if for those few hours, they had all fallen into a pocket of grace.

Then the usual chaos returned.

On Tuesday night, Christy and Katie had managed to set up a spontaneous video call. They talked fast, giving each other a summary of what their lives looked like lately.

"I'm heading up to the dining hall but keep talking," Katie said. "It's breakfast time here. And it's a really beautiful day, by the way."

The image on Christy's phone swooshed from a fixed shot of Katie's shoe to blur of the lush green lawn at Brockenhurst Conference Center. Jimmy was in a front backpack, and every few steps Katie took, Christy caught a glimpse of his bobbing head.

A tender ache roused itself in the corner of Christy's heart. In a week Todd would be there. He'd be strolling across the lovely grounds with Katie and Eli at the start of a beautiful day. He would be the one holding Jimmy and sending a photo home to Christy. Todd would be experiencing it all without her.

This hurts so much.

"By the way, newsflash," Katie said. "I burnt my fingers on the oven last night. You may have caught a glimpse of this jumbo cast."

She held up her first three fingers that were wound together with gauze and lots of masking tape. "Dr. Lorenzo went a little overboard, as you can see. We had no medical tape in the house so he used this. I don't know if it's painter's tape or what. It works. And it's helped me improve my saluting skills. Look."

Katie swooped the camera again so Christy could see her touching her bulbously wrapped fingers to her forehead and snapping them to her side. She did it again. "Yes, sir," Katie quipped. "I'll get right on it, sir."

Christy smiled. Katie always had a way of bringing a lighthearted tone back into any moment. "Speaking of your talented 'Dr.' Lorenzo, how is Eli doing?"

"He's doing pretty great, actually. Thanks to Todd. I wish all our teams that come over had a group leader that did as much as Todd has done. He's made our job here a lot easier." Katie turned the camera to her face again. "How are you feeling about his big trip? Are you ready for him to leave?"

Christy pushed back the ache and tried to keep her voice upbeat. "I hope so! He has a lot to do before getting on the plane with all those students. Tomorrow is graduation. Then he has a bunch of other stuff, and we'll have a big dinner at

Bob and Marti's the night before he leaves."

"What about you, Christy? Are you going to have enough help with the bambinos while he's gone?"

"I think so. I'll be fine." She realized how surfacey she sounded. But this was not the time to spill her guts to Katie about the emotional waves that kept washing over her. Katie was about to walk into a dining room full of people. Christy definitely didn't want her confession to be broadcast. Especially not a week before Todd would arrive and share breakfast every morning with the same people.

Christy turned to a convenient diversion for the last few minutes of the conversation. "I think a lot is going to depend on what happens with David and Fina. It could get really busy with them here while Todd is going. We just don't know."

"You said they were giving themselves a few days to pray through everything." Katie had stopped walking and was standing under a large shade tree.

Christy nodded. "They said they were going to go their separate ways for a couple days, but that was last Thursday. We haven't heard anything."

"Any guesses on what they'll decide?"

"I wish I knew. I've given up on checking my phone for messages. Todd says they'll come to us when they're ready. It's their future they're trying to figure out." Christy rolled to her side and got off the guest bed where she'd been stretched out talking to Katie. She had started on a new order for two aprons. All the pieces were laid out on the bed except the first apron string that was caught midstitch on the sewing machine.

"Some couples take a little longer to figure themselves out. I am, as you know, Christy, the primary example of a clueless woman who blinded herself to the gift of God that is

Elijah James Lorenzo." Katie had made the declaration loud and proud. Christy noticed in the background that her voice had startled a bird in the umbrella of branches above Katie's head. It flapped away and she looked up as if making sure she wasn't about to receive a small surprise on top of her head.

"The disadvantage of standing here under my favorite tree is the locals. I love this tree, but so do the birds." Katie started moving again.

"If you were to identify the primary reason you were so hesitant to open up your heart to Eli, what would you say it was?"

"Fear."

"I wondered if that's what you'd say."

"Why do you ask? Do you think that's what Fina is struggling with?"

"I think it is. Or, well, hopefully that's what it was. I had a chance to talk to her and pray about the fear. Todd talked with both of them, too. So like I said, at this point it's up to them to figure out what's next."

"You know how you and Todd were the ones who got me to wake up and smell the God-thing going on under my nose? I thought I wanted everything in my life to be safe, small, and predictable. That was my mother's voice in the back of my head. I'm so glad you guys pushed me out the door and challenged me to take a risk and get on that plane with Eli. I love him so much. And I love this little monkey so much, too."

Christy smiled as Katie tried to get a shot of Jimmy's face on the camera.

"Hey." Christy looked at her phone more closely. "Is it my imagination, or is Jimmy starting to look like he might have red hair?"

"I think he is. Eli's mom thinks it will turn darker like Eli's hair."

Katie zoomed the camera in so close Christy thought she was looking at a fuzzy shot of the moon.

"I'm at the dining hall. I need to go. I miss you, Christy. So much."

"I miss you, too." Christy blinked quickly. "Love you, dear Peculiar Treasure."

"Love you, too." Katie saluted with her bandaged fingers. "Signing off from the land of zebras, giraffes, and hopefully . . ."—she tilted the camera so Jimmy's head once again filled the frame—"ginger monkeys!"

The screen went blank. Christy was still smiling at the redheaded monkey comment. At the same time, tears were welling up. It felt like one of those moments when the sun was beaming through a cluster of clouds while those same clouds were raining on you.

Christy tried to brush away the sadness that folded in on her. She wished their call could have been longer. She wanted to tell Katie what she and Jennalyn had talked about and get Katie's thoughts on what it was like to be living out your ministry-woman passion on a day-to-day basis and still raising a child in the midst of it all. In Katie's situation, had her college education, call to full-time missions work, and motherhood all found a perfect balance?

Is what I'm doing enough? I still feel like I should be doing more.

Christy heard the anticipated siren alarm from her starving son and heeded the call without delay.

The rest of Tuesday continued to feel scattered to Christy. She took Cole in to the doctor for his two-month checkup and Christy's mom went with her to help out with Hana.

Christy determined ahead of time that she wouldn't be the one to start a discussion about Fina and David. Apparently her mom had made the same decision because neither of them said anything.

Cole's checkup went smoothly and while everything was fine, he was in the 90th percentile on the charts for his size and weight for his age. That news concerned Christy.

"Your brother was a big baby. So was your father." Her mom had such a comforting tone in her voice. "I don't think you should worry about Cole because we have some big folks on the Miller side of the family."

Christy knew that was true. As she was driving home she reminded herself that the pediatrician hadn't seemed concerned about anything related to Cole's development. Why should she fret about it?

Her mom stayed long enough to make some lunch for all of them and color with Hana in her puppy coloring book. Christy's mother had always been the opposite of her sister, Marti. Calm, sensitive, unobtrusive. She left without even dropping a hint as to what she knew about David and Fina.

As frustrating as that was, Christy had something else she was thinking about. When her mom left, Christy started looking up information online. She wondered if she was feeding Cole too much, too often, or too long. It perplexed her that if he was drawing so many calories from her, why hadn't her stomach flattened more, the way it did after Hana was born? Was her skin too stretched out?

Christy searched and clicked her way down the spiraling Internet cavern until she'd read herself into an anxious frazzle.

Todd had texted that the run-through for tomorrow's graduation was going overtime. As usual, Christy understood but at the same time she was growling inside. It had been a rough afternoon with so much crying from Cole and so much mischief from Hana interspersed with her competitive wailing, Christy was exhausted.

As soon as the children were settled, Christy flopped in bed without even brushing her teeth. She prayed a simple prayer for herself that God would take away the fear she had about Cole's health and development.

A calm settled on her. She slid under the blanket and prayed another simple prayer. This time she asked God to give her deep sleep. She closed her eyes, alone in her bed at eight thirty.

Early the next morning, Christy heard the details about graduation rehearsal when Todd was in the bathroom shaving. Details about the issues with the sound system and the way the principal kept changing the order of the program during the walk-through were only slightly interesting to Christy. The details she was hoping Todd had to share were any updates on David and Fina.

"Nope," Todd said when Christy asked him. "I haven't heard anything from them. Have you?"

"No. It's frustrating after the way you and I were included in all the details a few days ago." Christy leaned against the bathroom doorjamb and crossed her arm across her middle. "I feel like I owe my parents an apology for the way I didn't include them in many of the details in our relationship."

Todd put down the razor and looked at her in the mirror. "Don't you think it's important for a couple to keep those decisions between the two of them?"

"Yes. But I know you always say there's wisdom in a multitude of counselors."

"David and Fina have had plenty of counselors. They'll figure it out. You and I, we're just the Uncle Bob and Aunt

Marti players in this scenario."

Christy scrunched up her nose. She never wanted to be anybody's Aunt Marti. "Will you text me or call me if you hear anything today?"

"I'll try to. It's going to be a full day."

"Do you still have a little time off tomorrow?"

Todd returned his attention to the mirror and finished shaving. "Can I answer that tomorrow morning at this time?"

"Of course. Sorry. I know you have a lot going on."

"No need to apologize."

Todd left after Christy apologized to him a second time for not having his best shirt washed and ready to wear. He'd worn it on Sunday to baccalaureate and she hadn't begun to get caught up on laundry.

Todd didn't seem to mind wearing a different shirt, but Christy felt frustrated at herself. It seemed there were so many areas in her life right now that she couldn't quite get on top of.

The best part of the schedule that day was the 10:00 a.m. playdate she and Jennalyn had set up. Christy got the kids ready and realized this was the first time that she was meeting Jennalyn and she hadn't fretted about what to wear or whether her hair was a mess. There was no more pressure to perform or fit in or try to make sure she appeared to have it all together. Jennalyn was now a "come as you are" friend.

Oh, honey. Stop buzzing and just bee.

The busy-bee image that had softly landed in her thoughts the other night alighted again as Christy headed out the door. She had Cole in the sling and Hana in the beach wagon, clutching her Bunny Wuv and surrounded by sand toys.

Jennalyn had texted that she'd meet Christy down by the water so Christy headed out, trekking down the street and across the wide stretch of sand. To the right and to the left the beach was dotted with blankets, beach chairs, umbrellas, ice chests, and huge inflatable beach toys in the shape of dinosaurs and pink unicorns.

It felt so different when I used to come here as a teenager. All I ever brought with me was a towel and maybe a bottle of whatever fancy zero-calorie drinks Aunt Marti sent with me. Now it seems people come with enough gear to camp out for a week.

She strolled past a family group set up under a pop-up tent shade. They had a huge ice chest on wheels, and next to it was a BBQ grill on wheels. Christy counted eighteen beach chairs lined up in a row with only five older people sitting together at one end. The rest seemed to be waiting in readiness for when the rest of the group either arrived or returned from the water.

Christy settled in a few yards back from the invisible line where the tide raced up on the sand and then receded. She spread out the beach blanket, and Hana easily got herself out of the wagon and wiggled her toes in the warm sand.

"Aren't you a big girl," Christy said. "Can you get your toy?"

Hana knew the routine. With happy jabbers she did her funny little squat and went to work with a shovel and bucket. Her floppy, polka-dot beach hat created a butterfly wing movement as she bobbed her head. Christy realized she hadn't brought her phone so she couldn't take a picture.

Carefully lowering herself onto the blanket with Cole still wrapped around the front of her in the sling, Christy gazed out at the expansive deep blue. She'd felt the tug and pull from the gymnastic effort and tried to get comfortable. Cole had fallen asleep on the walk to the beach and continued dozing with his head pressed against his mommy's heart.

The ion-charged beach air enlivened Christy. She loved the steady rhythm of the waves. She loved the way they curled into a frothy burst and then stretched out across the sand. She loved the mysterious way the disbursed seawater would faithfully retract, returning to the ocean so it might once again spill itself out on the shore.

The ocean always had been and always would be a miraculous wonder to Christy. She closed her eyes for a moment, face toward the horizon, and remembered when she and Todd went to Maui for their honeymoon. The day they snorkeled in the clear turquoise water was a day she would never forget. Colorful tropical fish of all sorts swam all around them in a flurry of motion and beauty. Holding hands, she and Todd had explored the coral reef and kicked their fin-wearing feet in tandem as they followed a huge sea turtle. The sensation of being so buoyant in the warm water while peering in on another world was one of the most euphoric experiences Christy had ever had.

She opened her eyes and smiled, her heart drenched in golden memories. Swimming with angel fish and spending luxuriously long hours floating beside her true love seemed like it all happened a lifetime ago.

She sighed and gently patted Cole's back.

Be grateful, Christy. Be as grateful for what you have now as you are for what you had then. It's all grace.

Fourteen

The playdate was so successful Christy and Jennalyn decided to meet every Wednesday morning in the same area at ten o'clock. It lasted only an hour, but both of them agreed that the break in the middle of the week did wonders for them.

As they exchanged a hug in front of Christy's house, Jennalyn said, "If there's any chance you and Todd are free on Sunday, we'd love to have all of you over before he leaves."

"We'd love that," Christy said. "But we already have plans to go to my aunt and uncle's."

"No worries. We thought we'd ask." Jennalyn shifted Eden on her hip and added in a rather shy-sounding voice, "It's Joel's first Father's Day as a dad. Since we don't have family nearby, I think he wanted to cook something especially nice and have someone over to enjoy it. It's the Italian in him, I think."

"Why don't you guys join us at Bob and Marti's?"

"We couldn't do that."

"Of course you could. They love you guys. If Joel made some of the dinner, I know my uncle would love you even more."

"We wouldn't want to impose."

"You wouldn't be imposing at all. I want you to come. It's a going-away party for Todd."

Jennalyn looked skeptical. "It's also Father's Day."

Christy liked her idea so much, she wasn't going to let it go. "I say it's both. We can celebrate the fathers and have a send-off for Todd at the same time. It's perfect."

"Okay." Jennalyn still looked skeptical. "Promise me you'll ask your aunt about us first. If she's squeamish at all, we won't come and that's fine. Really. No hurt feelings."

"I'm certain she'll love the idea once I tell her about Joel's flourless cake. Todd was even saying he wanted one of those cakes for Father's Day. Actually, I think his exact words were that I should get the recipe and bring two of them to the Family Dinner on Sunday."

"That was an amazing cake, wasn't it?"

Christy was about to rave about it when Hana got tired of waiting for them to finish chatting and started to get out of the wagon.

"Oh, hold on, Hana. Let's go inside. Not in the street. This way." Christy reached for Hana's hand and gave Jennalyn a "gotta go" look. "I'll call you."

"Sounds good. Thanks for the playdate." Jennalyn waved Eden's arm. "Say bye bye. Bye bye, Hana."

Hana looked up and had to tilt her head way back in order to see Jennalyn from under her floppy hat. "Byeeeee."

"Byeeee," Jennalyn repeated, still waving Eden's arm for her.

It took Christy a while to get lunch together for Hana and get Cole changed. She was glad he was content to wiggle on the floor so she had time to get sleepy Hana down for her nap. By the time Christy was ready to nurse Cole, he was crying so she went for the closet location, which was the couch. All settled, she reached for a pillow to slide under her arm for support. When she moved the throw pillow, she saw her phone on the armrest.

"There you are. What did I miss while we were gone?"

The phone screen was covered with notices that she'd received a bunch of calls and text messages. Her heart lurched when she saw them all, hoping nothing bad had happened. As Christy scrolled through, she was relieved to see that actually something good had happened. Something very good. Everyone in her family wanted to chime in.

David and Fina were officially engaged.

Christy had oodles of questions. She listened to the phone message from her brother and another one from Fina and a third one from Christy's mom. None of them answered Christy's questions about how the take-two proposal turned out or what the next steps were.

Her heart was doing a happy dance as she pressed Fina's number, eager to hear all the details. The call rolled to voice mail, so she left a congratulatory message and tried David. His phone went to voice mail, too. Christy left another exuberant message and tried her mom.

No answer.

"Where is everyone and what are they all doing right now?"

As a last choice, Christy called Aunt Marti. Certainly Marti would have the whole scoop and be eager to share it. Plus, Christy could ask about Jennalyn and Joel coming on Sunday.

Marti answered on the first ring.

"Finally!" Christy said. "No one else is picking up. You didn't all go out to lunch to celebrate without me, did you?"

"Celebrate? What are you babbling about, Christy?"

Christy froze.

Oh no, oh no, oh no. What have I done? Marti doesn't know yet! What should I say?

With a nervous laugh Christy said, "I was trying to be funny. Mommy-life, you know. I picture everyone else is out there having little parties and going to lunch while I'm here changing diapers." She laughed another odd chortle and squeezed her eyes shut, as if she could make this panicky moment disappear.

"Are you all right, Christina? You're not being held at gunpoint, are you?"

Christy burst into a normal laugh. "No, I'm just . . . I'm fine. Why in the world did you ask that?"

"I read about a girl who was being held up at a fast-food restaurant. She tipped off the people in the drive-up line by repeating the order in her headset in a way that made no sense to the drive-up customers. They caught on and called the police. I believe they saved that girl's life." Marti paused and then in a lower voice asked, "Christy, should I call the police?"

"No. I'm fine, Aunt Marti. I'm not in any danger." Christy had collected her thoughts during Marti's social-media news report and was ready to ask about Jennalyn and Joel coming on Sunday.

"Joel would love to bring some or all of the food. You've had his cooking before, remember? At Todd's birthday party."

"We would love to have Joel and Jennalyn come. And their baby. That would be fine. Joel doesn't have to bring anything, though. Unless he'd like to make an appetizer or a dessert, perhaps."

"Should I ask Uncle Bob to talk to Joel? They can coordinate their efforts."

"Yes. That's a good idea."

Marti sounded pleased and Christy felt relieved.

"You know," Marti said. "It's probably a good thing Jennalyn and Joel are coming."

"Why is that?"

"We haven't seen David or Fina more than five minutes over the past week, and those five minutes were when we stopped by the other night with the flowers."

Christy took the diversion of the flowers and used it to thank her aunt once again for the beautiful bouquet.

"I split it up into four vases. It's been so nice having fresh flowers throughout the house."

"I'm so glad you're enjoying them. I do enjoy a colorful bouquet around the house in the summer."

Christy was ready to end their call and say that she'd see her on Sunday. Marti returned to the topic Christy was hoping to avoid.

"I'm actually a bit concerned about Fina. On Monday, as she was dashing out the door, she told us that her parents were at the airport for a few hours, and she was going there to meet them. I don't know which airport or how long their layover was. You know, her father is a pilot. I thought he might have arranged to stay a day or two. We could have put them up here, if they wanted. Did you know anything about that?"

"No. Nothing." It felt good to be able to honestly say she was in the dark along with Marti on this one. Christy put the pieces together and concluded that Fina's parents must have come down from Oregon for the day in order to spend time with Fina and possibly with David, too.

"Well, she certainly has been a butterfly lately. I'm looking forward to when her class finishes and she'll be home here for the summer. I purchased a set of Pilates DVDs because she and I were going to start working out together. She hasn't been home even long enough to take any of the DVDs out of their case."

Christy recognized so many familiar touch points in Marti's words. Marti was trying to connect with Fina in her world of fitness and being ignored. Fina was trying to figure out her future and do it in a way that didn't include Marti's input quite yet. And the most painful part of it all was that Christy knew that Fina would be leaving in a short time, but Marti didn't know.

"Well, I guess when we're all together on Sunday, we'll be able to get caught up and find out how Fina is doing." Christy knew her diplomatic skills were lacking. She had to be so careful not to tip the scales of Marti's curiosity in this conversation.

"That's my point, exactly. Based on how Fina's busy schedule has been lately, I can't guarantee that she'll make an appearance at our family dinner on Sunday. It's a pity, since it's Father's Day and Robert has such a fatherly affection for her. Not to mention that Todd will be leaving and your uncle and I will be going to Idaho and none of us will be together again until August, I suspect."

Christy was about to make another benign comment and try to get off the call when Marti added her final thought.

"So, it's a good thing we'll have Joel and Jennalyn. They might end up filling David and Fina's places at the table."

Christy had a pretty good idea that would not be the case. She kept her lips sealed and managed to end the call in what felt like a natural sign-off to her.

From then on, it was off to the races as Christy started texting her brother and Fina. She asked if they had plans to tell Bob and Marti soon.

Fina texted back almost two hours later and said, YES. TONIGHT. She added an emoji with big round eyes as if to say, "Eek!"

Over the next few days, Christy felt as if her life was caught in the same expand, recede motion she'd loved watching at the beach on their playdate with Jennalyn and Eden. Interesting information would come to her, like her mom explaining that she and Christy's dad had gone with David and Fina to LAX on Monday, and the four of them had spent most of the day with Fina's parents. She told Christy it had been a very special time, but Christy didn't know exactly what that meant. Was it somehow a group decision that the two of them should marry?

A few more details came out when Todd told Christy that he'd talked to David before the Gathering on Friday to make sure he was going to be available to run everything. David had told Todd that the conversation with Bob and Marti had gone "great" and that the family dinner planned for Sunday night had morphed into a small engagement dinner for them.

Apparently, Uncle Bob and Joel had put their heads together and come up with a fabulous menu. David and Fina had invited friends from school and work. Christy's mom had invited a few of their church friends from Escondido to come, and now it was going to be a grand event.

Christy felt so left out.

She knew this was all about her brother, of course. And she appreciated that her family was being considerate of the fact that she was limited in what she could help with, so none of them had asked her to do anything.

Like the tide, her routine with her children rolled in and rolled out. She napped when she could, fretted a little over what she was going to wear on Sunday night, and helped Todd get everything he needed for Kenya packed up on Saturday.

While he was downstairs on Saturday night having a playful wrestling match with Hana before her bath, Christy sat on the edge of their bed and pulled a small box of note cards from the drawer in her nightstand. She'd gotten them several years ago at the gift shop where she'd worked on Balboa Island. The cards had pen-and-ink drawings on the front of various familiar Newport Beach icons such as the Balboa Ferris wheel, a seashell, the Balboa Pier. There was even a card with a sketch of an orange surfboard on it. That was the image that had motivated her to buy the handmade note cards because Todd had always had an orange surfboard and he always called it *Naranja*, which was Spanish for "orange."

She wrote inside the cards quickly. She'd been thinking about this for a while so it didn't take her long to pen her heartfelt thoughts to her husband. Each card was a love note. Some included a verse. Inside the surfboard card she wrote, "Naranja and I miss you. Hang ten and hurry back to me and your favorite little grommets."

Two of the cards contained mushy sentiments. Inside the final card she bit her lower lip and took what was for her, a bit of a risky plunge. She wrote a sweet note and added a single line at the end that was something that conveyed an amorous sentiment that only she and Todd would understand.

Pleased and feeling delightfully secretive, Christy hid the cards in between the packed clothes in Todd's suitcase. She hoped that every time he found one and opened it up, it would make him feel loved and missed and very much desired.

Best of all, the evening unfurled in such a way that Christy was able to fully and freely express everything she felt for Todd. She had been determined to put aside all the aching feelings that were focused on how lonely she was going to be and how much harder it was going to be without his help with the children.

Her thoughts were all on Todd. How was he feeling? What was he thinking? What did he need?

Their expressed love for each other drew them closer than Christy thought they'd ever been before in heart and mind and body. There was nothing left to discuss or evaluate or explain. Todd was leaving in a day and Christy was staying. They were both doing what they needed and wanted to do, and even though they were going to be apart, Christy couldn't help but feel that their hearts were knit more tightly than ever.

Fifteen

The closeness and love Christy had felt for Todd on Saturday night threatened to unravel when Todd woke her on Sunday morning. Cole wasn't awake yet, and she was used to sleeping until her newborn alarm went off in the nursery.

"Do you want to get a shower before Cole wakes up?" Todd asked.

"Why?"

"It's Sunday. The team is being prayed for and dedicated during the first service. We need to leave in about forty minutes."

"Did you tell me this? I don't remember you . . ."

"I thought I wrote it on the calendar. Christy, this is really important to me. I want you to be there."

"I don't know if I can get the kids ready and get myself ready."

"I'll get Hana up and dressed and I'll make some breakfast. I really want you there."

Christy didn't know what to say. Todd rarely asked her to do anything lately. He didn't expect her to go to the Gathering on Friday nights anymore. She didn't go with him to baccalaureate or graduation. She hadn't accompanied him to a single meeting with the students who were going on the missions trip or any of the meetings with their parents.

Why in the world does he want me to go with him this morning?

Christy made a heroic effort to speed up the morning routine all around so she and the kids could be in the car and dash off to church with him. Todd waited in the church lobby for each student to arrive while Christy took Hana to the children's ministry room and signed her in. She was carrying Cole in his baby carrier, and she felt like her arm was going to cramp up.

Amazingly, she found a seat in the back, got Cole secure on the seat next to her, and stood with the rest of the congregation when the worship music began. She felt so flustered. She didn't know where Todd was. Most of all, she hoped the loud singing didn't prompt Cole to start crying.

Cole snoozed through the worship songs. Christy wondered if her theory of putting him down for a nap in the midst of normal, daily noise was helping to acclimate him more than his sister had been at this age.

Everyone sat down for announcements. The first announcement was the team from South Coast Believers Academy who were going to Kenya.

"We'd like to pray together as a congregation right now for these students," the pastor said. "And as they come up here onstage, would you remember their faces and remember to faithfully lift them up in prayer over the next three weeks?"

Todd led the way. A dozen students followed him and stood rather self-consciously in a line. None of them seemed to quite know what to do with their hands. One of the girls was much shorter than the other students and ended up in the lineup between the two tallest boys. She appeared uncomfortable with the random placement and slid behind everyone. A moment later she wedged herself in between two of the girls at the end. Christy was glad to see that the two girls made room for her with pleasant expressions.

One of the guys was large. He was at least six inches taller than Todd and had a solid build. All Christy could think of was the many youth group trips she had gone on with Todd when he was a youth pastor. Fitting students into busses and vans had always been challenging when some of the students had long legs or got car sick. She could only imagine how challenging it was going to be to fit this assortment of highly emotionally charged young people on the extremely long flights and bumpy van rides in Africa.

Oh, Todd. What have you gotten yourself into? I wish I was going with you. Or at least another adult leader. You are going to be mother and father, brother and coach, leader and shepherd to these young God Lovers for three weeks.

"Let's pray." The pastor placed his hand on Todd's shoulder, and all the students bowed their heads.

Christy prayed fervently. The trip just got real to her. Very real.

Her husband wasn't just going to be dealing with the physical labor in building the wells in the remote villages; he was going to be corralling all those impressionable, volatile personalities onstage, plus the few that for whatever reason hadn't managed to be there that morning.

She prayed and kept praying even after the pastor said,

"Amen." Christy would not let up praying for this group. The image of them on the stage had lit a fire in her belly. Her husband was a brave man. He was a servant and a warrior. She loved him so much.

Christy tried to tell Todd that afternoon how much it had affected her, seeing all the students onstage. She wasn't sure he heard her over the usual ruckus going on around them. It didn't matter. She knew she'd be praying for him, and he must have known the value of her coming to the church service because of the way he urged her to be there.

In the middle of Cole's afternoon feeding, Christy realized that it was Father's Day. She had done well that week by remembering to get a small gift for Todd and also for her dad and something for Uncle Bob. She wasn't sure if she should give Todd his gift now or take all of them to dinner tonight at Bob and Marti's.

Christy was reminded of Father's Day last year. It had been a difficult day. Katie was with them because her father had passed away unexpectedly a week earlier, and the funeral was in Escondido on Father's Day.

Did they even celebrate Father's Day in Africa, and if so, was it today? Her heart went out to her friend. Katie had gone through so much during the past year.

Christy sent her a text, letting Katie know she was thinking of her and loved her.

To Christy's surprise, a reply came back, even though it was the middle of the night on Katie's side of the globe. With her multitasking mama skills in place, Christy tapped out a longer message. The two of them went back and forth for a few minutes with fun quips and mama jokes.

Christy thought their fun touch-point moment was about to end, but Katie surprised her with what seemed like an out-of-nowhere text.

THINKING ABOUT MARTI LATELY.

AUNT MARTI?

COULD THERE BE ANY OTHER MARTI IN THIS WORLD?

Christy grinned. PROBABLY NOT. WHY?

Katie's response must be long because Christy had to wait for it to come through. She put a cloth in place and positioned Cole over her shoulder. He started squirming and working on one of his really good belly burps.

Christy's phone pinged. She picked it up and read the reply.

Katie said she had been thinking about how Marti had come to Kenya for Katie and Eli's wedding and had hand delivered Katie's wedding dress. She said all the recent updates about David and Fina made Katie wish she could be there for the fun of it all and to see how Fina was going to handle Marti's eagerness to be at the hub of the festivities.

Christy managed to reply with only a smiley face emoji because Cole was wiggling and starting to fuss.

Katie came back with a text that was pure Katie Weldon, redheaded feistiness.

AS MUCH AS YOUR AUNT LOVES WEDDINGS AND WOULD BE WILLING TO TRAVEL ALL THE WAY HERE FOR MINE, I'M GOING TO TELL HER SHE NEEDS TO GET ON HER KNEES AND SURRENDER HER LIFE TO JESUS BECAUSE THE WEDDING FEAST OF THE LAMB IS GOING TO HAPPEN! IT'S ON! HEAVEN IS FOR REAL AND SHE IS GOING TO WANT TO BE THERE AND TRUTH IS I WANT HER TO BE THERE BECAUSE SERIOUSLY SHE NEEDS TO BE THERE. AUNT MARTI NEEDS TO GO. TO. HEAVEN!

Christy shook her head. "Oh, Katie girl. You do love to

say what you're thinking. I can only imagine how my aunt would respond if you said that to her."

Christy thought about how to give the best diplomatic response. She considered reminding Katie how she had been praying for her aunt for over a decade, and how Marti had been so resistant to even talking about trusting Christ. Even after Uncle Bob became a Christian, Marti hadn't softened toward God Lovers, as Todd called them. If anything, she had become more critical and combative.

Katie's approach was not one Christy would recommend.

She sent a short reply. PROBABLY BEST THING WE CAN DO IS PRAY FOR HER.

Katie replied, I'LL DO THAT TOO. HEADING BACK TO BED. LOVE YOU.

Christy realized it had been a long time since she'd prayed for Aunt Marti. She started right then with a simple prayer focused on one word. The one word that immediately came to mind was heaven. It wasn't *salvation* or *redemption* or *repentance* or *forgiveness*. Those were all the messages Christy had felt she needed to try to express to her aunt in the past. She wanted Marti to know that she needed a Savior, and Christ was the only One who could make her right before Almighty God. She needed to repent and turn the controls of her life over to God.

None of those approaches had worked in the past. So the simple prayer she prayed right then for Marti was that she would come to Christ so she could one day be with Him in heaven.

The good thing about Katie's tactic of praying simple, one-word prayers was that with Christy's often fuzzy brain, she found she was able to remember the single word that was associated with the person she was praying for. It was as if her mind would pull up a head-shot picture of the person she was going to pray for and affixed the single word to their top like a name-tag sticker. In a fun way, her thoughts were keeping a yearbook of friends and family. She now pictured all of them wearing a single prayer-request word as a name badge.

At five o'clock, with all the usual baby gear loaded in the car, Christy and Todd drove over to Bob and Marti's. When they walked in, Christy was stunned. The house was decorated with cute triangle buntings strung everywhere. Standing clusters of white helium-filled balloons were tucked into corners like bobbing sentries in the entry, the living room, and in the kitchen. Lively music flowed inside as well as out on the front patio that faced the ocean. There was no doubt that a party was about to happen.

"Oh, good. You're here." Marti swished in from the kitchen wearing a sleeveless gold top and tight-fitting black pants. She wore a stack of gold bracelets up both arms that jangled every time she used her hands, which was often.

Marti linked her arm through Christy's. "I should still be furious with you, you know. I'm sure you knew all about this for weeks on end, and yet you didn't tell me. I admit I was angry. And hurt. Mostly hurt. No one wants to be the last to know when it's something wonderful and so important to the family."

"I know, Aunt Marti. I'm sorry. It's just that . . ."

Marti held up her hand. Her voice quavered. She was tearing up. It was so out of character for her to be this vulnerable in expressing her feelings to Christy.

Lowering her tone and still sounding earnest Marti said, "Fina explained to me how she had made you promise not to say anything, and I realized I need to respect your level of confidentiality. I hold nothing against you, Christy. This is a happy time for all of us."

Marti was still crying. Really crying. She was saying this was a happy time. But her tears seemed to be drawn from a well of some deep sadness. Christy didn't know what to do.

As might be expected, though, Marti's moment of genuine emotions did not disable the sergeant-at-arms feature of her personality. She lifted her chin, brushed her fingertips across her moist cheeks, and said, "Now. If you wouldn't mind helping with the candy. I put all the glass candy bowls out on the kitchen table. You need to fill them and place them in the living room, the family room, the dining room, and out on the patio. There are ten bowls. Could you do that for me?"

"Sure." Christy left Todd with both the children while she ventured into the kitchen.

She found Joel and Bob at work over the stove. Both of them were wearing official-looking, button-up chef jackets. The counter was covered with food and platters and cutting boards. The sight was a swirl of movement and precision as the two of them worked side by side.

"Try it this way." Joel took a whisk from Bob's hand and began furious stirring something in a saucepan on the stove.

Uncle Bob stood with his hands on his hips, leaning forward, and intently absorbed in the personal cooking lesson he was receiving from Joel.

"I see. Yes, that's it, isn't it?"

"Here," Joel said. "You try."

Before Bob took the whisk from Joel, he glanced over his shoulder and noticed Christy was watching them.

With a grin and a wink, her charming uncle said, "Livin' the dream here, Bright Eyes. Livin' the dream."

Sixteen

Christy smiled. The sight of those two, Joel and Uncle Bob, at work in the kitchen was a happy sight. *Good things are going to come of this. I just know it.*

The ten candy dishes had already been filled, so she started carrying them out on a large tray, ready to plant them as directed. She found Jennalyn in the dining room, smoothing a cloth over Marti's large table that had extended to its fullest length.

"Christy! Hi. What do you think?" Jennalyn motioned to the centerpiece on the table. It was undoubtedly a Jennalyn creation of fresh flowers and trailing vines in a long rectangle planter.

Most noticeable was the hand-lettered placard that rose from the center of the arrangement on a twig. On the sign Jennalyn had penned the names David and Josephina.

"It's beautiful, Jennalyn. All of it. I didn't know you were roped into doing the decorations."

"Don't worry. It was my idea. I volunteered. I love doing things like this. You've probably guessed that by now."

Christy looked again at the names. She couldn't figure out why Jennalyn had written *Josephina* instead of *Fina*.

"You're wondering about the Josephina, aren't you?"

"I guess I am. I'm used to everyone calling her Fina."

"I know. I asked twice. David said he wanted the sign to have her full name. He said she was named after her grandmother, and since it's her grandmother's ring that they're using for their engagement ring, he wanted it to be her full name."

"Oh. That makes sense. That's sweet." Christy hadn't realized that the ring belonged to Fina's namesake. It felt a little awkward to find out from Jennalyn.

"Remind me to tell you my own little story about her ring sometime," Christy said.

"Okay. I will. At our next Wednesday beach date."

Jennalyn's dark hair looked different. Christy was trying to figure out what it was. The style was the same cut that skimmed her jawline that she'd had done a little over a month ago.

Once again, Jennalyn seemed to be reading her thoughts.

"I know. My hair. I tried a deep conditioner I'd tucked away in the bottom of the bathroom cupboard. Joel thinks it looks purple." She made a grimace and smoothed her hand over the back, then fingered the ends for a moment.

"I was going to wash it again and not use any conditioner, but we ran out of time. What do you think? Is it gruesome?"

"No. It's definitely not gruesome. I barely noticed. It seemed something was a little different, but I couldn't tell what it was."

Now that Jennalyn had said it looked purple, Christy could definitely see the purple tinge. Or maybe it was so sleek and had such a sort of celluloid gleam to it that the shine was picking up the reflection of Jennalyn's magenta-colored top.

Christy was going to share her theory, but whenever something was off with her appearance, she'd rather have people not bring it up instead of try to explain what they saw or advise her on what she should do about it.

Christy had her own self-conscious thing going on that night with the single, long braid hanging down her back. They'd been in such a hurry to get out the door for church that morning, she skipped washing her hair because it took so long to dry now that it was nearly to her waist. She knew she could have looked fresher and a lot more styled if she had been able to wash her hair that afternoon and do something with it other than a clumpy braid.

But she didn't fit in a shower and so here she was, feeling a bit "less than" once again. It seemed to be her permanent condition more and more ever since Cole was born.

To move on so she wouldn't try to be sympathetic to Jennalyn's purple hair by discussing the condition of her own hair, Christy nodded to the end table by the couch. "What do you think? Should I put the candy over there or here on the table?"

"Either would be fine. The bowls are small. I know your aunt plans to use this table for the buffet."

"I saw the guys at work in the kitchen. Looks like we're going to have quite a feast."

Jennalyn's Italian roots seemed to sparkle through her smile as she said, "I love a good feast, don't you?"

Christy grinned her agreement and nodded. She loved having Jennalyn in her life. She loved that Jennalyn and Joel had made themselves so comfortable in Bob and Marti's home and were fitting in like family.

"I'll finish making my Easter Bunny deliveries," Christy said. "Then you can put me to work with whatever else you need help on."

Christy discovered Jennalyn's charming touches everywhere she went around the house. There were balloons, clusters of flowers and greenery, and lots of strings of colorful buntings. She found her dad in the family room. He was watching TV with the sound on mute because he had apparently also been given the job of watching Eden while she napped.

Christy went over to her dad in the recliner and gave him a peck on the cheek. He wasn't big on affectionate hugs or words, but a few months ago, Christy had decided that wasn't going to stop her from showing him how she felt about him every chance she had.

"Hi, Dad." She kept her voice low. "Happy Father's Day. I have a little sumpthin' for you in the diaper bag. I'll get it for you before you leave."

"In the diaper bag, huh?"

"Don't worry. It's not a diaper. It's a little gift for you for being such a wonderful dad."

"You didn't have to do that."

"I know. I wanted to. So, what do you think about your son getting married?"

Her dad's expression was about as mushy looking as it could be. His words, however, came out with steady logic. "He's made a good choice. The two of them have impressed your mother and me. I think they'll be just fine."

"I think they'll be just fine, too." Christy kissed him again and continued her rounds.

The doorbell rang and a couple Christy didn't recognize entered with a gift. Marti greeted them with effusive decorum and accepted the gift, saying that David and Fina should be here any minute.

Marti glided across the entryway and handed the gift to Christy. In a low voice tinged with panic, she said, "I didn't anticipate gifts. How did I overlook that? We need a place for guests to put them. Please, Christy. Could you arrange for a gift table?"

The assignment wasn't difficult. Christy cleared the small statue and bowl of flowers from the side table positioned up against the wall near the front door. She placed the gift on the table and took the statue and flowers into the family room and found a corner on the shelf for them.

Todd had joined Christy's dad, who was now holding Cole and had his feet up on one of the recliners. Todd was in the other recliner reading a book to Hana.

"Where's Eden?" Christy asked.

Her dad answered. "Your mother took her after she woke up. I think they went upstairs."

"Diaper change," Todd added.

"Are you guys okay in here?"

"We're good. Let us know if you need help with anything," Todd said. "I'll come find you when Cole wakes up."

Christy went upstairs to say hi to her mom. More guests were arriving and yet David and Fina weren't there, as far as Christy knew.

"Mom?" Christy could hear Eden crying. She followed the cries to Bob and Marti's bedroom at the end of the hall. The bedroom door was open, which was unusual since Marti protected her privacy in all things, even when she wasn't in her room.

Christy found her mom in the luxurious master bathroom, holding a damp washcloth to Eden's forehead.

"Everything okay?"

"She bumped her head. It's not bad. I think it frightened her." Christy's mom removed the washcloth.

Christy looked closely at the faint reddish splotch on Eden's forehead. "Poor baby." Christy stroked her soft cheek. "Are you okay, Eden?"

Eden stared at Christy with her dark eyes looking like two round drops of chocolate. Eden seemed to recognize Christy and stopped crying. She reached out her arms for Christy to take her.

As Christy held Eden she automatically fell into a mothering sway. Christy was glad for the chance to finally talk face-to-face with her mom about all the events of David and Fina's engagement.

Lots of the missing pieces became clear as her mom explained how she and Christy's dad had spent the afternoon at a hotel restaurant near LAX with David and Fina and her parents, Stephen and Genevieve, to talk through all that was necessary for David and Fina to take this big step to get married and also make the move to Indiana. Fina had found out that classes started for her on August 23.

"That's why they set the wedding date for August 6," her mom said matter-of-factly.

"Wait." Christy felt way behind on all these newsflash details. "They've set a date?"

"Yes. August 6. It's a Sunday. They want a sunset wedding on the beach. Small and simple. Then they're taking a week for their honeymoon, which will be good for them, I think. They plan to drive from here to Glenbrooke where they'll have a reception and then drive to Indiana."

"Wow." Christy shifted Eden to her other hip. "I'm so behind on all this. How did they finally decide to move ahead and get married?"

Christy's mom looked surprised. "They said it was because of you and Todd. The two of you helped them settle their concerns."

"Oh."

Her mom remained surprised. "Certainly you knew that."

"I knew they were taking time to think and pray and yes, Todd and I talked with them a couple times. But I hadn't heard the final conclusion. I didn't know David re-proposed, or whatever we should be calling it. I didn't know Fina had said yes. That's how far behind I am."

Christy's mom's expression changed. She tapped her fingers to her lips and seemed to be trying to remember something. "You know, Christy, I don't recall either of them saying anything about David proposing a second time or about her saying yes."

"Did David have the ring resized?"

"I don't know. We've hardly seen him since Monday. I guess we'll hear all the details tonight."

Christy heard a familiar sound wending its high notes up the stairs and all the way into the master bathroom. She checked the elegant clock on the bathroom counter. "Right on time. Cole's schedule is starting to get consistent." Christy also heard footsteps with a familiar gait coming down the hall toward the bedroom.

"I'll take Eden," Christy's mom said.

Todd entered with their wailing banshee and handed him over to Christy with an apologetic look.

"Do you think Marti would mind if I fed him on her balcony?"

Todd shook his head, although it seemed as if he hadn't heard what she said. Christy's mom pointed to indicate that she was going back downstairs with Todd.

Christy carried Cole out through the open French doors and selected the chaise lounge that was the easiest for her to lower herself into. The plush cushion felt luxurious as she stretched out her legs, leaned back, and fed her son in comfort and style.

Now that Cole was hushed, Christy could hear the sounds of the party downstairs. The doorbell rang, happy voices greeted each other, the lively music rolled through the house, and every now and then a burst of laughter would break out. She tried to imagine who had come and how they all knew her brother and Fina.

Marti's distinct voice in its best cruise director tone could be heard at the bottom of the stairs giving directions that the buffet was ready and everyone should help themselves. She could hear voices of the guests who had moved out onto the patio. They were surprisingly clear. It made Christy wonder if she had ever said anything while on the patio that she thought her aunt couldn't hear upstairs.

Christy recognized David's voice right away. He was telling someone that Fina had gotten a waitressing job at Julie Ann's Café for the next six weeks. "Tell her how it happened," he said.

Fina said, "It was completely unexpected. David and I had gone to Julie Ann's Café. We were talking to the waitress who said she was about to go on maternity leave. I asked if they needed a replacement for six weeks and before we left, I had a job."

"That never happens around here." The voice sounded like one of the young women Christy had met before who was part of the career group Fina and David went to at church.

"I know. That's why I saw it as a confirmation of everything David and I had been talking about. We were saying that since we had taken the step of faith to move forward, then we needed to trust God that He was going to provide everything we needed."

"That's cool," a guy's voice said.

"I start tomorrow," Fina said. "And work until a few days before the wedding. It's perfect."

"Won't you have a lot to do for the wedding between now and then?" The young woman asked Fina.

"Yes. But we have a secret weapon. She's right over there in the shimmering gold top."

"Is that David's aunt?"

"Yes. She's offered to help with everything. My mom will help, of course. And David's mom said she'll be able to do a lot."

David added, "I just talked to my brother-in-law, Todd. He said he could perform the ceremony."

"And we thought we'd ask Joel if he could be our caterer. He and David's uncle did the food for tonight."

"It's delicious," an unfamiliar voice said.

"Maybe we could ask Jennalyn to do the flowers," Fina said. "I love what she did tonight with the decorations. I feel like we've got everything we need thanks to David's family and friends."

Christy looked across the top edge of the balcony and focused on a thin bank of clouds that floated just above the horizon. At this moment she felt as distant and vaporous to her family as those clouds. It wasn't that she wanted to be at the center of things. She didn't like drawing attention to herself in any way. The hurt came from not being included on David and Fina's final decision to get married, and now the way she was left out of the lineup of women who were going to make this wedding happen.

I know everyone is being considerate since Cole and Hana require so much attention right now. Plus, Todd is leaving tomorrow. I need to let Fina know I'm available to do whatever I can.

"How did you guys decide to go ahead with everything?" Another female voice asked.

"When Fina was accepted into the graduate program, it put everything into motion," David said.

"I know, but how did you get Fina to decide so quickly? It's a big decision."

"It is," Fina agreed. "It's the biggest decision of our lives. The whole story is too long to tell. Plus, it's kind of bumpy and not very pretty. Let me just say that I wouldn't be here right now, so crazy in love with this guy and so much at peace about this being the right decision for us, if it wasn't for David's sister."

David's sister? That's me!

Christy felt as if a little jolt of lightning had passed through her and made her heart give a twirl.

"Christy was the one who took the time to sit and listen to me. I had so many doubts and fears. She helped me to see where the fear was coming from. After she prayed with me, that was the turning point."

"Same with me. My sister was the first person I went to when I knew I wanted to ask Fina to marry me," David said.

Christy felt touched. She wasn't an afterthought. She was part of this wild love story that was unfolding for her little brother.

Oh, David. I can hardly believe this is happening for you.

"I haven't asked her yet," Fina said, "but I'm hoping Christy will help me find my wedding dress. Actually, what

I'm really hoping is that she could make it for me."

Christy's jaw went slack.

Fina! You don't know what you're asking. The wedding is seven weeks from today! I make pillows and aprons. Not wedding gowns. We need to talk. Tonight.

Seventeen

Three days after David and Fina's engagement party, Christy packed Cole in the baby sling and Hana and her beach toys into the wagon. She chugged her way across the sand at ten o'clock for her Wednesday morning beach date with Jennalyn.

Jennalyn was already at the water's edge, sitting on a beach blanket with Eden in her lap. "Morning!"

"Hi!" Hana called out from her happy throne on the wagon. "Hi! Hi, Baby Eden!"

Christy was glad that Hana was focused on Eden. On other family treks down to the water's edge, Hana had been timid to get too near the shore break. The sound and the movement of the foamy waves seemed to frighten her, and she didn't want to even put her feet in the water with Christy.

Christy spread her blanket next to Jennalyn's to make a larger space for them together. It seemed they were just the right distance from the shore to avoid a squealing meltdown from Hana.

Hana carried her sand toys over to Jennalyn's side of the blanket so Eden could watch her scoop the sand and pound the plastic shovel on the bottom of the bucket. "Look, Eden. Look."

Jennalyn turned to Christy once she'd lowered herself to the blanket without bumping Cole around too much. She reached over and gave Christy's arm a squeeze. "How are you doing?"

"Okay."

"No, I mean, really. How are you doing? I was going to call after Todd left on Monday, but things got a little crazy. I've been thinking about you."

"Thanks." Christy took Cole out of the sling and let him kick and wiggle on the blanket in the shade of her shadow. She drew in a deep breath of salty air and turned to give Jennalyn a halfhearted smile. "Do want the honest answer?"

"Yes. That's all I want. Just the true stuff."

"It's been awful." Christy noticed in the sunlight that the tinges of purple were still coming through slightly in Jennalyn's hair. She didn't say anything, though, because she was pretty sure that wasn't the true stuff Jennalyn wanted to talk about right now.

"Have you heard from him yet?"

"Yes. He let me know they arrived safely. It's such a long trip. They had one suitcase that didn't arrive, but they were able to track it so it should be delivered to them at the conference center. He sent me a picture of him holding Jimmy just before I came down here."

"Jimmy is Katie and Eli's son?"

Christy nodded.

"Have you had a chance to talk to Todd yet?"

"No. Just a lot of text messages. But I understand. I really do. He has a whole herd to move around. At least they'll be at Brockenhurst for the next few days so he'll have phone and Internet access. That might change depending on where they end up going for the two weeks they're in the village."

"How was the good-bye for you guys?"

"Kind of fast and not as emotional as I thought it would be. It was good that he left so early. Hana didn't wake up when he kissed her good-bye. I was trying to make sure he had carried everything out to the airport shuttle when it was at the curb. We kissed and said good-bye and he got in and left."

Christy left out the part about how she'd leaked tears off and on through the day and how she felt like she was doing serious battle in her spirit not to entertain thoughts of plane crashes or African bus accidents or some sort of government coup while Todd was so far away from her.

"I'm glad we had this beach date planned," Christy said. "It helped a lot this morning to know that I had someplace I needed to be and a friend who would be there."

Jennalyn smiled. "I'm glad I can be that friend."

They watched their little ones do all their different variations of wiggles in the fresh air. Hana jabbered away in her own little language and seemed to be instructing Eden on how to make a sand pie.

"May I ask you a friend-to-friend question?" Jennalyn asked.

"Of course."

Jennalyn leaned closer and lowered her head. "Is my hair still purple? Be honest."

Christy pretended to be examining it for the first time, as if she had to look really close to see the color. "It's not entirely purple-purple. But yes, there are hints of purple."

"That's what I thought. I've washed it every day, and it's

not changing back to my normal color."

"It's pretty," Christy said optimistically. "Your hair is very pretty."

"Thank you for saying that."

"I mean it. The cut is a great style on you. I'm sure there are a lot of women who pay a lot of money to get subtle hints of purple in their hair."

"Yes, but I'm not one of those kind of hair women. I like everything in my life to be as close to the way it came from nature as possible." She sighed. "I think I'll have to go against all my natural convictions and get it colored."

Jennalyn's decision launched a conversation about hairstyles and how their skin and hair had changed so much during and after pregnancy. Finally Jennalyn said, "I'm going to do it. I'm going to make an appointment today. Otherwise, I'll be staring in the mirror for many weeks and cringing every time I see a purple hair."

She turned to Christy with a "lightbulb" look in her eyes. "Why don't you come with me?"

"To get my hair colored?"

"Or conditioned or cut or whatever you want. It would be so fun to go together. Moms Day Out. The salon is just down the street from Julie Ann's Café so we could go there afterward for a latte and say hi to Fina. What do you think?"

Christy agreed. It would be a lot of fun to do something carefree like that. She also needed to talk with Fina. The two of them had connected at the party on Sunday night only long enough for Christy to hug her and for Fina to show Christy that her grandmother's resized ring was now on the correct finger. Fina hadn't said anything about Christy helping with her wedding dress. She did ask if Hana could be their flower girl. Christy told her to come by so they could talk soon.

"What do you think, Christy? Should I call the salon and make appointments for both of us?"

"Okay. Sure. Let's do it. I'll see if my mom can watch Cole and Hana."

Jennalyn went to work on setting the appointments. She was able to get them both in on Saturday morning due to a cancellation. Christy made arrangements with her mom. Jennalyn lined up her usual babysitter, and the plan was set.

For the rest of the day, Christy contemplated what she wanted to do. A deep-conditioning treatment? A conservative trim? Highlights? Or a whole new look?

An unexpected complication set in for Christy when she was nursing Cole that evening. She had sharp, hot pain radiating on her left side so it made her bite her lip and squeeze her eyes closed just to get through a very short feeding on that side. She typed in her symptoms to a motherhood site she frequented and was inundated with information on clogged ducts, mastitis, inflammation, infection, and all the various cures.

That night Christy tried soaking a hot washcloth and holding it to the affected area. She had a breast pump she'd been given when Hana was born but had never used it. Christy pulled it out, read the instructions, fiddled with the pieces, and plugged it in. She hoped it would help unclog the left side. But it didn't.

Nothing seemed to help. She didn't sleep well, and by the next feeding since was crying as Cole nursed. Hana was finding ways to get into mischief while Christy was in her nearly paralyzed state trying to nurse Cole. Hana found a marker in a drawer and drew all over the front of the washing machine.

Christy went through the discipline steps she and Todd had agreed on. She got Hana in a time-out chair while Cole cried and then spit up what appeared to be most of the milk Christy had so painfully given him.

The chaos continued all day Thursday and into Friday morning. Nothing had changed. Christy was in great pain as well as utter frustration. She did what she knew Todd would tell her to do. She called her mom and practically fell into her arms when she arrived.

Christy's mom brought a heavenly calm with her, as usual, and helped Christy the rest of the afternoon with Hana, laundry, dishes, and rocking Cole so Christy could catch a very brief nap.

When Christy woke to Cole's wails and attempted another round of painful feeding late that afternoon, Christy's mom suggested a plan.

"When you called the advice nurse yesterday, she said the goal is not to get to where you've developed mastitis, correct?"

Christy nodded. "She told me what to take for the pain and the best infant formula I could try so I can give myself a rest. I just don't know if I want to do it."

"Honey, you won't earn a medal for getting an infection."

"I know. I wanted to try to do what I could naturally."

"That's what you have been doing. You gave it your best. What if you took the next step now? You can keep using your coconut oil and drinking the teas and everything else. You can substitute formula just for a little while so you can take the medication. You can pump, as the nurse suggested, and toss out your milk while he's on the bottle. Once you heal, you'll be able to go back to nursing."

Christy knew her mom was right. She gave in. The solution was time consuming and cumbersome and struck a blow to Christy's image of herself as a capable, womanly mother.

The consolation was that it worked.

Christy's mom made the trek to the grocery store to purchase the recommended medication, formula, two different kinds of bottles, and she also brought home a cherry pie.

"Everything in life seems better with a slice of pie," she said.

Christy appreciated her mother's Midwest approach to what had seemed like a defeating problem to Christy. She was able to rest and heal. Cole took to the formula with the help of Christy's mom coaxing him and finding a position that worked. That night all of them slept well. Christy's mom had stayed overnight in the guest room, and the next morning she was making eggs and buttermilk biscuits before Christy had rolled out of bed.

Cole was already fed and changed. Hana was dressed and lining up all the plastic mixing bowls on the kitchen floor, ready to use them for a private little drum solo.

"Mom? How did you do all this?"

Her mom looked surprised. "It's what you do every day, Christy."

Christy blinked as if she was standing outside her life looking in. "Oh, yeah. I guess you're right. Except for the biscuits. I can't remember the last time I made biscuits."

"How are you feeling?"

"Much better. I need to use this wonderful contraption, though." She went through the routine and hoped the hassle of pumping was going to be worth it in the end. If Cole decided he didn't want to change back after getting used to a bottle, she didn't think she'd like it.

The formula system did make it easy, though, when Christy left with Jennalyn at eleven that morning for their hair appointments. Christy thanked her mom profusely for being there for her over the past twenty-four hours and for watching Cole and Hana so she could go to the salon.

With a soft smile Christy's mom said, "A man may work from sun to sun but a mother's work is never done. You two go have a good time and relax. Everything here will be fine."

Jennalyn and Christy arrived at the small, brightly lit salon about five minutes late due to the challenge of finding a parking spot now that the summer crowds were arriving. Jennalyn was shown to a chair first.

Christy sat on the love seat in the waiting area and wished she'd worn jeans instead of a skirt. The air-conditioning vent was blowing her direction, and her bare legs felt chilled. Worse though, were all the mirrors in every direction. She had very few mirrors at home and wasn't prepared for the onslaught of her reflection. She was conscious of the rolls around her midriff.

I knew I shouldn't have worn this T-shirt. It's too tight. My bust is so large right now and this shirt is too clingy. I wish I'd worn jeans and a different top, but none of my jeans fit me yet.

She glanced at her left thigh in the bright lights. Her skin was covered with goose bumps and something worse. Christy drew her skirt up a few inches and what she imagined was confirmed. Another stretch mark, long and ugly, was visible on the side of her thigh.

"Christy?" An older woman motioned for her to come and sit in the chair next to Jennalyn.

Tugging at her skirt and hoping no one noticed her examination of her stretch marks, Christy walked over to the chair. The stylist fastened a large cape over Christy's top half, and she immediately felt a little warmer and more comfortable as she looked at her image in the well-lit mirror in front of her.

"All I want is a conditioning treatment."

The stylist nodded. She shifted from one foot to the other behind the salon chair, gazing at Christy's reflection in the mirror. With gentle strokes, the woman started brushing Christy's hair, examining it closely. "When was your last significant haircut?"

Christy tried to remember. "About fifteen years ago."

As soon as she said it, Christy vividly remembered how Aunt Marti had convinced her she needed a makeover and how willingly she'd said yes to the new clothes, makeup, and very short haircut. The experience had a significant impact on the way Christy viewed herself. She had dearly hoped that the radical change would help her fit in with the Newport Beach teens. Ever since that dramatic haircut, it seemed to Christy that she had been trying to grow her hair out.

Why have I been so determined to have long hair? It looks frazzled and messy most of the time. Even though it's long I hardly ever wear it down.

Christy shifted her eyes to catch glimpses of the other women in the salon. Most of them were Christy's age or a little older. All of them had hair that looked healthier, more stylish, and more flattering than Christy's mane of what seemed like seaweed in comparison.

"I changed my mind." Christy caught the eye of the stylist in the mirror. "I'd like you to cut it."

Jennalyn said, "Are you going to do it?"

Christy nodded.

"You'll love the way it feels cooler and easier to take care of. Good for you, Christy."

The stylist seemed pleased with Christy's decision as well. "What do you think? To about here?" She placed the comb at the top of Christy's shoulder.

"A few inches longer. Yes. Right there."

"Does she have enough to donate?" Jennalyn asked.

"I don't think so. The condition doesn't look as if it would meet the criteria," the stylist said. "Let's get you over to the washbowl for a shampoo and conditioning. I'll see how much I can keep."

Christy closed her eyes when she leaned her head back for the shampoo. She barely opened them until the stylist had finished the cut and said, "What do you think?"

It was the first time in many years that Christy could see the ends of her hair in the front when she looked into a mirror. The style was slightly tapered and a little shorter than she thought it would be, but her hair looked thicker and healthier.

Christy didn't want to commit to a final opinion until the stylist had finished blow-drying it, so she nodded and smiled in the mirror. After the loss of the many inches of weight, her hair had regained the natural wave it had when she was a girl. Her hair didn't dry straight and sleek but rather it had a lot of movement. She ran her fingers down the side and was amazed at how much softer and less frizzy it felt.

"It looks a lot better." Christy was offered a hand mirror so she could see the back. "I like it. Thank you."

"You have beautiful hair. It just needed some TLC. I wasn't able to keep enough to donate." The stylist held up a bottle of hair product. "This is what I used after the shampoo. It's my favorite conditioner for long hair. We carry it here at the salon."

"Christy! It's gorgeous." Jennalyn's voice carried over the sound of the blow dryer her stylist was using.

Christy was aware that other patrons were turning to look at her. She ran her fingers through her tresses and hoped she wouldn't regret this decision.

Christy and Jennalyn made their entrance to Julie Ann's with grins and a string of comments still going about how much they liked the other's hair. Jennalyn's color looked rich and warm without a single strand of purple.

They both waved at Fina who was behind the counter wearing an apron and carrying a big mug of something frothy. Fina smiled back and nodded, indicating they should go around the corner to find a table. The charming little café wasn't as busy as Christy thought it would be. They took the table for two up against the back wall and waited for Fina to come over.

"Christy, your hair looks great." Fina reached over and touched the ends as Christy nodded. "I love it. You look so much older."

Christy gave her an exaggerated frown. "Older? That wasn't exactly the look I was going for."

Fina laughed. "No, I didn't mean older like that. I meant, you look more sophisticated. That's what I was trying to say. You look womanly. Like a classy European woman. That kind of older."

Christy still wasn't sure if Fina had truly complimented her or if she was subtly telling her that her last tie to her youthful years had been severed.

She considered Fina's comment again the next morning when she washed her face and took a long look in the mirror. *Do I look older?*

Christy brushed her hair and felt that sudden end-of-the-road sensation every time the brush ran out of hair. She held it up in a ponytail and then let it fall and flipped it from one side to the other, trying to decide if she should twist it up on top of her head in the usual knot she'd worn daily for years.

Fina was coming over early for breakfast so she didn't

have a lot of time to decide. Down and flipped behind her ears was the choice she went with. She also took a moment to fish in the bathroom drawer for an eyeliner pencil and mascara. She brushed her teeth and rummaged for a tube of glossy lipstick, applying it with a pucker and a smack.

Evaluating the results, Christy decided it was the first time in a long time that she felt normal. Better than normal. She felt refreshed and less haggard than usual. The medication had helped her tremendously. She was healing up. Cole was getting on fine with the formula, and even though the pumping routine was her least favorite thing to do, it was working.

With one last smile at her reflection, she said, "Okay, big 3-0. I'm ready for you. Come and get me."

The spring in her spirit gave her cheery words for her son as she lifted him from his crib. She made up a silly tune for Hana when she started pouting over her breakfast. Hana missed her daddy. She asked for him every morning, every night, and at intervals throughout the day. Every time she asked, her little face seemed to cave in. She dipped her chin and jutted out her lower lip.

"I want my daddy" was becoming her mantra. Christy tried holding her and explaining that Daddy was on a trip with Aunt Katie and Uncle Eli, but that did nothing to cheer her. Hana had been too young last summer to remember Katie and Eli.

Christy tried a more nonchalant approach, thinking that if she didn't feed the sadness both of them were feeling over Todd's absence, it might diminish Hana's reaction every time. Christy simply said, "I know. I miss him, too. Should we color or play with a puzzle?"

None of her approaches helped. No matter what, Hana

would cry and cling to Bunny Wuv. Christy would do her best to comfort her until the wave had passed. Nearly every time Hana had a meltdown she would wail, "Sing." Todd's worship songs seemed to be the best touch point for her, so Christy kept her repertoire ready.

When Fina arrived that morning, Christy had already sung her way through the first meltdown of the day and changed not one but two major diapers. She indulged Hana with one of her favorite cartoon movies so Christy and Fina would have a chance to talk longer in the kitchen.

Fina entered with fresh muffins from Julie Ann's Café and two very large take-out cups in a cardboard carrier. "I thought we could use some fuel for all we need to accomplish this morning." She placed the goodies on the counter and added, "Don't worry, though. They're both decaf." She looked more closely at Christy. "You look really good. Your hair gives you an entirely new look."

"An older look?" Christy ventured.

"No. I'm sorry I said that yesterday. What I was trying to say was that your hair is really flattering. You have gorgeous hair, and when it's down like this, it's eye-catching. It shows off how beautiful you are."

Christy felt her face warming at the compliment. With all the pain from the clogged ducts, the insecurity she felt over her clothes being too tight, and the discovery of yet another stretch mark, Christy was thrilled that at least her hair was looking better than it had in years.

My mom thinks a piece of cherry pie can make the world a better place. For me, it's a kind word. And it's even better when it comes from the young woman who is about to become my sister-in-law.

Nineteen

"Fina?" Christy called out softly as she entered the dressing room.

"Down here at the end."

Christy saw a bare foot sticking out underneath one of the dressing stalls. She stood outside the closed door, not knowing if Fina wanted to keep the big-reveal moment a secret from everyone, or if she was eager for Christy to have a look and offer an opinion. "Well? How does it look?"

The door swung open and Fina was beaming. Her hands were at her sides where they disappeared into nearly invisible side pockets. The top was very flattering on her, and the length seemed to be exactly what she'd wanted. With her bare feet she looked like she was ready to skip down the aisle.

"Fina! I love it!"

"Me, too!" Fina's expression was bursting with joy, but her eyes were filled with question marks. "Do they make it in white? Please tell me yes. And tell me it can arrive in time."

Christy started nodding before Fina completed her plea.

"Really!" She grabbed Christy by the shoulders and did a Grace Kelly elegant sort of spin with Christy in the compact dressing room. She stopped and gave Christy a serious look. "You're sure they can get it in time?"

"They found a white one in your size at another store and said they could get it in two weeks, or if you want to pay extra, it can arrive in two to three days."

"I want to pay extra," Fina said solemnly. "Definitely. Two days would be amazing. And what do you think about a veil? I didn't know that I'd want a veil until a few minutes ago. I thought I wanted a wreath of flowers around my head like a crown like you wore. Your mom showed me your wedding photos the other night. You were such a beautiful bride, Christy."

"You're going to be a beautiful bride, too."

"I want to come down the aisle under a veil, like this." Fina imitated the motion of holding a bouquet and walking slowly without going anywhere. "I get to the front, my daddy gives me away, David smiles at me, we repeat our vows, and then . . . he lifts the veil and kisses me."

Fina playfully lifted her invisible veil and closed her eyes to kiss her unseen groom.

"Sounds perfect. I'm sure they have lots to choose from here. Should I find someone to help us?"

The next hour and a half was way up there on the fun and happiness scale of Christy's life. She treasured the chance to experience all of this planning between just the two of them. It might be her "only thing," but Christy was determined to do her best to make it one of Fina's most favorite things about planning her wedding.

For all the right reasons, Fina had ordered the dress to be

shipped to Christy's house. It arrived on Wednesday morning just as Christy was heading out for her playdate with Jennalyn.

"Guess what I have at my house?" Christy asked once they were settled on their blankets on the beach.

"A pile of dishes in the sink and a mound of laundry to fold?" Jennalyn gave Christy a smirk. "Because that's what I have at my house waiting for me. I'm so glad we have our set time each week. Otherwise, I feel like I would never get out of the house."

"I feel the same way. So, guess what I have? Besides dishes and laundry."

"I have no idea."

"Fina's wedding dress!" Christy dove into the whole story and said she was hoping Fina would be able to come over after work and try it on.

"That's such a big thing for Fina to be able to check off the list. When Joel and I got married, I had ten months to find a dress and it was torture. I ended up with a dress I didn't love when I got it, but on our wedding day, I decided I loved it. It was the right dress and it looked good in the pictures. I don't know why it was so stressful for me." Jennalyn stretched out her long bare legs and put Eden on her lap. "What about you? How stressful was the hunt for your dress?"

"I made it as challenging as possible."

Jennalyn looked intrigued. "How did you do that?"

Christy explained how she was so set on having an embroidered bodice to her dress after going to school in Switzerland and seeing lots of beautiful embroidered pieces, that she took on the task of hand embroidering the bodice during finals week of her senior year of college.

Jennalyn held up her hands. "You win. Most stressful

for sure. Now, what about your aunt? How stressful was it to have her involved in your wedding, and how crazy-making do you think it's going to be for Fina?"

"You know, I complained a lot about Aunt Marti at the time, but she was the one who coordinated everything and pulled together all the loose ends. She's really good at organizing. And she loves weddings. I think Fina will be glad that Marti is as involved as she is."

Christy had forgotten her sunglasses with the surprise arrival of the deliveryman at her front door. She squinted and said, "I can't believe how much you've volunteered to do for them. Let me know if you need any help with anything."

"I was thinking of having you embroider a flower on the corner of each invitation." Fina lowered her sunglasses and looked at Christy over the top of them. "Just kidding."

"Good thing, because I think my embroidering days are very limited. It's getting hard to even see the stitches when I'm using the sewing machine."

"Do you wear contacts?"

"No. I can't even remember the last time I had my eyes tested. I should make an appointment. I might need glasses and not even know it."

"I've worn contacts since high school. I can give you the name of my optometrist."

"Thanks." Christy stared out at the ocean, still squinting. "Turning thirty is rough."

"Thirty? Did I miss your birthday?"

"No. It's July 27." Christy thought about how Todd had told her a few weeks ago that she'd run out of "firsts." That wasn't the case with Jennalyn. She was discovering that the delight of making a new friend meant that everything was new information. It was the first time they could swap stories about their weddings and the first friend she'd ever shared beach dates with. Jennalyn didn't even know when Christy's birthday was. The firsts of discovery and sharing stories as this new friendship was sprouting brought their own sort of delight, Christy decided.

They chatted back and forth about how their husbands proposed and shared the most memorable moments of their rehearsal dinners and their wedding ceremonies. Jennalyn shared about a particularly distasteful shower gift one of her friends had given her and how she felt when she opened the gift in front of everyone.

"That reminds me," Christy said. "I want to have a shower for Fina at my house. I'm waiting for her to tell me what day she thinks would work best. I want it to be honoring to her, and I'm trying to figure out how to set it up to be a sacred sort of time."

"Do you think it might turn into a rowdy shower with some of her girlfriends from school?"

"I don't know. But I've been to showers like you're saying. They had games that were sketchy and gifts that were embarrassing. It didn't seem like the kind of celebration the bride deserved."

"So, how are you going to make Fina's shower more honoring to her?"

"I was thinking of having a little time before she opens the gifts where everyone goes around the circle and shares a favorite memory of Fina and then we could pray for her. Something like that."

"That would be really nice," Jennalyn said. "At the last few showers I went to, it felt like all the emphasis was on the jokes and games and like I said, the gag gifts. The focus wasn't really on the bride. And that's the point, right? To make her feel special and celebrated. At least to my way of thinking that's what the focus should be."

"I agree. I know that Fina is like me, well, like you and me, in the way we see marriage as sacred. There's something beautiful in an ancient way when women come around a young woman and bestow on her."

"Bestow," Jennalyn repeated with a laugh. "You may have lost me there. What do you mean? Bestow is such a quaint word."

"I know. I guess I'm trying to say I want to give to her lavishly and for her to feel like she's been honored and blessed."

"I'm all for that."

"I'm not saying it should be solemn or anything. It's a celebration. I just want to include some traditions. Fina values traditions and family heritage. You know how she's wearing her grandmother's ring. She's going to wear her mother's dress for the ceremony in Glenbrooke. I'd like to come up with a shower theme that highlights those values."

Christy and Jennalyn tossed a bunch of ideas back and forth. They concluded that the shower would be outdoors on Christy's deck in the evening with twinkle lights, lots of greenery, and colorful paper lanterns to add more ambiance. That's as far as they got before it was evident that their little ones had taken in as much sun and sand as they could.

"Let me know if you need help with anything," Jennalyn said as they walked home.

"Okay. I will. It's going to be a small group, so I'll probably be able to handle all the details once we come up with a date and I can figure out the theme. Besides, you have a lot on your plate."

"I know. But I love doing things like this."

Christy thought about the bridal shower all afternoon. Trying to create a special, memorable time for friends was something she loved to do. As Hana and Cole napped, she scoured dozens of Pinterest boards and saved all the ideas she liked the most. Her plan was to show them to Fina when she came over to try on her wedding dress. Whichever ideas got the best response, those would be the ones she'd incorporate.

Things got harried for Christy after Cole woke up. He was fussy and spitting up a lot. Hana wasn't happy about anything all afternoon and evening. She didn't want a snack and she didn't want to look at Pinterest with Mommy. All she wanted was to lay on the rug in the living room with her cheek on the rug, her round little bottom up in the air, and Bunny Wuv under her arm.

"Does your tummy hurt?" Christy asked.

"No." Hana's voice was small and sad.

"Do you want to read a book?"

"No."

"Auntie Fina is coming over in a little while. Do you want to see Auntie Fina?"

"No."

Christy was going to put a kids' program on TV for her sluggish little girl even though afternoons were usually playtime. Instead, Christy remembered the music recording Todd had mentioned. Christy set it up and Todd's voice came through the speakers, rolling over them and filling the room.

Christy sat on the rug next to Hana and together they listened to Jeremiah 31.

"Yes, I have loved you
With an everlasting love,
With lovingkindness
I have drawn you."

The song ended and the next one began with both Doug and Todd singing. The guitar intro was one of Christy's favorites. Hana got up, went fishing in her toy basket, and came back to the rug with her toy bongos. She plopped down on the rug and started tap-tapping along with the song. She didn't seem to have natural rhythm or an understanding of the tempo, but she did know all about being included and playing along with her daddy whenever he got out his guitar at home.

Christy captured a video on her phone before Hana realized what she was doing. After that, Hana wanted to see the pictures on the phone. She wanted to call Daddy on the phone. She wanted to see Daddy's face on the phone. Christy found herself saying, "No, not now. Maybe later" at least a half-dozen times before Hana curled up into a puddle of tears.

The doorbell rang and Fina called to Hana through the screen door. "Is that my Hana Girl I hear crying?"

Hana hopped up and tottered to Fina as she opened the door and came in. Fina scooped her up and started peppering her with little kisses all over her head and cheeks. Hana's tears soon turned into giggles and her melancholy was forgotten.

Fina looked over at Christy with bright expectation in her eyes. "Well?"

"It's in the guest room. I left it in the box. I thought you might want to have the fun of opening it."

"I'm so excited." Fina put Hana down. "Wait until you see my dress, Hana Girl. It's the most beautiful dress you've ever seen. You stay here and I'll be right back."

Fina dashed into the guest room, closed the door, and the usual bedlam broke out. Hana cried because she couldn't go into the room with Fina. Cole needed a diaper change, and in the midst of all the normal chaos, someone came to the front door and rang the doorbell three times.

Christy peered through the screen. "Aunt Marti!"

"Are you going to invite me to come in? I rang the bell, but I doubt you could hear me over the noise."

Christy had Cole balanced on one hip wearing only a fresh diaper. Hana clung to her other leg, peering around the side as if she were uncertain of Aunt Marti. Christy wasn't sure what to do.

"Do you need something?" Christy asked, still not opening the door. She realized how that sounded and quickly opened the screen door to invite her aunt inside.

"I told you I'd come by this week and give you the measurements for the new seat cushions I need for the patio."

"You did?"

"I thought I did. It may have slipped my mind. I've had so much to do." Marti stepped over a scattering of toys and sat on the sofa. "As you know, I had to cancel our vacation plans for Idaho, and your uncle had to withdraw from the tournament. There were so many details to take care of."

Hana let go of Christy, ran over to the rug, grabbed her Bunny Wuv, and held it up to show Aunt Marti. She smiled at Hana sweetly and leaned over to look at the bunny. Marti had never been good at showing any sort of demonstrative affection toward Hana. Marti's love was expressed through buying Hana things all the time. She would lean down and speak to her in a sweet-sounding voice. But Aunt Marti had never offered to hold Hana or give her a hug.

Todd had told Christy not to worry about it. He was sure Aunt Marti would take a keen interest in Hana as soon as she was old enough to enjoy the art of shopping or be willing to be dressed up in cute outfits so Marti could take her to lunch at one of her favorite posh restaurants.

"It's not that your uncle or I mind having to change our plans. We can always go another time. Not that it will be as convenient, since we're going to be losing our housekeeper."

"Don't you mean house sitter?" Christy corrected her.

"Yes. That's what I said. Our house sitter. Fina. Now that she and your brother have rushed their wedding, I've found it a daunting challenge to get everything accomplished in the short time we've been given."

"I'm sure you'll do a great job, Aunt Marti. You always do." Christy hoped her voice carried loud enough and that the words "Aunt Marti" made it into the guest room. If Fina heard her, she'd be able to decide if she wanted to pop out of the room and share this moment of the big reveal with Aunt Marti, or if she'd rather wait quietly and come out after Marti left.

"Now about the cushions. I'd like you to pick the fabric for me. I simply don't have time to do that."

Christy had an immediate red flag go up. First of all, she didn't remember her aunt ever mentioning new covers for the patio chairs. Secondly, she'd never attempted sewing cushions. They seemed easy enough if she could take apart one of the current ones and use it for a pattern. But she couldn't give an accurate idea of how long the new project would take.

The third and most important reason she was hesitant was because she did not want to be in the position of making the fabric selection. Too much potential for disaster, in her mind.

Marti charged ahead. "Now, I prefer broadcloth, neutral colors, but nothing too pale. Nothing gray. And nothing patterned. No tropical prints or stripes. I especially don't want stripes."

Christy looked at the paper Marti handed her and skimmed the measurements and other notes. "I think I can try this, but you should know I'm not experienced with cushions."

"You can sew anything, Christy. I'm sure of it."

"I'm willing to try, but I don't want to select the fabric. I need you to do that part of this project."

Christy's resistance didn't settle well with Marti. "Could you ask Jennalyn to do it? She has a good eye for color and style."

Christy stood firm. "Jennalyn is just as busy as you are, Aunt Marti. If you will select the fabric, I will attempt to sew the cushions. If you don't select it, I'll have to pass on the project."

Aunt Marti blinked at the surprising backbone Christy had demonstrated.

"You're coming into your own, Christina. You're speaking up for yourself." Marti stood up, let out a sigh, took the paper from Christy, and headed for the front door. "I suppose I should congratulate you on this new burst of independence. I just wish you'd waited until after the wedding before you demonstrated it so effectively." Marti let herself out and said nothing more.

Christy looked at Hana who was watching her mommy for a clue as to what all that was about.

"Who says I'm all out of big firsts?" Christy said calmly. "I just set a boundary with my aunt and she honored it. I think that was a first."

The guest room door squeaked as it opened a few inches. "All clear?" Fina called out.

"Yes, all clear."

"Are you ready?"

"Yes!" Christy moved to the center of the kitchen. She faced the guest bedroom door and held her breath.

Twenty

Fina emerged from the guest room with a huge smile. She spread her arms out and did a twirl for Christy. “It’s perfect. I can’t believe it! I love this dress. And look. The pockets. Aren’t they the best?”

Christy stood with her hands on her hips and a wide grin on her face. “You look stunning.”

“Where’s the veil?” Fina asked excitedly. “I want to get the full effect.”

“I put it in the guest room closet. Do you want me to get it?”

“No. Wait there. I’ll be right back.” Fina fluttered away like a garden fairy in her light-as-a-feather layered skirt. She returned looking every bit the happy bride in a perfect blend of winsome and elegant.

“I can’t believe how perfectly it fits you. You look radiant, Fina. You really do.”

“I’m so overwhelmed with how everything is coming together so easily. Ever since we decided to move ahead and get married and move to Indiana, it's like God has opened the floodgates. Everything we need is coming to us. I'm learning so much about trusting Him."

Christy smiled and nodded. "Life can be pretty amazing that way when God puts you on a new path. I love watching all the ways He's been blessing you."

Fina's excitement over the details and her tender heart toward recognizing that God was leading them made Christy even more motivated that the bridal shower should be something special. She showed Fina some of her ideas for the shower theme and asked what she wanted.

"I like it all. Everything you showed me is beautiful. I don't have a preference."

"I've been meaning to ask you something." Christy was standing and swaying with Cole in her arms. "Did David propose to you again? I never heard if he got down on one knee and improved on his first try."

"No, he didn't go down on one knee or come up with a romantic dinner date or anything."

"How did he ask you?"

"After he and I talked the day when you prayed with me, I gave him the ring and told him I was ready for him to ask again. He took it but he said he wanted to get counsel from both our parents first. I guess he took the ring in to be sized pretty quickly because on our way to the engagement party on Father's Day, he stopped at our bench. Neither of us said anything. We just got out of the car, walked hand in hand to the bench, and sat down for a few minutes, looking at the ocean."

Christy remembered how Fina and David had been among the last to arrive at the party.

"David pulled it out of his pocket, in a ring box this time, and he opened the box. He wasn't nervous at all. He said, 'For me, this means till death.'"

Christy hid her slight cringe. *Oh, David. That wasn't terribly romantic. It sounds like a line from a Viking movie.*

"I told him that it meant the same for me." Fina's matter-of-fact tone and her starry-eyed expression made it clear that for her, the words and gesture had been perfect. Christy could see that with Fina's athletic abilities and because of the way she respected strength on every level, David's warrior sort of transformation and his direct approach was what she responded to best.

Fina checked the time. "I've got to get going." She changed out of her wedding gown and was gathering up her things. "If you set the date for the shower any time after August 1, my mom and sisters will be here. I don't know if you want to wait until that close to the wedding to have the shower, but I'd love it if they could come."

"How about August 2?"

"Perfect! Once again, everything is falling into place. Thank you so much, Christy, for everything." Fina gave Christy a big hug and, as usual, dashed out the door. Christy checked on Hana and found her lying on the couch using Bunny Wuv as a pillow.

"Are you okay, sweetheart?" Christy felt Hana's forehead and was surprised at how warm she was. Christy went to find the baby thermometer, carrying Cole with her as she trekked up and down the stairs. She returned to find Hana whimpering and clutching Bunny Wuv's ear.

Hana's fever was slight. Her appetite was nil. Her energy was low and her tears were plentiful. The sneezes came on about an hour later, followed by a cough and lots of frowns.

Over the next six days, Christy experienced what it was

like to get a cold and flu bug and feel awful along with her child. The misery was enhanced by the fact that she had to care for her toddler and infant when all she wanted to do was curl up in bed and make everyone else go away.

Christy had no idea how they caught the bug. She told her mom to stay away just in case they were all contagious. Her days were filled with caring for Cole, who seemed to have miraculously avoided the bug, and lounging on the couch while Hana curled up in the snuggle chair with Bunny Wuv. They took turns napping and sneezing and watching every episode of every calming children's' show Christy could find.

Christy had been making a noble effort to get Cole off the bottle and formula and back to nursing. It was getting more complicated now that she was sick. Cole was such a big baby it seemed to Christy, based on what she was able to produce when she pumped and comparing it to how much formula he was taking, she wasn't producing enough milk anymore.

On the fifth day of her cold, Hana was back to normal, but Christy had reached a new low. After several consultation calls to the advice nurse, conversations with other mom friends, and a lot of reading, Christy finally resolved herself to the fact that she couldn't keep going the way she was with pumping because her milk had reduced significantly. Cole was fine. From here on out, he'd be a formula baby.

And that made her feel like a failure.

She didn't share those thoughts with anyone. Mostly because the cold bug had knocked her out so completely. The days melted into one long blob. When Christy came up for air the following Tuesday, she felt especially depressed. It was the Fourth of July, and her family had plans for a full day at Bob and Marti's with a beach picnic, volleyball with David and Fina's friends, and an evening of sparklers. She knew she didn't have enough energy to participate, even though she was starting to feel better.

It was the most uncelebratory Independence Day she had ever experienced. Being on duty for twenty-four hours all by herself with two children when she was sick was just about the worst thing she'd experienced since becoming a mother.

Todd had been able to text her and receive her e-mails and texts so he knew they had the "sniffles." Christy hadn't told Todd how sick she really was or how difficult everything had been. It would concern him, and she was certain from his clipped messages that he had way too much on his mind already. Todd mentioned in a couple of his messages that he hoped she was asking for help from her mom. Christy avoided answering with specifics.

By Friday, a full nine days after Hana had started with her symptoms, Christy felt like she was back on her feet. Hana had come through the quarantine with no problem. The only residual effect was that Hana had a craving for more TV time since they'd watched so much over the past week. Christy was determined to get back to their previous routine.

Cole was a formula baby now. The breast pump had been put away. Christy's body responded surprisingly quickly to the weaning process. She had told her mom, Jennalyn, and Todd. They all said she'd done the right thing, but she disagreed. It killed her not to be able to enjoy the same success in nursing Cole as she had with Hana.

It helped Christy's sense of defeat when she saw how Cole was more alert and interactive now. He stayed awake a little more each day as well as slept a little longer each night. In some ways, Christy felt the same way sort of stabilizing of her body she'd felt after making it through the first trimester of her pregnancy with Cole. What mattered most to her now, as it had during her pregnancy, was that her little guy was healthy and growing strong.

To break the homebound pattern, Christy packed up the kids on Thursday and headed to the grocery store. Her shopping list was long, and maneuvering through the process with two children was still challenging. So was unpacking the groceries once they got home. It felt as if that one minor chore took nearly all her strength. She made smoothies as an easy lunch for her and Hana and gave in to her daughter's relentless requests for more TV.

Christy pushed the *On* button and was ready to flip through to Hana's program so she could go take care of Cole. The image that appeared on the screen was the close-up of Rick Doyle in the *Diner Do-Overs* commercial. She stood frozen in place with the remote in her hand, watching the montage of Rick and Nicole living out their amazing life.

"Mommy . . ."

"I know, Hana. I'm getting your show for you. Be patient."

Christy couldn't stop thinking about Rick and Nicole as she was giving Cole his bottle. She missed Todd so much it felt in some ways as if he'd left her for good and she would never see him again. Her recovering body was still weary, and her emotions were as thin as tissue paper.

All the initial delight she'd enjoyed a week and a half ago as she helped Fina with her dress had passed once they accomplished the goal. She'd halted plans for Fina's shower when she got sick, and Christy hadn't had any communication with Aunt Marti since the patio cushion showdown.

Christy was just about to let a self-pity tear roll down her face when she heard a voice call out, "delivery" through the open screen door.

The small, flat package was from Tracy, her longtime

friend in Glenbrooke. Christy could tell it was a book when she opened it, even though it was wrapped as a birthday gift. Tracy had always done kind things for Christy on her birthday, starting with the summer they first met. Tracy and Todd had gone in together to buy Christy her first Bible, and Tracy had made a fabric cover for it. The pink floral cover had fallen apart years ago when Christy tried to wash it. She still had the Bible, though, and it was marked with dozens of notes and comments Christy had written in the margins over the past decade and a half.

Tracy's pretty handwriting on the card explained that this was a book she loved and hoped Christy would enjoy it, too. She wrote that she and Doug and their three children were planning a trip to Yellowstone National Park in the middle of July. She'd mailed Christy's birthday present extra early so she would have it in time.

"Fina is right. I do have the best friends."

She debated if she should open it now or wait until her birthday. Cole made the decision for her when he spit up on her shoulder. She hadn't covered herself with a burp cloth so a more thorough cleanup was needed. Additional spit-ups were part of the new normal with her formula-fed baby. The diapers were worse, too, in her opinion.

Christy's mom called as Christy was changing Cole into a fresh Onesie. She had called almost every day to check in. "Would you and the kids like to come over for dinner tonight?"

It had been weeks, maybe months, since Christy had been to her parents' apartment. Most of the time it was easier for them to come to Todd and Christy's house because everything needed for the children was right there.

"I think we're up for that," Christy told her mom. "It will

be nice to get out of the house, too."

"David and Fina won't be here. They have the Gathering tonight. It will just be you and the children."

Her mom's mention of the Gathering made Christy feel as if it had been a lifetime ago when she used to dash out the door with Todd every Friday night to get to the Gathering. She always took snacks. Over the years, she'd had some significant conversations with a lot of teens that started with them commenting on her homemade cookies or requesting that she bring brownies the following week.

I can't even remember the last time I made cookies.

The monumental changes in her life struck her once again. Christy felt very much alone and lacking in the area of purpose and worth.

Dinner at her parents was short. The conversation was focused entirely on the location for the rehearsal dinner and a list of other responsibilities of the parents of the groom that had flustered her mom and dad. Christy listened a lot and tended to her children like the single mother she'd become.

"Are you counting the days?" Her mom asked as Christy cut the evening short and got Cole buckled into the infant carrier.

"The days until the wedding?"

"No, until Tuesday."

Tuesday?

"Isn't that when Todd comes home?" her mom asked.

"Yes. Tuesday. Yes. Believe me, I can't wait till he gets home." Christy got her two little human treasures securely tucked in the car and drove the ten minutes back to her house.

Tuesday. Todd is coming home Tuesday. I've been so out of it, I've hardly known what day or week it is.

The reminder from her mom jolted her into action. Christy had many small projects she intended to do while he was gone, and none of them had happened. She felt a surge of motivation to do what she could over the next four days.

She started first thing on Saturday morning with cleaning up the master bedroom. She had a stack of clothes that needed attention due to spots or tears at the seam. Those were carried downstairs and placed on top of the dryer. She folded the towels from the dryer, started another load, went upstairs to get Hana up and dressed, and repeated the process for her baby boy.

The mommy two-step routine kicked in and she got nothing out of the ordinary accomplished the rest of the morning. When Hana went down for her nap, Christy put Cole in his infant carrier seat and set him up on the counter where he seemed to like watching all that was going on. Her plan was to clean the downstairs bathroom.

However, the birthday gift from Tracy caught her eye. It was on the counter right where it had sat for two days. Christy decided she didn't want to wait until her birthday. She pulled off the ribbon, peeled back the paper, and looked at the title. *A Pocketful of Hope for Mothers.*

The cover was a cute drawing of an apron with a bouquet of flowers spilling out of the pocket and apron strings flowing in the breeze. Christy flipped through the charming gift book, enjoying the interior art and the titles of the poems and stories in the book.

A piece titled "More Than" caught her eye. Christy started reading it and knew her bathrooms were going to remain the way they were for the moment. She carried Cole in his seat along with the book and settled in the shade outside on the deck. Christy stretched out in one of the low beach chairs. For the first time, she agreed with Todd's idea that if they could get a hammock on a stand out here, they'd use it a lot.

Taking her time, she read the piece as if these were the sort of words her mother would speak over her if her mother was an expressive person.

"I was wrong,
My darling daughter, I was wrong.
I told you that you were enough.
Enough woman, mother, chef, teacher, puppeteer . . .
Today I saw the deeper truth as I watched you accomplish heroic acts of everyday motherhood.
Now I know that you are not enough.
No.
The truth is,
you are more than.
More than
The length of your days
Or the breadth of your knowledge.
More than
Yesterday's accomplishments
Or tomorrow's goals.
You are more than you were when you started this journey into motherhood.
More than
A diaper-changing station
Or a twenty-four-hour concession stand.
You are more than you can see,
More than your thin emotions can feel.
You are more than the sum of all your parts.
More than what you saw in the mirror this morning.

More than what you told yourself three minutes ago.
Listen. Hear this and treasure it in your heart.
You don't have to
Do more
Be more
Give more
Try more.
You already are more.
More than you know.
You are
A song in the night
A gentle touch
A calm word
An assuring smile
A soft kiss.
You are not just enough, dear little mama.
You are more than.
In all things, for all day,
You are more than a conqueror through Him who
Handcrafted you
Unfailingly loves you
Continually guides you.

He is the One who placed on you the care of these eternal souls—

The Giver of all good gifts
The One who is
and was
and is to come.
He will give you more than enough to see you through.

"In all these things we are more than conquerors through him who loved us." —Romans 8:37.

Christy pressed the open book against her stomach and let the tears flow like cleansing rain. She wanted the words to plant themselves like seeds deep in her spirit and sprout. She wanted to stop repeating all her flaws and failings and believe the truth she had just read. There was something immensely valuable about being a "song in the night" and an "assuring smile". She could give her children something deeper, something more than what anyone else could give them. She wielded great power simply by being their loving mother.

I am enough. I am more than. More than a conqueror.

Twenty-One

Todd's homecoming was delayed a full day due to the group missing a flight out of Amsterdam. The anticipation and then deflation ripped into Christy much deeper than she would have expected. Hana didn't understand why Daddy wasn't home yet after Christy had talked about it with her for two days. They made a banner together that Hana helped color. The house was clean and ready. Christy had even made Todd's favorite Ritzy chicken and green beans for dinner.

When Christy tried to get Hana to settle in for bed that night, she kept saying, "Tomorrow, sweetheart. We'll see Daddy tomorrow." The days of the week still meant nothing to Hana, and all she wanted to do was cry for her daddy.

Christy cried, too.

She'd kept Todd's voice in the house for the last few days by playing all the worship music he and Doug had recorded. The immediacy of his familiar voice and the rich words in each song both soothed and knotted up Christy's stomach.

Three days earlier a flight out of Amsterdam bound for Los Angeles had made an emergency landing in Iceland due to a possible terrorist threat.

The details on the news were minimal. Just knowing that Todd and the team were flying out of Amsterdam as well made Christy anxious. Fear kept knocking on her door, and Christy kept repeating, *Jesus, it's for You. Jesus, it's for You.*

On Wednesday morning Christy woke at five forty-five in amazement. Cole had slept through the night!

She checked her phone and was relieved to see that Todd had texted her during the night. The flight he and the group were on had made it to Chicago. Unless their connecting flight to Los Angeles was delayed, he should be home before dinner.

Christy cancelled her beach date with Jennalyn for the second week in a row. Last week she'd still felt too sick to meet up. This week she was too excited to be away from the house.

"No need to apologize," Jennalyn had said when Christy called her. "I'd be doing the same thing."

"Thanks again for the meals you brought over for us when we were sick."

"It was our pleasure. Just to remind you, the invitations for the shower are finished. I was serious when I said I could address them and mail them for you, too. All I need are the addresses."

"I can do that. Thanks for offering. And thanks so much for making the invitations."

"No problem. I'll drop them off in a few minutes. I'm going to get Eden in the stroller and go for a walk."

Usually when Christy heard about all the things Jennalyn was creating or what she was harvesting from her compact garden, an immediate sense of comparison would come over her. Feelings of inferiority would rise in Christy's psyche as she thought about the lesser amount of projects she had accomplished that week. She always felt especially defeated whenever Jennalyn mentioned exercise of any sort.

Today it was different. She didn't know if it was the deep encouragement she'd been getting from reading *A Pocketful of Hope for Mothers* or if it was the fact that in a few hours Todd would be home, and that was all that really mattered to her right now.

Whatever the cause, Christy felt grounded. She was doing the best she could with the people and the time and the life that had been given to her. And that was enough.

No, actually, it was more than enough.

Today Christy felt like she was more than a conqueror. It reminded her of David's Viking-styled proposal. Love and life and raising a family required much more warrior-like strength than Christy ever realized. Maybe that's what Todd had meant over a month ago when he said that David and Fina knew too much. They were approaching marriage with the understanding that there would be times when they would have to fight hard against depression and debt, temptation and fear.

Christy had experienced a smattering of all the hard stuff over the last few months, and she was still standing, clothed and in her right mind, overjoyed that her husband would soon be home.

The hours sailed by. Christy got the invitations from Jennalyn, addressed them all, and managed to have them ready to hand to the mailman when he delivered the mail. While Hana napped, Christy kept her wide-awake son in his infant seat and set him up just outside the open bathroom door.

That way she could take a real shower that included shaving her legs and washing and conditioning her hair.

Cole was content, and the fact that he didn't start crying gave Christy another sense of victory. She spent a little extra time on her makeup and went through the options in her closet. The summer dress she'd worn to Jennalyn's Summer Soiree seemed like a good choice. She slipped it over her head and was surprised. The dress seemed to fit better than it had a month ago.

Cole jumped when she turned on the hair dryer. His big blue-green eyes watched all Christy's movements, and he kicked and flapped his arms as if he liked the sound.

Nearly finished with her hair, Christy wondered if the back seam had come out of the dress and that's why it felt so much looser. She closed the bathroom door, which meant she couldn't see Cole. For a quick minute she turned to the side and then the other side, studying her profile reflection in the mirror on the back of the bathroom door. When she found no ripped seams she dared to believe.

I'm losing weight! Even though I stopped nursing, I'm finally losing weight.

Stepping on the scale, Christy was surprised to see that the number wasn't as low as she expected. "Okay. Well, at least I'm losing inches. I'll take it!"

She swung open the bathroom door with a victorious expression as if she was going to make her announcement again to her baby boy.

Instead of her baby boy, it was her husband who stood on the other side of the door, larger than life, right there in the middle of their bedroom.

"Todd!" Christy squealed as if she were sixteen again and had thought she'd never see him again. In a dash, her arms were around him and their lips were reminding each other of where they'd left off three weeks ago.

Christy reluctantly pulled away. "I thought you wouldn't be here until this evening."

Todd flashed a lopsided grin on his unshaven face. "Do you want me to leave and come back tonight?"

"No!" Christy wrapped her arms around him and pressed her face against his chest. "Don't leave. Don't ever leave again." His clothes smelled like an exotic café to Christy. Smokey and sweet like black licorice and cloves. He needed a shower. That was evident. But she didn't care. He was home and in her arms.

"I didn't hear you come in."

"I think you had the hair dryer going."

"I'm so glad you're home!"

Todd pulled her close and kissed her again. As he drew back he murmured, "I missed you so much, Kilikina."

"I missed you more."

Cole, who had been watching them from his infant seat on the floor, let out a punctuated, singular wail that sounded a lot like he'd just said, "Hey."

Christy laughed. "I'm not the only one who missed you." She leaned over to get him out and let him join the reunion.

Todd's first words when he took Cole and lifted him up high were, "Whoa! Look how much you've grown."

"Can you really tell?" Christy asked.

"He's definitely heavier. Hello, my son. Were you good for your mommy while I was gone? I heard a few stories about you."

Christy tickled Cole's bare foot. "And they're all true, aren't they, Little Bear?"

"I take it Hana is still sleeping." Todd grinned broadly at

Cole and kissed him soundly on both his chubby cheeks.

"She's been down for about forty minutes. She'll be so happy to see you."

Todd handed Cole back to Christy. "Let me take a quick shower. I need one badly. Then I'll go in and surprise Hana."

Todd's surprise didn't seem to work as planned. After his shower, he slipped into Hana's room where she was still sleeping. As Christy watched, holding Cole, Todd placed his hand on Hana's back and started singing to her. She tossed her head to the other side and pulled away.

"I've been playing your music all week," Christy said in a low voice. "She probably thinks I've just turned up the volume downstairs. You know how much she likes her peace and quiet when she's sleeping."

Todd removed his hand, stopped singing, and prepared to exit. That's when Hana popped up like a baby bird in a nest made of stuffed animals. She sat up, looked around, and started crying.

"I'm right here, Sunshine." Todd went to her and lifted her up, kissing her with his still-unshaven face bristling against her cheek.

Hana, still dazed, pulled back and studied his face with a frown. She arched and leaned way back as if trying to get down so she could get back in her bed.

"It's me, Daddy. I'm home."

Hana acted as if she didn't want anything to do with him. Todd let her down on her bed and looked to Christy for an explanation.

"Hana," Christy came closer. "Hana, Daddy's home. Look! He's here. He wants to give you cuddles."

Hana sat in her safe bed, looking at Todd and Christy and Cole with a bewildered expression and tears forming in her sleepy eyes. She held up her stuffed bunny as if she was showing it to them.

Todd reached for the bunny and said, "Do you want me to hold Bunny Wuv?"

Hana pulled it back, clutching it closely, and shouted, "My Bunny Wuv!"

"Yes," Christy said. "That's your Bunny Wuv and this is your daddy."

After a few minutes of coaxing, Hana was willing to let Christy hold her while Todd carried Cole. The four of them went downstairs, but Hana kept her distance from Todd as if her little mind wasn't yet convinced of who he was. She was a little more affectionate when Todd put her to bed a few hours later, but she wanted Christy to be in the room while Todd sang to her.

When Christy and Todd were finally in bed together that night, cuddled up as close as they could be, Todd stopped midkiss and said, "Do you think I permanently damaged our daughter by being gone so long?"

Christy's thoughts were elsewhere at that moment. It was one of the few, very few times during the past three weeks that she had not been thinking about their children. She kissed Todd, hoping he'd remember what they were doing. "She will be fine."

He kissed her back. "Are you sure?"

"Yes." She inserted a kiss. "Very sure."

Todd let Christy kiss him again, but he didn't respond with equal fervor. "I never thought about that downside of the trip."

Christy pulled back. Clearly, Hana's wary responses had hit him hard. "She'll warm up to you, Todd. Don't worry. She knows who you are. She's just finding her way back after missing you so much. We all missed you."

"I missed all of you so much. I thought of you constantly."

Christy stroked the backs of her fingers across the side of Todd's gruff face. "We thought of you constantly, too. Hana had a rough time while you were gone, but she'll be okay. You'll see."

"What about you?" Todd's expression in the shadows of their bedroom light appeared serious. "How difficult was it around here for you?"

Christy hesitated before answering. All her text and e-mails had purposefully been written to sound as if everything was "okay." Not great, not catastrophic. Just okay. It was a cloaking mechanism she'd put into play months ago and had perpetuated the "okay" theme during the final weeks of the school year and even more so while Todd was in Africa.

"Tell me," Todd said softly.

She thought about how Jennalyn had influenced her to talk about "just the true stuff" and decided the time had come to say more than she usually did. Now that her world was once again as it should be, with Todd in her arms, she should tell him the truth.

"It was one of the most difficult things I've ever done in my life." She paused, making sure the weight of her words felt right.

Todd waited for her to say more. "Running a family alone is all-consuming. Especially since the kids are so little. I have felt overwhelmed since Cole was born. Actually, even before he was born. The last trimester was really rough with potty training Hana and being so pregnant that it was impossible to get comfortable enough to sleep at night."

Christy paused again, wanting to make sure she wasn't overloading him with her deepest feelings and ruining the moment for good.

"Go on," Todd said.

"When you left, I had a hard time sleeping. Cole's demands were constant, and when I got the clogged duct, I thought I was going to lose my mind. Then Hana got sick and I got sick and we were both down. I mean, really down. The cold lasted for over a week. Switching Cole over to formula was incredibly deflating to how I started to view myself as a mother. I cried a lot while you were gone. I prayed a lot, too. It was hard. Really hard."

Christy felt like she'd purged her thoughts fully and took a deep breath. "I have no regrets about you going, Todd. I really don't. And I'm not saying any of this to try to start a pity party. You asked, so I wanted to tell you. That's what my life has been like for about the last six months. I wouldn't want to change anything except my heart. I want my heart for you and our family to always be soft and kind."

Todd smoothed his hand over Christy's silky hair that flowed smoothly over her bare shoulders. He continued to stroke her hair, breathing in and out, thinking.

"Thank you." His voice was a tight whisper.

Christy began to cry. She knew that her husband recognized what his response to following God's call on his life had cost her. She didn't think he'd fully considered how all the responsibility had rolled back onto her throughout the year of planning, fund-raising, and during the trip itself.

She leaned in closer and kissed his cheek. Her lips unknowingly caught a salty tear. Not her tear. The tear was Todd's.

He knows. He understands. That's all I wanted. It's not that I think he should never go on another outreach like this again. I have just longed for him to see and understand how much I give so he can fully be the man God has gifted him to be.

No further words were needed. The years of uncluttered intimacy in their marriage had cultivated the precious gift of communicating well without saying anything. Tonight their actions spoke louder than any words.

Twenty-Two

It took a few days before Hana's shyness fell away and she was her "Daddy-Daddy" squealing self. Aside from Todd working off his jet lag by being up at odd hours and dead asleep on the sofa in the middle of the day, everything at the Spencer household was wonderful. Christy hadn't anticipated how peaceful and happy the tone would be with him home all day for days in a row.

They went out to breakfast one morning at Julie Ann's and enjoyed having Fina as their waitress. Fina was fun to watch. She was energetic and glowing as she moved from table to table. The staff and many of the regular customers seemed to all know she was getting married in a few weeks. The ones who didn't know soon found out because Fina didn't hesitate to announce her news to the coffee-sipping customers.

"It was my grandmother's." Fina held out her left hand and proudly modeled the ring for the two women at the table next to Todd and Christy's. "I'm named after her. Josephina.

Her family history goes back over three hundred years all in the same region of Switzerland."

Customers appeared interested. They also appeared to be more generous in their tips, as if they were contributing a little something extra to the upcoming wedding.

When Christy and Todd stopped in to see her parents afterward for a quick hello, Christy mentioned Fina's outgoing approach with the café guests. Her mother looked concerned.

"Do you think what she's doing is pressuring people to leave more tips?" Christy's mom asked. "I know she told us the other day that she's been making more at the café than she thought she would."

"You wouldn't think that if you saw her," Todd said. "She's being herself."

"She's very natural and not at all pushy," Christy added.

"Fina has no guile. She is who she is. Honest and forthright," Christy's dad announced. He'd been fixing a wobbly screen-door hinge on a neighboring apartment when Christy and Todd arrived with Hana and Cole. His position as manager of the small apartment complex had been an ideal job change for him several years ago. He was a natural handyman, and the complex grounds were immaculate with every shrub trimmed and lots of coastal variety flowers blooming in sequence year round.

Christy's dad didn't usually have a lot to say. This pronouncement seemed to be the highest form of praise for his new daughter-in-law-to-be. He pointed at Todd. "You're the same way. No guile. It makes a man proud to see his children marry their equals."

That evening as Christy and Todd walked along the beach with Hana and Cole, Todd said, "I think your dad likes me."

"Of course he likes you."

"There have been times when I've wondered."

"I'm sure you're not alone there. Fina seems to be bringing out a little more tenderness in him. He's always worked so hard and been intent on doing what was right in every situation. I think it must feel like it's a reward in a way to see that his children married well."

Christy looped her arm through Todd's and tried to balance while Hana was on Todd's shoulders and Cole was bumping along in the front sling. The sand was too uneven so she went back to using both arms to support Cole.

"Your dad's words were that his children married their equals. That's high praise for all of us. Especially since he values integrity so much."

Christy made a mental note to add the single word integrity to her simple prayers for Hana and Cole. As they strolled together feeling the cool sand on their bare feet, she whispered a simple prayer that springboarded from the word that had been on her mind for the last twenty minutes. "Joy."

Thank You, Father, for these sweet moments of joy that Todd and I have been able to share ever since he came home. Thank You.

Todd and Christy set up a routine of walking along the beach together every evening at sunset. Todd always wore his swim trunks so he could take in a quick swim while Christy rocked Cole and Hana played in the sand. One evening Hana wanted to join him. Todd was elated. He carried her out until he was waist deep and the water splashed against her legs. Hana laughed and clung to her daddy's neck, calling out, "Again, Daddy! Again."

Christy knew this had to be a dream come true for Todd. She had her phone in the pocket of her shorts and pulled it out quickly so she could capture a string of photos. After so many unsuccessful attempts by both Christy and Todd to get Hana to not be afraid of the water, Christy had a feeling this was the moment when Hana was at last making friends with her daddy's beloved Pacific Ocean.

The happy moment continued, and for more than a week it felt to Christy as if they were on vacation. A staycation in their own beach cottage. They'd unexpectedly meandered into the endless summer she'd once dreamed of with cupcakes and pinwheels. The dream was real and the sense of being cherished and cared for was off the chart.

On many nights during those midsummer days, Christy and Todd spent long hours around the fire pit on their deck after the kids went to bed. Under the string of café lights with their bare feet warmed by the fire, Todd told Christy story after story about the students, the villages, the people he met, the food they ate, the many God-things that happened.

Todd had some fun stories about Katie in her new role as a mom. It sounded like she had warmed up to the position and was enjoying every little new trick Jimmy could do. The most recent was that if Katie got close and blinked her eyes at him quickly, he would attempt to blink back.

"I remember when it was like that when Hana was first born," Christy said. "Everything was new and also pretty frightening, to be honest."

"You're a lot more at ease with Cole, aren't you?"

Christy nodded. "It's getting easier."

She took a sip of the tea that Katie had sent back with Todd for her. The birthday card Katie had included with the tea leaves said it came from the tea fields they had explored together almost six years ago before Katie and Eli's wedding. The same tea field where Katie had given birth in a tent.

Christy loved the tea and had been drinking a cup every day. It made her feel even closer to Katie and to the rich, green, rolling hills of Kenya while Todd shared his stories with her.

"We have two beautiful children," Todd said.

"Yes, we do." Christy didn't add anything about how she was more in agreement with that statement now than she had been over the past month. Todd had heard her when she said how exhausting her days had been. If she put herself in the role of a martyr, there was no grace in her love for him. They had settled their understanding of her sacrifice his first night home.

"I've been thinking," Todd said.

Christy smiled and took another sip of tea. She knew that could mean he was about to throw out a possibility of something wild, or he could simply say, "We should have tacos tomorrow." With Todd, it could go either way so Christy always prepared herself.

"There might be something else for us." Todd presented his thought as a statement. Each word was spoken with the same tone and pace, as if he'd inserted a period between each word.

Christy waited for him to continue. When he didn't, it seemed to her that he was pausing so she would invite him to explain what he meant.

The deepest part of her that, according to her dad, had no guile, wasn't sure she wanted him to tell her what that something else might be. For the first time in such a long time, Christy finally felt settled and grounded in this new season of life.

Do I really want to know right now if God has been nudging Todd to move to a remote corner of the globe or have another baby or adopt more children or . . .?

These were all discussions they'd had in the past when Todd's opening line had been, "I've been thinking."

Christy knew she had waited as long as she thought would be considered polite. With reluctance she asked the question he undoubtedly was waiting for.

"What is the something else that is out there calling to you, my adventurous husband?"

Todd studied her calmly. "You don't really want to hear it right now, do you?"

She shook her head and offered a timid smile. "It's not that I don't want to hear all about it eventually. It's just that right now, right here, at this moment, I'm not ready to dream of greater things or consider any new possibilities. All I want for now is this. Us. Here."

"Okay. Understandable."

A quote from the book Tracy had given her came to mind. She'd read it many times and had copied it in her Thankful journal. Christy leaned her head back and recited the quote.

"'Do not spoil what you have
by desiring what you have not;
Remember that what you now have
was once among the things you only hoped for.'"

"Where did that come from?" Todd asked. "Did you just make it up?"

"No. It was said by some ancient wise person. I don't remember the name. But I like the thought."

"Well, I like you." Todd leaned over and kissed her on the cheek.

Christy had a pretty good idea of how this night would end, and she liked the notion very much.

The next time she and Todd spent the evening on their deck was the following Wednesday night, for Christy's birthday. With all the planning for the big wedding, no one in Christy's family had keyed in to the fact that Christy was turning thirty only a week and a half before David and Fina said their "I do's."

Todd picked up on the oversight and put some party plans into motion. He invited the clan along with Joel and Jennalyn to come for a barbeque and told everyone to bring only themselves. He was taking care of everything else. Christy enjoyed watching Todd do what Christy was usually the one doing. He swept the deck, set up chairs, went grocery shopping, came home with balloons and flowers, and had hamburgers on the grill by five thirty as everyone started to arrive.

The sweetest gesture, Christy decided, was that Todd had brought home two big boxes from the grocery store bakery. Inside were cupcakes with a rainbow of frosting colors and, best of all, tiny pinwheels on top. Christy's immediate thought when Todd did his "ta-da" moment and opened the lid was that he had ordered them as if this were a party for Hana or for a youth group event.

"Cupcakes and pinwheels. Isn't that what you said your endless summer dream was?" Todd watched her expression, waiting for her to make the connection with his little surprise.

"Yes. You are so wonderful. Thank you." Christy gave Todd a big kiss.

Aunt Marti arrived ahead of Uncle Bob. She explained that she'd been working on wedding details and made it a point to say that she had to go pick up the cushions she'd had made for the patio chairs. "They charged me a fortune, but at least they're done in plenty of time."

Christy took the subtle jab. It didn't hurt, though. She

knew she couldn't have completed the project with all that had happened over the past few weeks. And even if she had made a heroic effort, she was pretty sure they would not have turned out to her aunt's satisfaction. She was glad she hadn't tried. Keeping up with her apron and pillow orders was all she wanted to take on for the time being.

"These need to be chilled." Marti handed Christy two bottles of wine. "It's an especially nice white."

Marti always brought wine when they had their monthly Family Night Dinners, and she was often the only one who drank much of it. This was the first time she'd brought two bottles. Perhaps it was part of her usual way of expressing her care for others by being generous with gifts.

Christy filled a large mixing bowl with ice and inserted the bottles of white wine, hoping that would be up to Marti's standards. She didn't have time to find out her aunt's opinion because Joel and Jennalyn arrived with Eden. Joel placed a covered cake plate on the counter and caught a glimpse of the colorful cupcakes.

"I wasn't sure if you'd have enough sweets." He lifted the lid and Christy's mouth began to water. Joel had made her a flourless chocolate-amaretto cake and piped "Happy 30th" across the glossy dark chocolate on top.

"I see you have cupcakes, though," Joel said.

"Don't worry," Christy said, giving Joel a hug. "Your gift will not go to waste."

Todd entered the kitchen with Cole in his arms and said, "It might go to my waist, though."

They all laughed and Todd handed Cole over to Christy. "I need to go flip some burgers."

"Need some help?" Joel asked.

"You know I do." Todd welcomed the master chef out

on the deck, and a moment later Joel strode into the kitchen looking like a man on a mission.

"Do you mind if I have a look in your fridge?" Joel asked.

"It's all yours." Christy had a feeling Todd's basic youth-ministry level burgers were about to be taken up a few notches, depending on what sorts of seasonings Joel might find in their limited supply of condiments.

Aunt Linda arrived about the same time as Uncle Bob, who had brought David and Fina with him. Christy's parents followed, and the handwoven basket Todd had brought back from Kenya for Christy filled up with birthday cards. Todd had let her know that in his invitation to everyone he'd suggested that instead of a gift, if they could all pitch in a little money, it would allow Christy a chance to enjoy a spa day or treat herself to something she wouldn't normally get for herself.

Jennalyn glanced out at Todd and Joel on the deck. "We sure have cute husbands," she said to Christy.

"Yes, we do."

"Cute?" Marti echoed. "I don't believe I ever in my life referred to my husband as 'cute.'"

"Well, you should," Fina said, reaching for a potato chip from the bag on the counter. "Your husband is very cute." She cast a grin at David who was in the living room playing cars on the floor with Hana. "And soon, I will have a very cute husband, too."

Jennalyn had been standing next to Bob around the counter. He had taken Eden from her and was holding her like an experienced uncle.

"We all think you're very cute, Bob," she told him playfully.

Bob took a little bow. "You can thank God for my naturally debonair good looks and thank my wife for my impeccable manners."

Marti had opened the white wine and was pouring herself some into a glass she'd taken from the cupboard, since all Todd had put out were plastic cups. Marti never drank from a plastic cup. She tossed out her opinion of Bob's clever quip by saying, "I'm not sure you should give the Almighty complete credit for your appearance. I think you'd agree that I've had a little more than a bit of influence in that area."

"Yes, you have. And I'm all the better for it, my love."

Christy saw Todd motioning for her from out on the deck. She slid away from the others to go see what he wanted.

My uncle has to be the most patient, loving, and forgiving man on the planet. He has put up with so much from Aunt Marti, and he just keeps on loving her. My marriage is a breeze compared to what he's endured.

"We're ready," Todd said. "Do you want to tell everyone to grab a paper plate and come get their burger?"

"We've got them sorted by medium rare, medium, and well-done," Joel explained.

Christy smiled at the way Joel was turning her birthday barbecue into a gourmet affair. She turned to Todd who still had a long spatula in one hand and a knife in the other. Leaning in, she went for his lips and gave him a right-on-target, I-mean-this-with-all-my-heart kiss.

"Thank you for making my birthday and my life wonderful. Absolutely wonderful."

Todd's eyes locked on hers and a happy-hubby sort of grin widened his freshly kissed lips.

Christy headed back inside. In the reflection of the sliding glass window, she saw Joel giving Todd a fist bump. She hoped she'd always remember to find ways to honor her husband in public and never tear him down in front of others. Especially in front of their family and friends.

Twenty-Three

Christy's birthday was just about perfect. The food, the family and friends, the weather, the music and the conversations were all just right. That was, until the end after everyone had sung to her. She'd blown out a candle and her puff of breath managed to turn the pinwheel on top of the cupcake. That launched a competition as the others took a cupcake and tried to see how fast they could get their pinwheels to spin. The laughter and spontaneity especially between the guys kept Christy smiling.

Then she looked over at Marti.

Marti wasn't participating in the pinwheel contest. She seemed to be the only guest who was enjoying the white wine during the evening. She caught Christy's eye and came over to sit beside heron Narangus, the patio bench Todd had made from his original orange surfboard and the backseat of his VW Bus, Gus.

"I have not been myself this evening," Marti said. "It's because of that redheaded dervish of a friend of yours."

"Katie?"

"Of course, Katie. How many redheaded dervishes are you friends with?"

"What did Katie do?"

"She wrote me a letter. A long letter. Handwritten on cheap notebook paper, stuffed in an envelope with four stamps. It was the most uncouth invitation I've ever received."

"Invitation? To what?"

"To heaven."

Christy gave her aunt a confused look. She thought the wine might be making Marti sound a little crazy. "Are you sure that's what it was?" Christy asked cautiously.

Marti was indignant, but in slow motion. "Of course I'm sure. I should show it to you. It was absurd. She said she wanted me to come to heaven and was inviting me, but the only way I could RSVP was if I repented. That's the word she used. *Repented!*"

Christy cringed. Until this moment she'd forgotten about Katie's text several weeks ago and how she said she was going to tell Marti she needed to get on her knees and surrender her life to Jesus. Apparently, Katie had followed through with her passionate idea.

"Your husband told me once that the only way I could be made right with God was if I asked God to forgive me for all my wrongs and to receive me as His own child." Marti huffed in disgust.

Well, actually, he's right.

"Apparently, that's your Katie's aisle . . . I'll . . . idea of how humans are supposed to get to heaven also." Marti took another long sip of her glass of wine. "Tell me. Is that what you believe, Christy?"

Without hesitation Christy nodded. She doubted her aunt would remember this conversation in the morning, but regardless, if Marti wanted to talk about how to become a Christian, then by all means, Christy was ready to speak up. After all, Katie had broached the subject already.

"Yes. That's what I believe. That's God's plan for how to bring us back to Him. The message is all the way throughout the Bible. We've all wandered far away from Him. He wants us back."

Marti studied Christy closely. "Have you done that? Fallen on your knees and repented?"

The way she said the words it sounded mocking, as if no intelligent, respectable person would ever lower themselves to such a moment.

"Yes. I have. On my knees and everything."

"When?"

"It was at your house, actually. The summer I turned fifteen and came to stay with you. I was in the guest room the morning after I went to Disneyland with Todd, and I just knew."

"Knew what? Knew that you loved God, like Fina and David said they just knew they were right for each other and wanted to be married right away?"

"Something like that. It wasn't that I loved God, truly. Not then. I do now. But back then, I was overwhelmed with the realization that He loved me. He wanted me. And I knew I wanted Him. I committed my life to Him. Like a covenant bond in marriage."

Marti was studying Christy's face. Tears had formed in Christy's eyes, and a soft smile drew her lips upward. Christy meant every word she was saying.

"I guess you could say, Aunt Marti, that that moment in

your upstairs guest room when I made that summer promise, it was the beginning of my love story with Jesus."

"I thought only nuns did that. Vowed to marry themselves to God alone."

"No. I did that. In a sense. And I'm not a nun."

"No, you're certainly not." Marti sniffed and adjusted her position.

Christy waited to see how this might go. Marti was looking around at the other guests on the deck. She tilted her glass, draining the last swish of wine, and peered at Christy again.

"Todd has done that, too, hasn't he? Surrendered his life to God."

"Yes."

"I know Robert did all those years ago. He has told me more times than anyone should have to endure." Marti shook her head as if she thought she deserved a medal for "enduring" so much from her husband. She seemed to be taking note of all the guests at Christy's birthday party and one by one realizing that she was adrift in a sea of God Lovers and had been for many years.

Marti raised her empty glass to Todd's Aunt Linda across the deck. "At least there's one person here who shares my political views."

"Having a right relationship with the Creator of this universe really has nothing to do with a person's political views."

Marti looked stunned by Christy's comment. She also looked as if she'd had enough of this discussion.

"You certainly aren't the person I want to talk to." Marti pushed herself to a standing position with an unsteady sway. "I simply wanted to point out that your Katie has gone too far this time. Whatever couth I put in that wild child was lost in Africa."

Marti started to inch her way around the fire pit. She stopped and turned to Christy, pointing her long finger nail somewhat in Christy's direction. "I have never been so insulted in my life. Tell her. I am not sending a reply."

Uncle Bob, who seemed to have been watching the conversation from a few feet away, stepped in and graciously offered to take the glass from Marti before she dropped it and it shattered everywhere.

"I was just about to call it a night," Bob said calmly. "What about you?"

Marti kept a grip on the glass and waved her hand in the air. If there had been any more wine in the glass, it would have spilled over the coals in the fire pit. "I'm done." Marti's voice was the loudest it had been all night. "I'm done with all this." Her wrist did a dramatic twist and the glass slipped. It fell directly into the fire pit, sending up a flash of red sparks and resting several large pieces of shattered glass on top of the coals.

"Let's go." This time Bob's words carried a firmness instead of a tone of suggestion.

"My glass."

"I'll get it, Aunt Marti." Christy had jumped up when the sparks landed on her legs. She'd brushed them off without injury. "Don't worry about it."

Uncle Bob had his arm around Marti and was saying his polite good nights to everyone as he ushered her to the front door. Christy was sure that she wasn't the only one who had never witnessed Marti in quite this way. Marti had been outspoken and fuzzy-thinking on other occasions. This was the first time she seemed to have let herself get so fully separated from her usual controlled self.

The rest of the family rallied to make sure Christy felt this night was still about her. Jennalyn cut Joel's cake into narrow wedges, and Christy told everyone they needed to try a piece. The enthusiasm was unanimous.

Fina turned to David with evidence of how much she enjoyed it still dotted on her upper lip. He grinned and pointed to the chocolate. She pressed her lips together and then said, "What do you think? Chocolate cake instead of cheesecake for our wedding?"

"You were thinking of having cheesecake?" Aunt Linda asked.

"We both love cheesecake with fresh strawberries. That's what we asked Joel to make for us."

Linda still looked surprised.

"Our wedding is not going to be traditional," Fina explained quickly. "The vows will be, but the rest of it is going to be . . . us!"

"I can make both, if you'd like," Joel offered. "The chocolate one can be the one you cut together, that is, if you are keeping that tradition for the pictures."

"Yes. We're going to do the slicing of the cake and feeding each other a bite. I love that." Fina looked to David for affirmation.

He was grinning, as he had been all night whenever he looked at Fina.

My baby brother is smitten. Completely smitten. I love it.

David's expression shadowed over for a moment. "But no smashing the cake in each other's faces. I hate it when I've seen that done."

"I think it could be fun and playful," Fina said.

David shook his head.

"Okay. No smashing. That won't be a problem because I

don't want to waste even a crumb of this decadent chocolate cake."

Todd had just returned to the group after putting Hana to bed. Christy's mom was holding Cole, and he looked like he might fall asleep in her arms. It was an image that made Christy so grateful for the way her mother had so serenely and unobtrusively wound her way through life. It made sense that she'd developed such a calm demeanor after growing up with Marti for a sister. Christy could only imagine what kind of drama Aunt Marti had brought to every family event when she was growing up.

As soon as Todd realized they had sliced into the cake without him, his expression turned slightly frantic. Christy pointed to the counter. "I saved you a big slice, Mr. Spencer."

Todd didn't waste any time digging in and enjoying his piece. As everyone else was starting to head out, Todd went to Christy and held out his plate. There were three big bites of cake left. "For you, birthday girl."

She smiled her everlasting gratitude and said, "I am honestly too full. It's all yours."

"Then I'll save it," Todd said in a low voice. "We'll share it later."

Christy was still grinning when Joel and Jennalyn, who were the last to leave, stopped at the front door. Joel had their sleeping daughter in his arms and Jennalyn was rummaging in the large, colorful beach bag she used as a diaper bag and purse combo.

"I almost forgot!" Jennalyn handed a wrapped gift to Christy. "Go ahead and open it now. I want to see your face."

Christy pulled off the wrapping from the thin box and burst into a smile when she saw what Jennalyn had made for her. "I love it! Thank you!" She wrapped her arm around

Jennalyn's neck and gave her a big hug.

Todd took the framed piece of graphic art from Christy and read the words Jennalyn had written in her lovely script.

Oh, Honey. Stop buzzing and just bee.

"It's perfect, Jennalyn. I love it."

Todd looked at Joel. "I'm guessing this means something to the two of them."

Joel played along. "It must. But I've gotta say, all the cuteness gives me the hives."

"Oh, that's a stinger," Todd added.

The two guys started cracking up. Christy and Jennalyn stared at them.

"Is it just me," Jennalyn said, "or do they sort of remind you of the two old guys who sit up in the balcony in all the Muppet movies?"

Christy laughed and now it was the guys' turn to look at their partners with feigned indignation.

"We better go before my husband and yours tell us what we remind them of." Jennalyn gave Christy another hug. "Happy birthday."

"Thank you." Christy closed the door and turned to Todd who had started cleaning up the kitchen. "Thank you for a wonderful birthday, Todd."

"Glad it turned out nice for you, in spite of whatever was going on with Marti."

"I think what she was saying was what was really rolling around inside her. It was like she was running out of defenses or something." Christy held up the picture and walked around the downstairs trying to decide where she wanted to hang it.

"So, what's the story behind the bee stuff?"

Cole had been fussing on his blanket on the rug in the living room. Christy put the picture down and went to him to tend to her little one. She told Todd about the night she'd sat on the deck by herself when he was gone and she was struggling with lots of anxiety.

"It was one of those moments when I prayed and it was as if God answered in my thoughts. You know how people say they can see something in their mind's eye? I felt like I heard this line in my mind's ear, if that makes sense. Like an echo in your heart. It's not audible, but you recognize it as the completion of the thought you just sent to the heavens."

Todd had joined her on the sofa and was nodding as she was talking. "I know what you mean. Deep calls to deep. That's how I've always seen thoughts like that."

"Well, I don't know if my thoughts are all that deep sometimes, but this line is what I heard. I told Jennalyn about it on one of our beach dates."

"Where are you going to hang it?"

"I don't know. Someplace where it will be a good reminder for me to stop sometimes and just be thankful for everything God has done for us."

"It's Psalm 46:10," Todd murmured.

Before Christy could catch what he'd just said, Todd started singing.

"Be still,
And know
That I
Am God;
I will be exalted
Among the nations,

I will be honored
In the earth."

When he finished Christy said, "I don't recognize that one. Is it a new song?"

"Yeah. It came to me the first day we were at Brockenhurst. I was on that bench on the way to the dining hall. You know that one under the big tree that looks like a giant umbrella."

"Yes. I remember that tree." Christy loved the thought that the first thing Todd did when he finally made it to Kenya was to sit down and write out a song from such a perfect portion of Scripture.

Both of them had been meditating on the same thoughts around the same time, thousands of miles apart. Todd interacted with the thought by composing a worship chorus. Christy pictured it in a winsome, artistic way, which Jennalyn had brought to life.

"God's Spirit is so alive," Christy said. "He communicates with us in such personal ways."

"Is that what you think was happening with Aunt Marti?"

Christy hadn't expected Todd to say that. She'd been thinking about the song and the cute little bee saying. Maybe God's Spirit was communicating with Marti in a way that she'd respond to, as crazy as that sounded. Marti was comfortable with being argumentative. Apparently that's the approach Katie had taken with her. Marti loved a party. She loved weddings. She loved RSVPs and being included.

Could it be that the best way for the Lord to get Marti's attention was through a feisty invitation to go to heaven? The ludicrousness of it messed with all the teaching Christy had ever received on how to effectively share your faith with someone.

"You have one more gift," Todd said, breaking into her thoughts. He handed her a small box. She hadn't seen him bring it over to the couch when he came. It wasn't wrapped, and he quickly apologized, saying he didn't know where they kept the wrapping paper and ribbons.

"Todd, you didn't have to give me anything. The party was perfect. And all the baskets and things you brought me from Kenya. You . . ."

"Just open it."

Christy adjusted her position with Cole in her arms so she could hold the jewelry box. She was immediately flooded with memories of when Todd had given her a gold ID bracelet for Christmas when she was fifteen. He'd had the word *Forever* engraved on it. All through their bumpy dating years, that gold ID bracelet held deep meaning for both of them.

She just knew that if Todd was giving her another piece of jewelry as they entered this next season of their lives and of their love, it was going to be something very special.

Christy slowly opened the lid. Inside was a small gold heart with delicate etching around the edges.

"It's a locket," Todd said. "Here. Let me take it out for you." He undid the long chain of the necklace, and with a little fumbling, he managed to open the heart and hold it up for Christy to see. Somehow he'd fit a tiny picture of Cole on one side of the hollowed out interior and a tiny picture of Hana on the other.

"I hold you in my heart, Kilikina." He dangled the locket from his fingers. "I know you hold me and hold our children in your heart. I wanted you to have a way of always treasuring that thought." He turned the locket over and said, "I wanted to add Phil.1:7 so I asked the jeweler to inscribe it here on the back."

Christy felt overwhelmed by his thoughtfulness. A gift like this had taken time to plan and prepare. During all those weeks when Christy felt like Todd was so wrapped up in school and the missions trip and too busy to even think of her, he had somehow managed to plan this very special gift for her.

"Todd." Christy couldn't speak. In a tiny whisper she said, "I love it. I love you. Thank you. Thank you."

He leaned over and fastened it around her neck. Christy's tears fell on Cole, on Todd's hand, and on the locket, baptizing all of them into the first day of her thirties.

Twenty-Four

The days of cupcakes and pinwheels, lockets and raging aunts paved the path to all the final preparations for David and Fina's big day.

The bridal shower was set to happen on Wednesday afternoon, and things were aflutter at Christy's nest. An unexpected wind had come in from the desert, raising the temperature and threatening to stir up trouble on the deck where Christy had set up the food table, extra chairs, and had strung lots of colorful paper lanterns.

The decision was made to move the party inside, and Todd went to work to make it happen. Christy's mom had come early to help with the kids while Christy took a very quick shower and dressed. She hurried back downstairs and found Todd buckling both kids in the car.

"Call me if you need me," Christy said.

"Your dad and I will be fine. Hope everything here goes well."

Todd looked nervous. Christy was nervous, too. She looked around at the state of her kitchen and knew she couldn't fret about Todd and Cole right now because the first guests had just arrived as Todd was pulling out of the driveway. Christy wasn't ready and that flustered her.

With quick steps around her kitchen, Christy got the rest of the appetizers on the island counter and gave her mom directions on how to arrange the extra chairs in a circle in the living room. The women seemed to all arrive in a bunch. When Fina's mom and two high school-aged sisters arrived, Christy knew it was too late to try to dash upstairs and put on any makeup. At least she felt like her hair looked nice. It was so much easier to manage now that it skimmed her shoulders.

She thought about how Todd had been so stunned and upset when she cut her hair while he was gone. Once he was home and realized she was wearing it down a lot more now that it wasn't so long and easily tangled, he had told her a couple times how much he liked it.

Christy adjusted her slightly loose-fitting summer dress. She considered changing since she didn't know what the other women would be wearing.

Would a skirt be better? Or maybe jeans with a long summer top? I have that one with the cute crisscross in the back.

Her eye caught on the picture Jennalyn had given her that she'd placed in a cookbook stand on the counter near the sink. Christy stopped "buzzing" and took a deep breath.

The focus is on Fina, remember? Grace. Peace. Do everything you can to make her feel celebrated, and don't fret for one more minute about yourself.

Aunt Marti was the last to arrive. Her gift box was the largest of all the others. It was tied with a huge pink bow. She placed it in a position of prominence in the living room. As soon as Marti returned to where the other guests were clustered around the island counter, she removed a large glass bottle from her bag and placed it next to the glass pitchers of strawberry lemonade and mint iced tea.

"I've brought my own mineral water. Lesson learned." She chuckled and looked around. "You see, I'm on strict orders from my doctor not to drink anything that might interact in a negative way with the allergy medication I'm taking."

Christy and Fina exchanged glances, and both pressed their lips together. They knew exactly what Marti was trying to declare, and it really didn't need to be revisited.

The morning after Christy's birthday party, Marti had sent a group text to everyone who had been at the party. It was a long text asking them to understand that she had no idea that the cold pill she'd taken before she came would interact with the wine and cause such a "delirium."

Marti had added that she wasn't accustomed to the particular brand of cold medication, but seeing as Christy had been so ill prior to the party, she had trusted her doctor's orders to protect her delicate system, especially since Todd had just returned from Africa.

Christy had privately picked apart the inconsistencies in the text, starting with the fact that a warning label appears on all such medications not to drink alcohol while taking the medication. Along with the fact that Christy and Hana had been sick weeks earlier and had been quite well and recovered far past the possibility of them carrying contagious bugs. As for Todd returning from Africa, he was certainly healthy and showed no signs of carrying an infectious disease.

When Fina called later that day to ask what she should do, Christy's best advice was to say nothing. She told Fina to be kind and just nod when she got home, and Marti would inevitably bring up the topic. "Whatever you do, don't try to correct Aunt Marti. You'll never win," were Christy's final words on the subject.

Marti, though, seemed to think the topic needed to be the headliner at Fina's shower in order to clarify to all in attendance that she was not responsible for her actions at the last family gathering. She had capably become her own savior by providing her own beverage this time.

Jennalyn was the one who managed to single-handedly return the rightful focus of the shower back onto Fina. She did it in a way that even surprised Christy.

"Fina, I made a little something for you for the shower." Jennalyn reached into her Mary Poppins' style beach bag and carefully pulled out a beautiful wreath of fresh flowers with thin ribbons streaming down the back.

All the women drew in a breath of awe at the same moment. Jennalyn held the wreath and said, "I heard that you considered wearing a wreath like this for your wedding because you saw the pictures from Christy's wedding and you liked it."

"I loved it on Christy. But I decided on a veil," Fina said.

"And you look stunning in the veil," Christy added. "Absolutely stunning."

"So I thought," Jennalyn said, "that since the veil is perfect for your wedding day, then the wreath of flowers would be just right for your shower day."

All the women seemed sweetly and deeply touched as they watched Jennalyn hand the wreath to Fina's mother, Genevieve, and say, "Would you like to crown your firstborn? It only seems right that you should be the one to welcome her into the circle of women who know the deep beauty of what it means to make a vow with all your heart."

Genevieve entered into the moment with a spirit of honor and sacredness that Christy had told Jennalyn weeks ago she wanted to be the hallmark of this shower. Christy didn't know if Jennalyn had prepared Fina's mom ahead of time, but what came out of Genevieve's mouth was awe inspiring.

"I crown you, my daughter, my beautiful, beautiful Josephina." Genevieve got teary eyed and so did Christy. "I crown you first of all a daughter of the King of kings. I also crown you a warrior woman. You have everything you need to fight to keep your love alive and to honor your marriage vows for the rest of your days. Josephina. My firstborn. My grown child."

Genevieve lowered the crown onto Fina's head. She looked Fina in the eye and Fina returned an unveiled gaze. It was clear that the two of them had a very close relationship. Both of them were crying silent, rolling tears as Fina's sisters dabbed the corners of their eyes and pulled out their phones and took lots of pictures.

The women in Fina's family weren't the only ones choked up by the extraordinary moment. Christy reached for a napkin and shot a smile at her mother, who was gazing at Christy with her trademark gentleness.

Christy couldn't imagine her mother ever saying the sorts of things Genevieve had spoken over Fina, nor could she picture herself being nearly nose to nose with her mother for a full minute of peering into each other's eyes and not feel silly and self-conscious. But Christy felt a tightening of the bonds that were there between her and her mother in all the ways that the two of them had come to relate to each other.

Christy gave Jennalyn's arm a squeeze, silently communicating that the theme of the shower had been set perfectly and Christy was so grateful.

The next two hours, with the food and the conversation and the opening of the gifts, carried the same lovely tone. Then came the opening of Marti's gift, the last box Fina reached for. With a slightly nervous glance at Christy, Fina folded back the tissue paper and lifted out a long, silky white negligee complete with white feathers across the bodice. Along with the floor-length negligee was a matching white satin robe with lots more feathers around the collar and down the front.

Christy watched Fina to see her reaction. The gown was elegant and expensive but looked like something a movie star would wear in a classic black-and-white noir mystery. Fina appeared to like it, or at least she did an Oscar-winning performance of accepting the opulent gift from Aunt Marti.

"I wanted to get something special for you, Fina. Everything your mother said is true. You are a beautiful woman. I wanted to give you something that would make you feel especially beautiful."

The reaction around the room was touching. Even though it didn't appear to be the sort of nightwear a no-fuss young woman like Fina would ever want, the intent behind the expensive gift was noted and honored.

The guests lingered, but not too long. There were lots of things to do now that Fina's family was here to help with the final details.

Genevieve slid up beside Christy and wrapped her arm around her. She gently rested her head on Christy's shoulder. It was a tender, motherly gesture that warmed Christy.

"Thank you, Christy. Everything about this shower was beautiful. Thank you."

"It was my pleasure. Truly."

Genevieve pulled back and placed both her hands on Christy's shoulders. "If I could have hosted a bridal shower for Fina in Glenbrooke, I would have wanted it to be exactly like this one was today. You are a gifted hostess, Christy. I felt welcomed the moment I stepped inside your home. You have created a beautiful haven. There's peace here. And much love."

"Thank you, Genevieve. That means a lot. I feel so blessed to have Fina in our family. And to be part of your family now, too! "

Christy and Genevieve exchanged a spontaneous hug. It delighted Christy to see the eager sprouting of this new relationship with Genevieve. When she was in Glenbrooke last summer she admired the closeness she saw in the women there. They shared a sense of sisterhood and community in a way that Christy hoped she could foster in her little corner of the world. It was something she and Jennalyn had talked about often. Today the two of them had worked together to produce those results and it made Christy's heart soar.

When Fina thanked Christy and gave her a big hug, she held on a little longer and said, "I think I'm allergic to feathers."

Christy caught the meaning immediately and whispered back, "Let me know if you need help returning it. I can help."

"Thank you!" Fina pulled back and gave Christy a wink. "We'll see you at the rehearsal dinner on Saturday, if not before."

Everything was on target for the next family gathering at the rehearsal until a little after five thirty on Saturday evening.

Todd had left at three thirty and was doing a walk-through of the ceremony with David and Fina and the parents. He'd taken Hana with him and that gave Christy a chance to shower and dress for the rehearsal dinner at six o'clock.

Christy was dressed and had timed everything so that Cole would have his bottle before she drove to the Five Crowns Restaurant in Corona del Mar. She knew she'd be a few minutes late, but that was understandable. She was seated on the living room sofa and Cole was about halfway through his bottle when he started coughing and immediately threw up all over Christy. It was unlike any other spit-upping Cole had ever done. There was so much dripping all over Christy and the sofa, it appeared the poor little guy had nothing left inside him.

Christy reached for a blanket to wipe down the front of her while standing and holding Cole up to her shoulder. He coughed again and issued whatever was still left in his tummy all down the back of Christy. She could feel it trickling down her skin and sliding underneath her bra.

"Buddy, what is going on? Are you okay?"

All consideration of her own discomfort aside, Christy got Cole into an elevated position in her arms. She checked his forehead. He wasn't feverish. He was a sloggy mess, but he wasn't crying and he didn't seem to be in any discomfort.

"Are you okay, Cole? Does your tummy hurt?" Christy pressed softly, but the gentle pressure on his stomach didn't seem to affect him.

Christy wrapped him in the blanket and, since she was the only one home and the front door was closed, shimmied out of her dress and wrapped it up in a ball so she wouldn't keep dripping on the floor.

Cole kicked and seemed content on the blanket on the floor. Christy left him for a few minutes in only his diaper so she could get cleaned up and changed and find something else for him to wear.

"We are really going to be late. But that's okay. It has to

be okay."

Christy was embarrassingly limited on options of what she could wear. With all the help she'd given Fina on the wedding dress, the advice she'd given her mom on what to wear, and the greatest challenge of buying a new suit for Todd, Christy had put herself on the bottom of the list and assumed that whatever she had in her closet would be fine.

She peeled off her underwear, gave herself a speedy washcloth bath, and started over with a top that was way too casual for the event and the only pants she could fit in, which was a pair of black pants she'd worn the first six months of her pregnancy.

This is so humiliating.

Even though she knew that no one there would be looking at her, and certainly no one on the planet would have any clue that these were her fat pants, Christy knew. And it was rough trying to reframe this as anything other than what it was.

Cole was on the blanket where she'd left him, but he was not the same as she'd left him.

"Did you just roll over? Cole!"

He raised his head like a blue-eyed lizard and Christy clapped at his achievement. The clapping stopped when she spotted what was coming out the sides of his diaper.

"Oh, sweetheart, you are blowin' out on both sides. What is going on?"

It took Christy over twenty minutes to get Cole fully cleaned up and in another outfit. She needed to get another bottle ready because he was bound to be starving as soon as he realized there was nothing left in him.

With her fresh and friendly baby boy on her hip, Christy scooted around the kitchen, getting the formula ready, pouring it in the clean bottle, and then holding it up to the light, just to make sure it looked right. If there had been some sort of problem with his last bottle, she didn't want to repeat the problem.

As Christy was holding up the bottle, Cole's right arm flailed up, catching it just right so that the entire thing came down on Christy's hair.

She stood at the sink with her wiggly boy in her arms as the formula dripped down her forehead, making smear marks with her mascara as it obeyed the laws of gravity.

Christy burst out laughing. She could do nothing else. This was ridiculous!

The first thing she thought was that she couldn't wait to regale the entire episode to Katie. Katie would understand completely. This was something that would happen to Katie, not to Christy. At the moment, she felt like Katie and somehow wished the last twenty minutes had all been videoed.

Reaching for a paper towel to start the next round of cleanups, Christy checked the clock. It was later than she thought. If all she did was wash her face, not reapply any makeup, dab her hair, and go with the formula fragrance as her eau de toilette for the evening and not worry about her damp shirt or her soon-to-be-starving baby, Christy figured that with Pacific Coast Highway traffic, she could be there by seven twenty at the earliest. The dinner part of the evening would be over. People would be visiting, and she undoubtedly would be trying to get her crying baby to take his bottle and hopefully keep it all down this time. If he didn't, well, that would be another Katie adventure, only this time at Aunt Marti's favorite posh restaurant and in front of all of her brother's soon-to-be relatives.

She tossed the paper towel in the trash and that's when she knew. She couldn't make it to the rehearsal dinner. None of this was funny anymore. The thought made her stomach clench.

Christy went hunting for her phone and saw that she'd missed three calls from Todd. She got a hold of him, explained the whole situation, and with the clench in her stomach tightening, said, "I feel terrible about it, but I honestly don't see how I can make it happen."

"Don't worry. Everyone will understand. We've already started eating here. I'll ask the waiter to box your dinner. It's really good."

"Todd, I don't really care about the food. I only care about my brother and Fina."

"Yes, of course. But listen, what matters most right now is that you take care of yourself and Cole so that by tomorrow at this time, you'll be at the wedding, smiling for your brother and Fina and enjoying every moment."

Christy was trying to warm another bottle for Cole as she talked to Todd. "Are you sure they'll understand?"

"Yes. Everything here is focused on David and Fina as it should be. They are in the center of the bull's-eye and the rest of us are the outside ring. I'll explain to everyone. Don't worry. Really. It will be fine."

Christy was only slightly convinced. Cole started wailing, just as she'd predicted. Christy sat in the chair in the living room and got Cole positioned so he could take his bottle without going too quickly and possibly gagging himself, in case that's what happened last time.

She had her phone with her and thought that if she could balance the bottle just right and also keep Cole's head in the right position, she could send a group text and make her apologies to everyone in the extended family group, who had been busy texting back and forth for the last few days.

After two attempts with the auto-correct on her phone coming up with ridiculous words for the ones her pointer finger had tried to type, she gave up trying and just fed Cole.

In the quietness that surrounded her, Christy put her phone down and gazed at her beautiful son. She refused to cry about all this, even though everything in her wanted to break down and sob.

After all, she had only one brother. She knew how much her parents had spent on this very special dinner for the two families. Fina's family had welcomed her and Todd to a beautiful family dinner around the table at their café last summer. For many weeks now, Christy had seen the rehearsal dinner as the Miller family's opportunity to return the favor.

All that had to be let go. Her life was here. With Cole. This was all she could do right now.

With a sigh of resignation, Christy put aside thoughts of her only brother and cared for her only son with all the love her aching heart could muster.

Twenty-Five

The golden morning sunlight came pouring through the upstairs bedroom of Christy and Todd's beach house, announcing by its faithful presence that God's mercies were new once again.

Todd had convinced Christy that everyone understood her predicament from the night before. Marti had pointed out that if Cole was, by chance, coming down with something contagious, that it had been especially considerate of Christy to keep from exposing all of them.

Cole was fine. So was Christy and so was Todd. It was a great day for a wedding.

Hana was fine until that afternoon when she fussed about being woken up after her long nap. She liked that she got to take a bath in the middle of the day but then fussed that she had to get out of the tub so quickly and fussed the most when Christy tried to get her into her pretty little frilly flower-girl dress.

Once her daddy entered, wearing his new suit with his clean-shaven face, Hana turned into a little doll. She wanted Todd to dance with her and carry her downstairs and sing to her.

Todd obliged gladly. He kept Hana joyful up until the moment when they all arrived on time at the beautiful canopy pavilion that had been set up on the sand in front of Bob and Marti's house. Several guests were already in the rented chairs set up on either side of the white runner, which led to a metal arch at the very front, radiating with frilly green fern fronds and big, brown-eyed sunflowers. Jennalyn's interpretation of Fina's idea of a celebratory summer garden altar was stunning.

Hana had lost her happiness because she wanted to walk down the aisle right then with her basket of white rose petals the way she had done at the rehearsal the night before. Todd patiently explained that she had to wait. She burst into tears and Todd carried her over to Bob and Marti's patio to have a talk with her.

"How's the little man today," Uncle Bob asked, coming up alongside Christy. He looked dashing in his suit with a snazzy bow tie.

"All better. I don't know what was going on last night. It was crazy." Christy reached over and straightened Uncle Bob's tie. She grinned, remembering the Christmas Bob had given David a fancy battery-operated bow tie just like the one he had. The two of them kept the family entertained all day by squeezing the button in their pockets and making the silly things light up.

"What are you smiling at, Bright Eyes?"

"You." Christy leaned in to give him a solid kiss on the cheek. "You are one of the finest men I've ever known. I love you so much. Thank you for always loving me and all the people that I love."

Bob teared up. He gave Christy's arm a squeeze. "You've always been my favorite niece, you know."

Christy smiled at the inside joke they'd played on each other over the years. "I also happen to be your only niece, you know."

He didn't reply with his usual comeback of, "Minor detail, my child." This time he said, "About an hour from now that will no longer be true." He put out his hands, silently asking for the baby.

Christy grinned. She loved that her family was receiving Fina with so much acceptance and love. She handed Cole over to him along with a large receiving blanket. In the diaper bag over her shoulder she had more burp cloths, wipes, clothes, and diapers. She was prepared for whatever antics this little guy might try on them today.

Aunt Marti appeared in a stunning, shimmering gold dress with an elegant corsage pinned to the right side. "Robert, he'll ruin your suit!"

"Let him try," Uncle Bob said with a playful growl in his voice.

Christy's parents came in from the side and were seated. Other guests were chatting and filing in. Christy decided she'd go sit beside her dad and reached to take Cole back.

"I've got him." Bob nodded. "Save me a seat."

Music began filling the open air under the shaded canopy. The rest of the seats were filled. Bob came over and sat beside Christy, holding Cole and saving the seat on the end for Marti who was busy arranging people on the patio.

Christy watched over her shoulder as Todd gave David a shoulder-to-shoulder guy hug, and David strode across the sidewalk and through the sand to take his place in front of his parents under the tent. He stood in front of them looking like a fully grown man with his tender heart showing in his gleaming eyes and his jaw set like flint, ready for his bride.

Jordan, Sierra's husband, was taking photos with a camera that had a huge lens. Sierra hadn't been able to come down for the weekend after all, but Jordan had a list of open dates when they could all get together for a weekend in the near future. Christy looked forward to that reunion whenever it happened.

She looked over at Bob and Marti's house and saw Todd coming across from the patio next, carrying Hana. He put her feet down on the runner and handed her the basket of white petals. Hana's big blue eyes were wide with fright as if to say, "Who are all these people? They weren't here last night when we played this game, Daddy."

Hana turned to Todd, holding up her arms, waiting for him to pick her up. Christy bit her lower lip. She knew it was a huge risk putting a two-year-old in a wedding. Fina said she didn't mind, but at this moment, Christy minded. She knew the look on her daughter's face. This was not going to go well.

For a moment, Christy considered getting up and crouching at the end of the runner so she could coax Hana to play her role. The sound of Jordan's camera clicking away and the muffled chuckles of the guests kept Christy from providing them with awkward photos and more to laugh about. She watched with a grateful heart as Todd took Hana's hand and walked down the runner with her taking small steps and speaking tenderly to her all the way.

Tears welled in Christy's eyes as she caught a moment-in-time image in her mind of the day when she would be sitting on the other side of the aisle in the front row and this walk would be reenacted, only Hana would be the bride and her daddy would be walking her down the aisle to be united with her groom.

Christy reached in her bag for a tissue and watched as Hana made it all the way to the front with a big smile. Then, because she'd forgotten all about strewing the petals along the way, she stopped, lifted the basket over her head, and as Jordan zoomed in, she dumped the entire contents over herself in a rain of pure elation.

The tone was set. The groom was ready. Here came the bride.

Fina looked resplendent in her elegant, playful gown. She wore dainty satin shoes that made her look like Cinderella. The veil was dancing in the ocean breeze, and the opulent bouquet of white flowers was gorgeous. Fina held her father's arm and fixed her eyes on David, who had not looked at anything else but Fina from the moment she emerged from Bob and Marti's living room.

Todd took his position, holding a Bible that had belonged to Christy and David's grandfather. Hana climbed up on Christy's lap to receive all the cuddles and whispered sweet words Christy had to give her. But then she wanted to sit on Paw Paw's lap. She climbed onto Christy's dad's lap, and there she sat contentedly for the fifteen-minute ceremony.

Todd's words were articulate and woven together just right. Fina and David repeated the vows they'd agreed on ahead of time, both of them incorporating the phrase that had become part of their love story, "For me, this means till death." They understood the power of their vow. Theirs was not an airy "happily ever after" but rather an oath to fight to the finish for what they had as a married couple.

Todd prayed over them and then with a grin he said,

"David, Fina, will you now seal your vow with a kiss?"

David lifted Fina's veil, very much like the way she'd acted out the moment when she was in the dressing room with Christy. He smoothed it back over her head, gazed into her eyes, and then like a magnet, they came together and kissed each other tenderly.

Christy started crying and didn't stop until David and Fina were down the aisle to the jubilant words to one of their favorite songs. Aunt Marti had already slipped out the side and scurried over to the house where the reception would go into full swing. The guests rose, all smiling and nodding to each other and moving through the sand over to the house. Fina's mom and dad linked arms, smiling, sharing a kiss, and whispering something that made both of them draw even closer as they walked to the house.

"We've got Hana," Christy's mom said.

"I'll take the little man," Bob said.

Christy stayed where she was in the chair, smiling at her husband as he stood gazing at Christy under the arch bursting with greenery. He stepped toward her, held out his hand, and drew her up. The song was still playing. Everyone else had gone to the house. Todd pulled Christy close and began to dance with her on the beach where they first met.

Christy pressed her cheek against the serge lapel of his new suit and hummed along with the song. Todd never danced with her in their early years. This was something new. Another first in this new season. Something she hoped they'd repeat many times together until one day they'd dance at their daughter's wedding, and their son's wedding, and as Todd had often said, "At the wedding feast of the Lamb."

Christy remembered when she wanted him to ask her to her high school prom, and he had said the getting dressed up, the dancing, and celebration was all a poor imitation of what it will be like in heaven one day when we are all gathered together at the wedding feast of the Lamb. She also remembered being at the dinner table one night when Todd had showed an argumentative Marti where the wedding feast of heaven was talked about in Revelation. He also showed Marti a passage that said that Jesus would sing over us and referred to Christ as "The Great Wedding Singer," with all respect.

"I love you, Kilikina," Todd whispered in her ear and drew her back to the temporal yet so eternal moment as the wedding recessional song ended.

"I love you."

They kissed, a lingering forceful kiss that seemed to convey, at least from Christy's perspective, that she was ready and willing to renew her commitment to Todd and fight through all the forces that came against them in order to keep their love alive.

With their arms around each other, they joined the rest of the happy wedding guests inside the house.

The transformation of the interior of the house that Marti had achieved was quite stunning. She had arranged all the furniture so it provided the maximum amount of space for people to sit throughout the downstairs. Guest were already finding where they wanted to sit in the inviting clusters, while others were standing with beverages in their hands, circled around Fina and commenting on her dress.

One of the changes Marti had agreed to make at the last minute was to clear the patio so it could be used as a dance floor after sunset. David had arranged the mix; Fina had requested café lights like the ones on Christy and Todd's patio. The large patio table had been removed, and Marti's chairs with the new cushions lined the far side for those who'd need to take a breather.

Joel had prepared all the scrumptious food, and servers had been hired to move among the guests with platters of whatever he had just produced in the kitchen. It was a much more exciting buffet than if all the options were lined up at the same time on a big table. The music was fun, everyone was chatting, Hana had found her way up into Uncle David's arms, and Fina's sisters were playing peekaboo with her.

Jennalyn came up to Christy with a smile and a hug and told her how great she looked. "Really cute dress, Christy. I don't think I've seen it before."

"I haven't been able to fit in it for a while. You look great, too. And the flowers were so gorgeous!"

"Thanks. I loved how it all turned out, too."

Their chitchat was interrupted by the piercing cry that Christy knew by heart.

"Do you want me to get him?" Todd asked.

"No. I'll take him upstairs. He's ready to eat." She had no trouble finding her chunky monkey, who had terrified one of the guests who'd asked Bob if she could hold him.

Christy carried Cole up the stairs and stopped halfway when she heard her name. She turned to see Todd looking up at her. "Let me know if you need anything."

Christy nodded and smiled. The setup of where the two of them stood at that moment was so familiar. She couldn't believe that all those years ago, she had stood on this same step, taken off her woven sandal, and heaved it at Todd because she was so furious at him. She'd stomped up the rest of the stairs to the guest room, thinking that her handsome prince had just turned into a toad.

She didn't think that now.

Christy was going to go in the guest room, which had

been Fina's room for almost a year. Then she remembered how lovely it had been during the engagement party to sit out on the balcony of Bob and Marti's master suite and watch the sunset and listen to all the conversations going on below.

She got Cole's bottle out of the bag, got it ready, and settled in one of the lounge chairs, enjoying the view of the big orange ball of sunshine that was about to lower itself into the sea.

Christy had just gotten her position settled and locked eyes with her baby boy when the bedroom door opened and someone was coming toward her. When she looked over her shoulder and saw that it was Aunt Marti, Christy felt the instant urge to apologize for not asking if she could be in Marti's private space.

Marti spoke first, though. "Okay, I'm ready." She sat on the lounge next to Christy and looked at her waiting for a reply.

Christy was nervous about taking the bait, but she did anyway. "Ready for what?"

Marti put her feet in front of her, leaned against the back of the chaise, and in a small, unhurried voice she said, "I am ready to send my RSVP."

"For what?" Christy asked.

Marti looked at her as if it should be obvious to Christy and to the whole world. "For heaven."

All the previous conversations came tumbling over Christy, and her jaw went slack. "Aunt Marti, are you saying you want to surrender your life to the Lord?"

"Yes. That's what I'm saying."

"You understand what this means."

"I'm repenting of all my sins, as Katie so eloquently explained in her letter. The girl has no idea how long the list is."

"But God knows." Christy didn't realize she'd said the

words out loud. She quickly followed with, "And He still loves you. He wants you to be made right with Him. He wants you back."

Marti let out a slow breath, looking straight ahead. "I have avoided His love for too long."

Marti's voice didn't carry the "poor me" tone Christy had often heard over the years. She didn't sound haughty or bossy, either. She sounded young. Like a teenager coming to terms with the fact that while the world is filled with so many terrible hurts and injustices, God is still there and His love never changes.

"I want what all of you have. I want to get on my knees and repent. I want to pray and I want you to be the one who tells me what to say."

Christy's heart was racing.

"The words don't matter, Aunt Marti. God already knows what's on your heart. Just tell Him."

"I don't have to repeat a vow?"

"No."

"What about kneeling?"

"Only if you want to."

Marti thought for a moment. The sun was highlighting her face in this golden hour, and it seemed to Christy that a softness was spreading across her expression.

"I want to kneel." Marti got up, moved the lounge to the side, and lowered herself in her elegant gown with the beautiful corsage, facing the radiant sun.

"Go ahead." Christy's voice was just above a whisper. "Tell Him what's on your heart."

The eternal weight and glory of this moment came over Christy in a heart-stopping breath.

Aunt Marti was about to make her own summer promise.

"Father in heaven, I ask that You in Your great mercy would forgive all my wrongs and receive me into Your family. I want to know You closely. I commit myself to You. Amen."

Marti turned to look at Christy, but her gaze rose to meet someone else. It was then that Christy realized Todd was standing behind her and next to Todd was Uncle Bob. Todd reached out both hands, helped Marti stand, and wrapped his arms around her. "Welcome to the family, Aunt Marti."

Bob reached for his wife and drew her close. She seemed to melt in his arms.

"It's about time," Uncle Bob said in a choked voice.

They all laughed softly, even Marti.

Marti wiped her tears and leaned her head against Bob's shoulder. "You know I said I never would do this. Well, I was wrong."

"There's a first time for everything." Bob's eyes were filled with tears. His voice broke as he looked at Marti lovingly like a patient groom. "You don't know how long I have waited for this, my darling."

Marti let loose with her tears and cried like Christy had never seen her cry before.

Christy couldn't stop crying either. Her tears fell silent like a gentle rain as she held Cole close and marveled at what had just happened. New life. Deep love. Grace upon grace. It was almost more than she thought her heart could hold.

"Come," Todd said, drawing Bob and Marti out onto the balcony where the four of them and baby Cole formed a tight cluster, all holding hands, watching the sun as it began to dip into the ocean.

Todd rolled back his shoulders and lifted his chin. Like a jubilant wedding singer he opened his mouth and the rich notes rolled out, knitting them together as one.

May the Lord bless you and keep you
May the Lord make His face to shine upon you
And give you His peace.
And may you always love Jesus first, above all else.

Todd's blessing covered them like a sunset lullaby, ushering out the end of the day, the end of an era and welcoming a new beginning for all of them.

Forever.

Christy and Todd

The Baby Years

Join in the adventures of
parenting with
Christy & Todd in this
3 book series

BookShop.RobinGunn.com

Christy and Todd

The Married Years

Follow Christy and Todd's first few years of marriage in this 3-book series

BookShop.RobinGunn.com

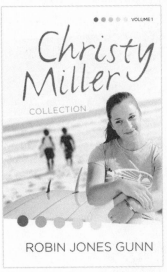

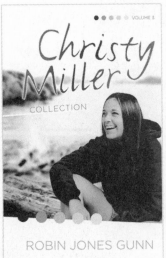

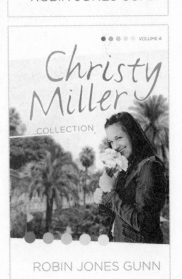

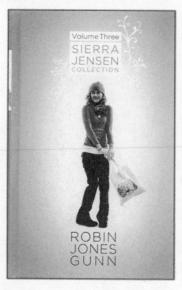

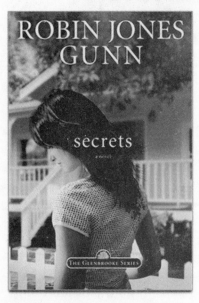

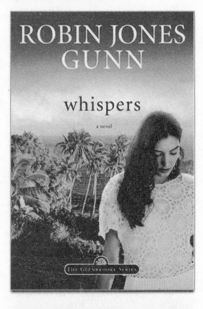

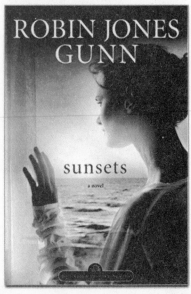

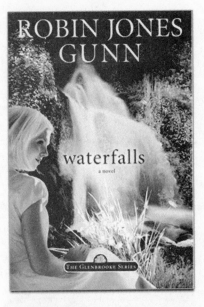

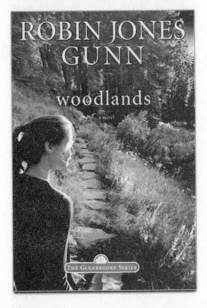

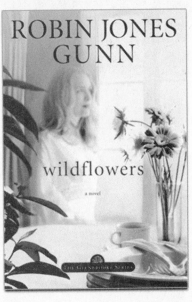

Non-Fiction

Go deeper with your reader friends with these book club favorites.

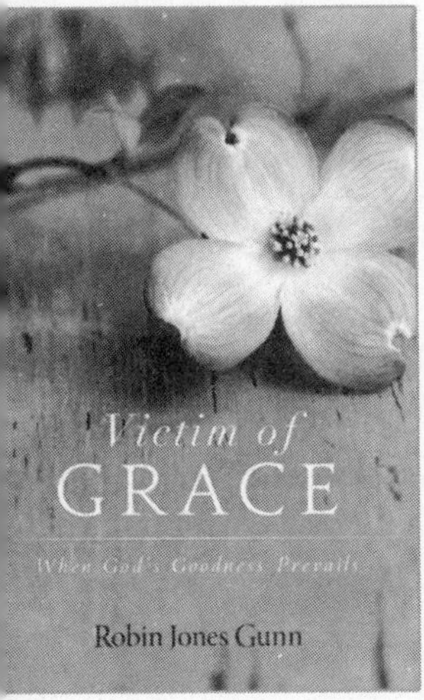

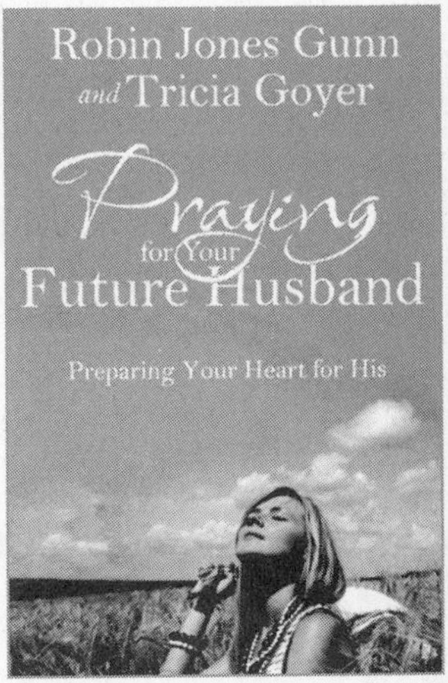

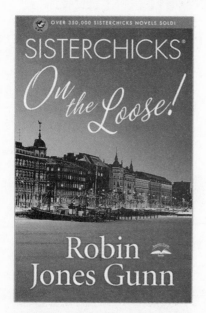

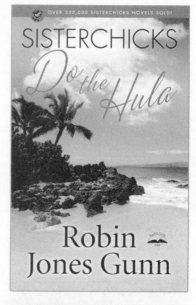

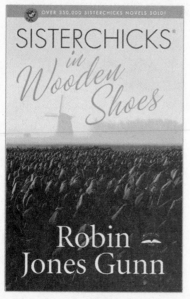

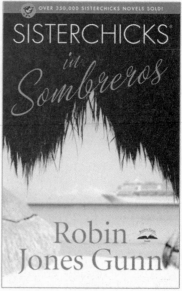

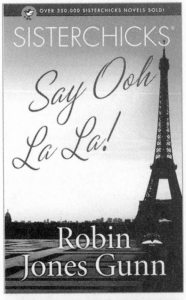

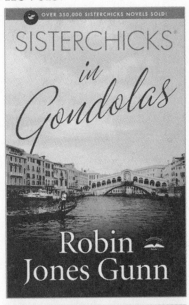

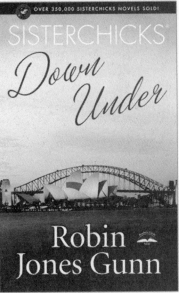

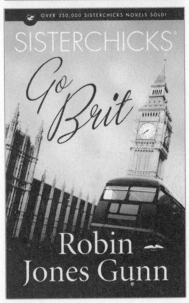